frantic

frantic

JERRY B. JENKINS
TIM LAHAYE
with CHRIS FABRY

TYNDALE HOUSE PUBLISHERS, INC.
WHEATON, ILLINOIS

Visit areUthirsty.com

Visit Tyndale's exciting Web site at www.tyndale.com

Discover the latest Left Behind news at www.leftbehind.com

Frantic is a special edition compilation of the following Left Behind®: The Kids titles:

Published in association with the literary agency of Alive Communications, Inc., 7680 Goddard Street, Suite 200, Colorado Springs, CO 80920.

Designed by Jenny Swanson

Library of Congress Cataloging-in-Publication Data

Jenkins, Jerry B.
    Frantic / Jerry B. Jenkins, Tim LaHaye ; with Chris Fabry.
       p. cm. — (Left behind—the kids) #6 Vol. 20–22
    Special ed. compilation of the following three works previously published in 2002:
A Dangerous Plan; Secrets of New Babylon; Escape from New Babylon.
     Summary: Four teens battle the forces of evil when they are left behind after the Rapture.
    ISBN 0-8423-8356-5 (hc)
    [1. End of the world—Fiction. 2. Christian life—Fiction.] I. LaHaye, Tim F. II. Fabry, Chris.
III. Title.
    PZ7.J4138Fr 2004
    [Fic]—dc22   2003022986

Printed in the United States of America

09   08   07   06   05   04
9   8   7   6   5   4   3   2   1

1

VICKI Byrne lunged for the crib and swung a board at the hovering locust. She missed, but the beast veered away, screaming, "Apollyon!"

"More are trying to get in!" Darrion yelled.

"Stay there," Vicki said. "I'll get this one!"

The locust dove at the baby again. Vicki's stomach turned at the hideous face of the creature. She swung again and connected. The locust bounced off the wall and fell into the crib.

"Don't let it hurt my baby!" Lenore yelled from above.

"Shut the door!" Vicki said, peeking over the edge of the crib. The baby cried and kicked at his cover as the locust lay a few inches from his feet.

"It's OK, Tolan," Vicki said. "I'm going to get this bad thing away from you."

Tolan smiled. Vicki picked up the locust by one of its

legs and held it upside down. The body was shaped like a miniature horse armed for war, but where a mane should have been was long, flowing hair. On its back were wings. Vicki flipped the locust over and saw a human face, but the front teeth were like a lion's.

Lenore trembled. "Don't let it hurt my baby."

"Keep the door closed," Vicki said through clenched teeth. "If this thing gets upstairs it'll sting all of you."

"Put it under the door before it comes to," Shelly said.

Vicki dropped the locust, and Shelly kicked it against the wooden door, then mashed its body into the mud.

"Another one's getting in!" Darrion shouted.

Before Vicki could react, a locust skittered by and flew toward the crib. Its wings twitched furiously with a metallic clicking as it rose toward Tolan. The child reached for it and laughed.

"Apollyon," the locust wailed.

Vicki raced for the crib, but the locust disappeared over the edge. Tolan squealed. The locust flew at the child's face, its teeth bared. But it stopped each time, unable to get closer than a few inches from Tolan. The locust darted up, turned to attack, but stopped in midair. Venom sloshed in its tail as it screamed in its high-pitched voice, "Apollyon!"

Tolan stared at the locust, then looked at Vicki.

Lenore shrieked, eyeing the door above. "Don't let it get my baby!"

Vicki swung at the locust, but the beast darted behind the crib.

"Get back upstairs, Lenore!" Vicki said.

"We're not letting her back up here!" Melinda shouted. "She won't keep the door closed."

Shelly and Darrion tromped on the floor to keep other locusts out. Vicki helped Lenore up, but the woman fell back, horror on her face.

Vicki turned and saw the locust, its mouth dripping with venom, heading straight for them.

Judd Thompson Jr. was somehow calm in the middle of so much chaos. Their plane sat on the runway in Jerusalem, trapped by thousands of swarming demons.

The pilot scowled at Judd. "Why aren't you afraid?"

"They won't attack a believer in Christ," Judd said.

"You're crazy."

"I am not," Judd said. "Let me help."

"I can't let you go out there."

Judd put a hand on the pilot's arm. "Anyone else goes out, they'll get stung. Open the door and those things will swarm in. If I can get the gate attached, there's a chance these people can get inside the terminal."

The pilot looked out and studied the locusts. "This section of the terminal is isolated."

"Please," Judd said.

The pilot turned to the flight attendant. "Get the crash ax. We'll cut a hole in the baggage compartment."

"Wait," Judd said. "Those things will get through the hole you make."

Something skittered above them. A high-pitched sound followed. "Abbadon!" a locust proclaimed.

"How are they getting in?" the flight attendant said.

The pilot picked up a phone. "Jim, close the manual override to the outflow valve. Now!"

Judd heard locusts scampering overhead. "How thick is that tubing?"

"It's plastic and thick enough," the pilot said. "They can't chew through." He clicked on the intercom. "Ladies and gentlemen, please be seated. There's no way the bugs can get into the cabin. Please stay calm as we work on getting you out of here safely. A young man has offered to help, so clear the aisles and stay in your seats."

Applause greeted Judd as he stepped into the aisle and followed the pilot. The man lifted the edge of the carpet and pulled a yellow tab. The carpet tore along a seam, revealing a small door.

"This leads to a compartment under the plane," he said, grabbing a ring in the floor. "It's tight, but you'll fit."

"The locusts will come in when you open it," Judd said.

The pilot twisted the ring and turned a bolt on the hatch door. "Not if you do it right. It's an access bay. You get inside and we seal the top. Open another door at the bottom and you're outside. No way they can get in."

The pilot showed Judd how to move the jetway into position once he was outside the plane, then opened the hatch. "I hope you're right about them not attacking you."

Judd wriggled to the bottom and found a latch with a weird handle and a button. He pressed and turned it, bracing himself as the hatch opened. Locusts flew into

4

the hole, but Judd kicked at them. Finally, he let go and dropped to the ground.

Judd felt both relief and horror. The fresh air felt good, but the locusts sickened him. The plane's wings were full of the horrid creatures scratching and biting at the fuselage. Some hovered near the windows, shrieking as they tried to get at the passengers.

White fluid dripped from a burned-out engine. Somehow, the locusts had shattered a rotor and had flown right through the engine. If those locusts had survived, there was no way to kill the beasts.

Lionel Washington stood at a window in the terminal. He had lived through an earthquake and the other judgments sent by God, but nothing compared to this.

Sam Goldberg stood beside him, looking equally shocked. Lionel, Sam, and Judd had planned to return to Illinois, but now the world had turned upside down.

"My father," Sam said. "What happens when he is stung?"

Lionel pointed to an airline worker writhing in pain on the runway. "He'll hurt so bad he'll want to kill himself. But he won't be able to."

Sam groaned. "If only he'd listened."

A woman ran screaming through the waiting area and beat on the glass doors. A security guard ran toward her. "You can't go through there, ma'am! It's for your own safety."

"My daughter's in there!"

Lionel saw locusts were on the other side of the glass swooping and attacking as people ran from side to side. Some people cowered in corners. A few tried to hide near pay phones. Others ran for rest rooms and locked themselves inside.

Lionel felt helpless. The only hope for these people was the truth, but they were too frightened to listen.

Sam tugged on Lionel's arm and pointed toward the runway. "Look at that!"

Lionel gasped when Judd crawled out from under the plane and moved toward the terminal. He disappeared beneath the jetway in a swirl of angry locusts.

"We have to help!" Lionel said.

Mark was elated that his new friend, Carl Meninger, had believed the message and was now a follower of Christ. The locusts seemed to know he had stolen a victim.

Mark fired up the motorcycle and the two rode away. He slowed to a crawl because of all the locusts buzzing around them. "We get hit with one of those and we're dead."

After a few miles Mark pulled to the side of the road. "I can't drive in this. We'll have to wait until they thin out."

He pushed the motorcycle through a grove of trees and into a clearing. The locusts buzzed through the trees looking for more victims. Mark found a spot in the shade and took out food and drinks from his knapsack.

"You saved my life," Carl said. "That's twice some-body from your family has done that."

Mark smiled. "Getting stung hurts, but you wouldn't have died."

Carl took a drink and sat back against the tree. "I have a confession. I said I wanted to meet because of your cousin John. But that's only one reason I came up here. I don't think you're going to like the second."

Vicki had dropped her wood plank when she helped Lenore up. Now, with a locust bearing down on them, she swung and smacked it with her hand. Vicki recoiled in pain, like she had hit a metal baseball. Her hand throbbed and swelled.

The locust hurtled backward and hit the wall. It shook its head, sputtered, then resumed the attack.

"Another one's getting through!" Darrion yelled.

Tolan sat up in his crib and cried for his mother. Vicki joined hands with Shelly and Darrion and they surrounded Lenore, huddling close as three locusts circled menacingly.

"Pray!" Vicki said. "Hurry!"

"God, protect Tolan's mom from these things. Don't let her get stung."

A locust swooped in, brushing Vicki's hair. "In the name of Jesus," Vicki said, "keep them away. God, protect her like you protected your friends in the boat."

"Apollyon!" a demon hissed.

The girls moved closer together, arms linked, heads touching as they stood against the locusts.

"Jesus is King and Lord," Darrion shouted.

"Apollyon!" the demons called out.

"Jesus!" Darrion screamed back. "Jesus is the Christ, the Messiah, the Lamb of God! Get out of here!"

Two locusts hovered over Tolan's crib but moved no closer to him. They clicked their wings and joined the other in midair.

"Let's face them," Vicki said, arms still clasped with Shelly and Darrion.

The hovering locusts looked straight at Vicki. She summoned her courage and looked into their ugly faces, tongues sticking out of gnashing teeth.

"Leave this woman and her baby alone," Vicki said, her teeth clenched. "In the name of Jesus, I command you!"

Over and over the locusts repeated the name of the chief demon, "Apollyon!"

"Jesus has authority!" Shelly said.

"Jesus is the Mighty God," Darrion said.

The locusts seemed to look at each other while Lenore whimpered, her hands covering her head.

Suddenly, Charlie opened the door above and peeked into the room. Vicki yelled, but before the boy could close the door, the three locusts darted up and through the crack. Melinda and Charlie screamed.

Vicki locked the door from the inside. Darrion snatched Tolan from the crib and brought him to Lenore. The woman grabbed for him, and he hugged her neck tight.

"I've never seen anything like that," Lenore said. "They were awful."

"And more are trying to get in," Shelly said.

Panting, Lenore scanned the room.

"Settle down," Vicki said, kneeling before her. "This ought to show you what we're saying is true."

Lenore tried to catch her breath. "I know . . . you kids are religious . . . but I don't know what to do. . . ."

"Jesus is God," Vicki said, pulling Lenore's face toward her. "Do you want to know him?"

Lenore nodded.

"Tell him."

Lenore trembled and bowed her head, her face in her hands. "God, I need you. I know I've done bad things and I'm sorry. Forgive me. I know you're real, and you mean what you say in the Bible. I believe you died for me and that you're coming back after all this is over. So come into my life and make me a new person."

Shelly and Darrion knelt beside Vicki and the woman. When Lenore took her hands away from her face, Vicki saw, forming on Lenore's forehead, the mark of the believer.

2

JUDD moved past the screaming ground crew and carefully followed the pilot's instructions. He positioned the jetway and picked up a phone.

"These people are going crazy," the pilot said. "We need to get off now."

"Too many of these things buzzing around," Judd said. "Let me clear them out."

"Hurry."

Judd found a fire extinguisher, and to his surprise, the locusts flew away from the white spray.

Something pounded behind him. Lionel was at the door. Judd ran toward him and gave him a thumbs-up. Sam Goldberg stood behind Lionel, waving.

"We've kept them out of this end of the terminal so far," Lionel yelled.

Judd nodded. "Get as many fire extinguishers as you can find and meet me back here!"

As Lionel and Sam scampered away, Judd tried to clear the jetway. There was a gap of a few inches between the plane and the jetway. As he turned the hose on the demons, they flew down the ramp and clustered on the plane door. Judd hit them with another blast from the fire extinguisher, then maneuvered the jetway as tight against the plane as he could.

"We're almost ready," Judd phoned the pilot. "Don't leave the door open long. Let the passengers out about ten at a time. Do you have a fire extinguisher?"

"Yes."

"When I bang on the door, open it and shoot the extinguisher as the passengers get out. Tell them not to stop running until they get to the terminal."

"Got it."

"On my signal," Judd said.

He ran toward the terminal, where Lionel and Sam waited with several fire extinguishers. Lionel opened the door and Judd jumped in quickly.

"Wait here for the passengers," Judd told Sam. "If you see locusts, don't open the door. We can't let those things in here."

"Man, we're fighting a losing battle," Lionel said, grabbing fire extinguishers and following Judd. They blasted several locusts that had flown in while Judd was gone.

"Stand there," Judd said, "and when I knock on the door, blast your extinguisher around the hole. If I'm right, those things will head straight for these people."

Judd rammed his extinguisher into the plane door

12

twice. It opened a few seconds later as Judd and Lionel
sprayed around the opening.

"Go! Go!" the pilot screamed.

A dozen people darted through the spray, whimper-
ing and screaming. "Keep running!" Judd yelled. When
the final person was through, Judd rammed the door
closed and ran backward, calling Lionel to follow. They
sprayed the extinguishers in the air, hoping no locusts
would follow.

The group reached the terminal and collapsed on
chairs, coughing and sputtering.

"So far so good," Lionel said. "Let's get the next
group."

Judd went through the same routine, but this time
more than a dozen streamed out of the plane. People
shoved through, ignoring the pilot's instructions.

Lionel's extinguisher emptied first. As he reached for
another, a wave of locusts poured through the opening
between the plane and the jetway. A few flew into the
plane. Passengers screamed and ran toward the back,
scrambling to get away.

Judd backed up, his extinguisher pointed toward the
ceiling. He ran past the last few people scrambling toward
the terminal door. "Close it now!" Judd yelled to Sam.

When the last person was through, Sam slammed the
door shut. Judd and Lionel raced down the jetway and
found the plane door open. Judd rushed in first. What he
saw would stay with him the rest of his life. People lay on
top of each other in the aisle, writhing in pain. Locusts
flew at people's heads and arms as they flailed to keep the

beasts away. One woman toward the back knocked a demon away with her purse, only to have another fly at her from behind and sting her neck.

Judd opened the cockpit door and found the flight crew slumped over and moaning. The normally calm and collected flight attendant was hysterical. She had been stung on the arm and pushed through the sea of bodies screaming for the first-aid kit.

"What do we do now?" Lionel said.

Judd shook his head.

Vicki ignored the pain in her hand and helped Shelly and Darrion plug the hole by the door. Lenore and Tolan huddled in the corner.

Vicki took the piece of wood and the baby's blanket and opened the door to the room above them. The locusts clicked and buzzed around. Melinda sat on the floor in the middle of the room, and Charlie cowered in the corner. Vicki stunned the three locusts and wrapped them in the blanket. She called for Conrad. "I'm holding three trapped demons. Can you open the door?"

The locusts inside the blanket were awake now and trying frantically to bite through. Finally, Conrad opened the door, grabbed the bundle, and threw it in the next room.

"Thanks," Vicki said. "Get a couple of beds ready."

"What happened to your hand?" Conrad said.

Vicki waved him off. She closed the door and ran back downstairs. She rolled Melinda over and found she had been stung on the leg. Vicki tried to make her comfortable, then moved to Charlie.

Charlie scooted back into the shadows when Vicki came close. "Are those things coming after me again?"

"It's OK," Vicki said. "They're gone now."

Charlie looked around the room. He still didn't have the mark of the believer, but he wasn't in pain either. "I'm sorry about opening the door," he said, "honest. I just wanted to see what was happening. Before I knew it the three of them flew in, and I thought they were going to kill us."

"You weren't stung?" Vicki said.

"They tried," Charlie said. "Two went after Melinda and one came for me. It was ready to bite when it just stopped. Couldn't get closer. And it was screaming and stuff was dripping off its teeth."

Vicki tried to make sense of it. The baby and Charlie had escaped the locusts without the mark of the true believer. Melinda and Janie hadn't. And Lenore was clearly a believer now.

"Help me carry Melinda upstairs," Vicki said.

"Sure, if you promise those things won't bite me."

"I think you're OK," Vicki said.

Charlie carried Melinda on his shoulder and put her on a bed near Janie. The two moaned and begged for something to relieve their pain. The strongest medicine Vicki could find was aspirin. The girls gulped them down and tried to sleep, but there was no relief.

As the day wore on, the locusts thinned out and the kids gathered with Lenore and Tolan. Lenore told her story to Conrad and thanked Vicki and the other girls for praying for her. "I don't know what I would have done without the three of you."

Conrad suggested they write a message to Tsion Ben-Judah and ask why the locusts hadn't stung Tolan or Charlie. Vicki nodded. "And ask him how long this is going to last."

Mark studied Carl. Was this guy leading the GC to them by mistake?

Carl broke the silence. He told Mark about meeting John Preston and training him aboard the Global Community ship *Peacekeeper 1*. John had caught on fast and learned most of the equipment in half the time it took most recruits.

"How did you survive the meteor?" Mark said.

Carl held up a hand. "Let me finish. Your cousin talked about his friends back in Illinois, but he didn't tell me anything about the God stuff until the last day."

"When the meteor hit?" Mark said.

Carl nodded. "When he knew we were all sunk, he got me alone and tried to tell me the truth. I wouldn't listen. So he gave me his spot on the sub."

"What? John could have survived?"

"The captain drew names. He called John's, but John gave up his seat for me." Carl sighed. "Now I finally understand why he did it."

Mark looked at the ground and took a deep breath. He had tried to imagine what John's last hours were like.

"He gave me this as I was getting into the sub," Carl said, handing Mark John's Bible.

Mark opened it and saw John's handwriting on the inside cover. It included an e-mail address for Mark and *John 15:12-13. I hope you discover the truth, Carl. God bless you on your journey. John.*

"I could never figure out what those numbers meant after his name," Carl said. "Is that some kind of secret code?"

Mark smiled. "It's a Bible reference." He flipped the pages to the New Testament Gospel of John. His voice caught as he read the words to Carl. "This is something Jesus said to his followers. 'I command you to love each other in the same way that I love you. And here is how to measure it—the greatest love is shown when people lay down their lives for their friends.'"

Carl grabbed a handful of grass and threw it into the wind. He scratched his chin. "That's what John did. Gave his life for me."

They sat in silence. Finally Mark said, "Can you tell me anything else about him?"

"We kept our sub's monitor on the ship's frequency. John must have barricaded himself inside the command center and preached to everybody on deck. It sounded like the captain was really ticked, the way they were pounding on the door. The sub's skipper made me turn it off. We were all pretty much freakin' out."

"That's the last you heard from him?"

"Yeah. I'm sorry. If I'd have refused his offer, he'd be here with you right now."

Mark shook his head. "No, he wouldn't. He'd have found somebody else who didn't know God and given up his seat to them."

Carl nodded. "You're probably right."

"What happened in the sub?"

"We went down as far and as fast as we could go," Carl said. "We were carrying a few civilians we'd rescued from a drug ship. One guy had seen way too many of those movies where the submarine ruptures and everybody dies. It was all we could do to keep them calm and not use up all the oxygen.

"The navigator took us as far away from the splash-down site as he could. We heard the impact and braced. It took a couple of minutes for the wave to reach us, but when it did, it just took control. Even as far down as we were, it picked up that sub like a toy and brought us to the surface in seconds."

"You could've died," Mark said.

"A lot did," Carl said. "All but two of the civilians. Six of us from the *Peacekeeper 1* made it out alive. I was in the hospital for a long time. That's why I didn't get in touch with you sooner."

"Why didn't we hear anything from the media about this?" Mark said. "It should have been big news."

"The GC kept it quiet," Carl said.

"Must have been hairy inside that sub."

Carl took a breath. "I'll never forget it. People screaming. Everybody yelling, asking God to save them."

"Why'd you wait until now to believe what John told you?"

"That's what you're not going to like," Carl said.
"When I finally woke up in the hospital, a GC security
guy was there asking questions. I told him everything. I
told him about John, about what he'd said about God—"

"That was stupid!"

"I know that now. I thought I was doing the right
thing."

Mark stood. "John saved your life and you wanted
to sell us out?"

"They asked me to get as much information as I could
over the Internet," Carl said. "I didn't know what to do.
They figured anybody mixed up with somebody like John
had to be another religious fanatic. So I wrote you."

"And you led them right to me," Mark said. "Conrad
warned me not to—"

"That's not why I'm here!" Carl shouted. "When I was
trying to get in touch with you, I started reading some of
the stuff John gave me. But I got stuck and I wanted to
ask you some questions."

"And report to your friends in the GC!"

"I'm not going to do that. I know the truth now and
you helped me see it. But you have to know something
else."

"What?"

"The GC is gearing up, getting information on people
like you—I mean, like us, all around the country. Around
the world."

"We've known for a long time that the GC doesn't like
followers of Tsion Ben-Judah—"

"But they're getting organized," Carl said. "The GC

has names and addresses of people who visit the rabbi's Web site. They haven't acted yet, but they're going to."

"What are you saying?"

"Take me to your hideout and teach me everything you can," Carl said. "I want to learn about God. Then I want to go out and warn those people before it's too late."

3

JUDD backed out of the plane and walked up the jetway with Lionel. Everyone in the plane had been stung and were wailing and moaning.

The sight inside the terminal wasn't much better. Locusts had burrowed through ceiling tiles and attacked people at will. A woman carrying a baby ran screaming. The locusts attacked her but left the baby alone.

A man stood in the corner holding a bottle of water. When the demons flew at him, he threw the bottle toward them. As water poured onto the floor, it turned bright red.

"Blood!" Lionel said as the demons hissed even louder and stung the man.

"We've done all we can here," Judd said. He found a stairwell and led Lionel and Sam outside. Suffering people filled the roadway. Some had their windows rolled down when the locusts attacked. They were slumped behind steering wheels. Others had crashed trying to avoid the beasts and were attacked when they got out.

Judd tried to flag down a taxi, but even those sitting still wouldn't open their doors in fear of the locusts.

"Where are we going?" Sam said.

"No way we'll get a flight out," Judd said. "Let's head to Jamal's place."

Lionel shook his head. "I don't think he'll be too happy—"

"He'll be thrilled when I tell him about Africa." Judd briefly explained how he and Mr. Stein had discovered a remote tribe in the country of Mali. When Mr. Stein had spoken, the village had understood every word. "He stayed to talk to more tribes."

"That's a great story," Lionel said, "but Jamal was really ticked off after what happened with you and Nada. He seemed pretty glad to get rid of us."

"Let's just head back to Jerusalem and figure it out from there," Judd said.

While Judd and Lionel talked, Sam wandered into the traffic. A few moments later he called for them. "This man's a believer and says he can take us as far as the Old City," Sam said.

The three hopped in, and Judd told them more about what happened in Africa. They were surprised at how God had cared for the details of their trip and prepared the hearts of the tribe.

The driver turned to Judd. "I was here to pick up a friend who is also a believer. His plane was diverted to Tel Aviv, but I'm sure things won't be any better there."

As they neared the Old City of Jerusalem, the driver offered to take them wherever they wanted. "My friend will wait."

"Thank you," Judd said. "We can walk."

"God bless you," the driver said.

They passed a hospital where hundreds stood outside. Locusts buzzed around them, attacking people on the street and fluttering near doorways and windows, hoping to sting more victims. One man draped a heavy blanket over himself and crawled across the street, but the locusts finally flew inside and stung him.

Judd realized they were close to the Wailing Wall and motioned Lionel and Sam forward. As they neared the site, Eli and Moishe yelled their message to a small crowd of believers who lay flat on the ground. Unmanned cameras and microphones recorded the event.

"You rant and rave against God for the terrible plague that has befallen you!" Eli said. "Though you will be the last, you were not the first generation who forced God's loving hand to act in discipline.

"Listen to these words from the ancient of days, the Lord God of Israel: I also withheld the rain from you, when there were still three months to the harvest. I made it rain on one city; I withheld rain from another city. One part was rained upon, and where it did not rain the part withered.

"So two or three cities wandered to another city to

drink water, but they were not satisfied; yet you have not returned to me."

Eli spoke again. "I blasted you with blight and mildew. When your gardens . . . increased, the locust devoured them; yet you have not returned to me. I sent among you a plague after the manner of Egypt; your young men I killed with a sword . . . yet you have not returned to me."

Judd moved closer and noticed several people who had been stung by locusts. They moaned and cried softly as the witnesses continued.

"Forgive me," one man said. "I didn't listen and I'm paying the price."

Though his pain continued, the man immediately received the mark of the true believer.

Eli continued. "Prepare to meet your God, O Israel! For behold, he who forms the mountains, and creates the wind, who declares to man what his thought is, and makes the morning darkness, who treads the high places of the earth; the Lord God of hosts is his name.

"Thus says the Lord to the house of Israel: Seek me and live. . . . Hate evil, love good; establish justice in the gate. It may be that the Lord God of hosts will be gracious to the remnant of Joseph.

"Though you offer me burnt offerings and your meat offerings, I will not accept them, nor will I regard your fattened peace offerings. Take away from me the noise of your songs, for I will not hear the melody of your stringed instruments.

"But let justice run down like water, and righteous-ness like a mighty stream."

24

Later that day, Vicki called a meeting to read an e-mail message from Tsion Ben-Judah. When the kids were seated, she began.

> "Dear Friends of the Young Tribulation Force,
>
> "Thank you for telling me of your encounter with the locusts predicted in Revelation 9. As you know, these creatures will not harm grass or plants or trees, but will attack people who do not have the seal of God on their foreheads.
>
> "As for the baby, Tolan, he is protected by the same love God had for the infants taken in the Rapture. God would not allow these beasts to plague a little child like this. His love and mercy continue, even in these dark times.
>
> "I rejoice that because of your prayers, Lenore has been spared and has actually believed in the message of the gospel. This is the first time I have heard the locusts were hindered by the prayers of believers. I pray Lenore will learn much of God's word through you."

Vicki paused and looked at Charlie. He sat on the edge of his seat, tapping his foot.

"Does it say somethin' about me?" Charlie said.

Vicki nodded.

> "Keep praying for Charlie. I don't know why the locusts didn't attack him, but we have to believe that God's love is at work in his life just as it is in Tolan's."

Charlie smiled.

*"Scripture indicates the locusts will seek out victims
for the next five months. From my reading, I believe the
effects of the sting will last five months as well. Therefore,
unbelievers will be secluded or suffering for many months.*

*"This is a great opportunity for us. I believe we must
use this time to move about and network with other
believers for the terrible time that is to come in the future.*

*"I continue to receive incredible response to my Web
site. Many teenagers have written with questions, and
I am unable to respond personally to them. Judd told
me of his trip to Israel, and I know he cannot answer
as many as he would like. Would any of you be able to
respond to these questions?*

*"Thank you for your service to the King of kings and
Lord of lords. May God bless you as you tell others about
his love.*

"Sincerely in the love of Christ,

"Tsion Ben-Judah."

Conrad held up a hand. "Why can't we have a Web
site? We could post the most-asked questions and the
answers and call it theunderground-online.com.

"We could have a link to Dr. Ben-Judah's Web site,"
Darrion said.

Vicki said, "Wouldn't that put us in more danger from
the Global Community? Supreme What's-His-Face says
anybody who visits the Ben-Judah Web site will be fined
and imprisoned."

Conrad laughed. "If that's true, they're going to have
to build a lot more prisons. I think he's just trying to
scare people."

"A lot of kids are asking questions," Shelly said. "We
could reach millions this way."

Vicki weighed the risks. It seemed like God was giving
them more opportunities every day, even from this
remote place.

"OK," Vicki said, "start working on it. But I want
to talk about it with Mark when he gets back."

Lenore approached Vicki after the meeting and said
she was excited to start learning more about the Bible.
"I want to do anything I can for you kids. Cook. Clean.
I can even give some medical help if you need it."

"Medical?" Vicki said.

"I was studying to be a nurse just before I got married,"
Lenore said. "I was a little more than a year away from
graduation when Tolan was born."

Vicki unrolled the bandage from her hand. She
winced when Lenore held her hand.

"It doesn't look broken, but you've got a bad bruise
there. Better get something cold on it fast."

Vicki nodded and led Lenore upstairs to see what she
could do for Janie and Melinda.

Mark didn't know whether he could trust Carl. Mark
knew the boy was sincere about his faith. That was as
clear as the mark on his forehead.

"The GC knows about Dr. Ben-Judah, but they can't

find him," Carl said. "There's even a reward for any GC officer that finds information about where he's located."

"A bounty?" Mark said.

Carl nodded. "And there are other rewards for people who bring in rebels—people like us. It's very secret, but the operation is new."

"How much would they offer for someone like you?" Mark said.

"I don't even want to think about it," Carl said. "They found one group in South Carolina just before I left. They were set to move in on them."

Mark looked at the sky. The locusts had moved north to more populated areas. The two got back on the motorcycle and drove away slowly, but Mark still had questions. Should he take Carl to the hideout?

Judd, Lionel, and Sam walked through the Old City streets. From windows and doors came the screams of people who had been stung by the locusts. The sound of the winged creatures was like a thundering herd of horses.

"Will anybody not get stung?" Sam said.

"Everybody without the mark is fair game," Judd said.

"Why?"

"I'm thinking of my father," Sam said. "If he avoids these things, perhaps he'll listen."

Judd convinced them to go to Jamal's house, so they backtracked to the right street. When they turned the corner and saw the apartment building, Judd gasped.

28

Three Global Community squad cars were in front of the building, lights flashing.

Judd, Lionel, and Sam raced to the front entrance and buzzed. Several uniformed officers were on the floor inside, writhing in pain. A woman who had been stung managed to open the door for them.

"What are they doing here?" Judd asked, pointing toward the officers, but the woman was in too much pain to answer.

Judd ran toward the elevator. He stopped in his tracks when an old man cackled.

"The GC's going to get them!" the man said, talking through a crack in the door. "I told the GC what the people upstairs were teaching." The man squinted at Lionel. "*You're* one of them too! I saw you down here speaking against the potentate."

A locust buzzed nearby and the man slammed the door. Judd ran to the elevator. The man behind the door yelled, "They're taking them away! I hope they get the whole group!"

"Jamal and his family!" Lionel said.

"I hope we're not too late," Sam said as he stepped into the elevator. A locust flew inside, then tried to get out, but the elevator door clanged shut. The locust buzzed around the lights above and finally came to rest on the floor, panting. Judd took off his shirt and trapped the creature.

"What are you doing?" Sam said.

"We may need him," Judd said.

When the elevator reached the twelfth floor, the three

ran down the hall. They took the stairs two at a time and reached Jamal's door. Judd smacked the demon locust and tried to keep it quiet, but the thing kept yelling a muffled, "Abbadon!"

Judd listened closely at the door. Someone was yelling questions at Jamal and his family.

"The fire escape leads to our room," Lionel said.

Quickly they took the stairs to the roof and climbed down the fire escape. Judd opened the window easily and climbed inside. Lionel and Sam followed, closing the window before any locusts could get inside.

Lionel put the trapped locust under a mattress and sat on it. Judd put a finger to his lips and opened the door slightly. Jamal, his wife, and Nada sat with their backs to Judd, their hands cuffed behind them. The GC officer paced in front of them, barking questions Jamal didn't answer.

"I know this guy," Judd whispered to Sam and Lionel. "He was with your dad when they questioned me."

"Deputy Commander Woodruff," Sam said. "He's pretty tough."

Judd listened closely. Two other GC officers were in the apartment.

"We know you have illegally housed people who are against the Global Community," Woodruff said. "We know from inside sources that you have spoken out against Potentate Carpathia and the Supreme Pontiff."

"We have only spoken the truth," Jamal muttered.

Deputy Commander Woodruff leaned close. "Then tell us the truth about where Rabbi Ben-Judah is hiding."

As Judd listened, he noticed something familiar about Woodruff's voice. Judd was sure he had met the man before the questioning. *But where?*

Jamal and the others remained silent. The deputy commander sighed and walked across the room. Another officer spoke and called attention to the locusts outside.

"Since you know so much about the future, you must know a way we can avoid these ghastly creatures."

"*I* do," Nada said.

"Tell me."

Nada sat straight in her chair. "Believe on the Lord Jesus Christ and you will be saved."

Deputy Commander Woodruff slapped her. Jamal struggled to get up, but the man pushed him back, sending his chair to the floor. Jamal's arms were pinned behind him. He screamed in pain and opened his eyes, looking directly at Judd.

Judd put a finger to his lips.

"Shut up!" Woodruff said.

Suddenly, Judd remembered where he had heard Woodruff's voice. A chill went up his spine. Judd knew exactly what he had to do.

4

JUDD motioned to Lionel for the locust. Lionel slid off
the bed and pulled the shirt from beneath the mattress.
The locust screeched and tried to click its wings. Judd
held it tightly and listened as Deputy Commander Woodruff told the two GC officers to check the first floor and
see if the locusts were still there.

"Good thing we didn't stay in the hall," Lionel whispered.

Judd told Lionel and Sam to stay out of sight from the
door. If they needed to run, he'd give the signal.

Woodruff approached Jamal and hovered over him.
"Tell us what you know about Ben-Judah and we will free
you. Keep playing games and I'll be forced to act. First
against your wife, then your daughter."

Judd fumed. When Woodruff yelled, Judd pieced the
clues together about the man. Judd had vowed revenge
against him.

"You can't treat us like this," Jamal protested. "The Global Community would not allow—"

"Do you see any witnesses?" the deputy commander said. "Either you tell me what I want to know or—"

Judd opened the door. "There *are* witnesses. Just like there were witnesses when you killed those two in Tel Aviv."

Woodruff turned, surprised. "What are you talking about? Who are you?" Woodruff yelled for the other officers.

Judd took a step into the room. "I was on the phone when you killed my friends Taylor and Hasina. You said they resisted arrest and you were forced to kill them. You lied."

"Judd, get out of here!" Nada yelled.

"Judd?" Woodruff said, reaching for his gun. "That wasn't the name you gave at the station."

Judd stood his ground. "I was on the other end of the phone when you killed my friends. I said you wouldn't get away with it, and you won't."

"I should have dealt with you while I had the chance," Woodruff said. "If it hadn't been for Goldberg and the people at headquarters, you'd still be locked up."

"I'm going to give you the chance you never gave my friends," Judd said. "Walk out of here and leave these people alone."

Woodruff shook his head and moved a step toward Judd. "You're in no position to bargain."

Judd held up the shirt. "Abbadon," the locust said.

"This is the next judgment from God," Judd said. "These locusts will sting those who don't believe and they'll feel incredible pain. You'll want to die, but you won't be able to."

Woodruff scoffed and held up his gun. "You can't scare me with your little animal."

"You can't kill it," Judd said.

The elevator doors opened in the hall. Footsteps approached quickly.

Woodruff leveled the gun at Judd. "Now you'll see what a mistake you made coming here."

Judd opened the shirt, and the locust skittered into the air, disoriented. It looked at Jamal and his family, then spotted Deputy Commander Woodruff. "Abbadon," it screamed, its teeth dripping venom.

Woodruff jumped back, terror on his face. The locust darted toward the ceiling. Woodruff shot and missed.

Judd ran for the front door and locked it. The other officers shouted outside.

Judd turned and the locust dived for Woodruff. The man fired wildly and missed again, the bullet lodging in a wall. Then the locust was on him, biting his forehead.

"Deputy Commander!" an officer screamed outside the door. "What's wrong?"

Woodruff swatted at the locust but it was too late. The venom immediately entered the man's bloodstream. He thrashed and yelled in pain. His gun rattled to the floor.

Judd stepped over Jamal and his family and knelt beside Woodruff. The locust flew toward the front door.

"Get it off me!" Woodruff screamed, swatting at the locust that wasn't there.

Judd grabbed keys from the man's belt and quickly unlocked the handcuffs. The officers outside kicked at the door. Lionel opened the window, and a few more locusts flew inside.

"I wouldn't come in here if I were you," Jamal shouted. "There is a gang of locusts waiting for you."

The pounding stopped. The men yelled for their leader, but he was still thrashing and moaning on the floor. Lionel and Sam helped Jamal's wife and Nada to their feet. Sam grabbed the gun and stuffed it under the mattress in the next room.

"We have to hurry," Judd said to Jamal.

One by one they climbed onto the fire escape. Judd was the last one out the window. As he crawled outside, the front door splintered. Then came the frightened cries of men who were now face-to-face with evil.

Vicki and Lenore tried to help Melinda and Janie but nothing worked. The girls were just as miserable as when they were first stung.

"We have to make them comfortable and leave it at that," Lenore whispered as she and Vicki left the bedroom.

The other kids complained about the moaning and crying upstairs. "This is going to get spooky if it keeps up through the night," Darrion said.

As evening approached, the kids gathered to eat and talk about what had happened. Everyone had questions about the locusts and what was ahead. Charlie drank in every word. Conrad found an Internet news outlet and turned it up so everyone could hear. The news anchor had locked himself inside the studio to keep the locusts out.

"We can't estimate the millions of people who have been stung," the anchor said, "but reports are flooding in from throughout the world. All modes of transportation have come to a standstill. Hospitals are jammed with patients, but in many there is no one to treat the wounded. Doctors and nurses have been stung as well."

The anchor spoke by phone with a scientist in Philadelphia who had miraculously escaped the locusts.

"These creatures seem to be a hybrid," the scientist said, "between a horse, a lion, a human being, and an insect. I've looked at the venom closely, and this isn't like any other I've ever seen. It attacks the central nervous system and causes severe pain. The good news is, the sting is not fatal. The bad news is, there seems to be no letup to the pain."

The anchor continued. "That diagnosis seems to be true. With all the reports of locust attacks, we still haven't been notified of anyone dying because of an attack."

"I wonder if Nicolae Carpathia will get stung," Shelly said.

"The locusts are probably too scared to go near the guy," Conrad said.

Instead of heading to the schoolhouse, Mark took Carl toward the suburbs of Chicago. They made it to Z's gas station by nightfall, and Z's father led them downstairs.

While Carl grabbed something to eat, Mark explained why he was there. Z listened and scratched his neck.

"If he's got the mark and the locusts haven't stung him, that's proof he's one of us."

"I'm scared to take him back to the hideout," Mark said. "He could lead the GC to us."

Z nodded. "I understand. He could lead them here, too. Did you think of that? But where else is he going to get the kind of teaching you guys can give him?"

Z took Mark to his office and showed him how much money he had made from the coins the kids had found. "I've already sold almost half of them." Z pointed to a figure on the screen.

"Incredible!"

"With that money, plus what I get for the other half, we should be able to buy lots of food and supplies to send to believers around the country."

"How are you going to ship the stuff?" Mark said.

"A couple of pilots I know will take care of the flights overseas," Z said, "and I've already got drivers lined up for the States and Canada. I think you know one of them."

"Who?"

"Guy named Pete."

"The biker?" Mark said.

"Yeah. He's supposed to be coming here with a rig from down south. He's got an amazin' story."

"I can't wait to hear it," Mark said.

———————————

Judd and the others crammed into Jamal's car and drove away. The GC squad cars were still in front of the building, their lights swirling.

Judd told them what had happened at the airport. Jamal wanted to hear about Mr. Stein and their trip to Africa, but Judd said he would tell them later.

"We will not be able to return to our home," Jamal said. "We are fugitives."

"What about our things?" Jamal's wife said.

Jamal shook his head.

Lionel told them about the man downstairs who said he contacted the GC.

"We knew it was dangerous trying to help others in the building," Jamal said. "A few of them have believed our message. For that I am grateful."

Locusts buzzed the streets. People who had been stung moaned and screamed along the sidewalk. They passed a few cars. Everyone who hadn't been stung was staying inside.

"Look out!" Jamal's wife shouted as they drove through an intersection.

A woman stepped in front of the car. Jamal swerved, but it was too late. They hit the woman at full speed, smashing the right headlight. The woman flew through the air and landed with a sickening thud on the pavement. Judd and Nada ran to help.

Judd felt the woman's neck for a pulse. "She's still alive!"

The woman groaned and rocked her head.

"Why did you do that?" Nada asked.

"I don't want to live!" the woman screamed. "Please, I can't take the pain."

Jamal phoned an ambulance, but there was no answer.

They helped the woman to a nearby bench. When another car came near, she leaped from her seat and ran into the road again.

Jamal brought Judd and Nada back to the car. "She won't die. But there's nothing we can do for her now."

They drove to the home of Yitzhak Weizmann, the man who had helped Judd, Lionel, and Mr. Stein find a place to stay when they first arrived in Jerusalem. Yitzhak welcomed them with food and listened to their story. "Don't worry. You will stay here."

Jamal motioned for Judd to join him in the living room as everyone pulled out blankets and pillows for the night.

"I promise I won't be a problem," Judd said.

Jamal looked hard at Judd. "Nada told me everything. I was . . . stern with you. Too hard. I would be grateful if you would accept my apology and my thanks for saving our lives this evening."

Judd smiled. "Apology accepted."

The last time Mark had seen Pete, he was heading south with some of his gang. The rattle of Pete's 18-wheeler shook Z's gas station. Mark reached to shake hands, but Pete grabbed him in a bear hug, and Mark could hardly breathe. Pete was still big, but it looked like he had lost some weight.

Mark and Carl helped Pete unload supplies and stash them deep in Z's hideout. When they finished, Z's father had dinner ready. Mark couldn't remember when he'd had a better meal.

Mark brought them up to date on the kids and introduced Carl. Pete was surprised that Judd and Lionel were in Israel, but he was glad Mr. Stein had been able to attend the Meeting of the Witnesses. Pete asked about Vicki and the schoolhouse. Mark told him about Taylor Graham's death.

Pete hung his head. "I hoped Taylor would become one of us."

"My cousin John also died," Mark said.

Carl explained what had happened.

Tears came to Pete's eyes as he listened. "I'm glad you came to the truth, son."

Z asked about the condition of the roads.

"It's pretty rough in places," Pete said. "With a cycle it's a breeze, but with the 18-wheeler you have to take it slow."

"Where you going next?" Mark said.

"I head to Florida tomorrow. We hooked up with a believer who can get us food that won't spoil. I'll take it north and put it in a warehouse, then head back this way."

"How did you get into trucking?" Mark said.

"I've met a lot of people over the years," Pete said. "Sometime ago I was through Alabama and Mississippi and hooked up with some good friends. I left to find them and tell them the truth."

"What happened?"

Pete smiled and took another bite of pie. "I had

hoped everybody I talked with would become a believer. Didn't happen. A few believed, though. We even started a church at one of the truck stops."

"How'd you get the truck?" Mark asked.

"An older guy I know got hurt in the earthquake. Said he wanted me to drive his rig. I told him I wasn't interested, but he wouldn't take no for an answer. Said he thought God wanted me to have it."

"Another driver down south told me about Pete," Z said. "We talked and he agreed to come on board."

"This is the perfect time to store provisions," Pete said. "With all the locusts attacking people, it's like we're the only ones on the road. The GC won't be able to keep track of us."

Carl told them about the GC plans to find believers throughout the country. "I'm not going back to active duty. I have to warn those people."

Pete scratched his chin and looked at Carl. "You might want to rethink that. I don't pretend to know everything, but maybe God wants you to stay on the inside. That could be a big help."

"But dangerous," Mark said. "If they catch you—"

"I don't care about that," Carl said. "I wanted to get more teaching and make sure we warn as many as we can."

"I'll drop you off at the schoolhouse tomorrow," Pete said. "You'll get a crash course there and then you can decide."

Carl nodded and stared at his plate. Mark knew whatever Carl decided would be dangerous, but if it meant saving the lives of believers, he was ready.

5

THOUGH he was exhausted, Lionel couldn't get to sleep. When he closed his eyes, images of frightened people on the plane flashed in his mind. He saw the locusts, teeth bared, attacking the passengers. He thought of the woman inside the airport terminal and wondered if she had found her daughter. So many needed help.

Judd and Sam slept soundly, which increased Lionel's frustration. He tossed and turned until the wee hours of the morning, then gave up and went to the kitchen for a drink. He found Yitzhak at the kitchen table pecking away at a laptop computer.

"Every morning I thank God for a new day to live and be part of this adventure," Yitzhak whispered. He pulled out a chair for Lionel. "I could very easily be in heaven right now. The GC could have killed me while I was locked up there, but they didn't. So God must have something for me to do."

Yitzhak turned. "Do you realize we have something other believers have never had?"

"What's that?" Lionel said.

"We know when Jesus will return! Believe me, I wish I had recognized the Messiah, but even though we are going through terrible times, each new judgment from God is a sign that he is real and he keeps his promises."

Yitzhak had logged on to Tsion Ben-Judah's Web site and read it carefully. "Tsion believes, though he admits it's only a guess, that the locusts need bite a person once, and then they move on. I haven't seen one up close yet."

Lionel shook his head in disgust. "I have and it's not a pretty picture."

"I'm glad they're working for God and not against believers."

"What do you mean?" Lionel said.

"If Tsion is right that these are demons, these creatures must be going crazy. They hate believers. They must want to kill us, but they are under instructions from God to torture only unbelievers."

"What Satan means for evil, God is using for good."

"Exactly," Yitzhak said.

Lionel looked out the window. Yellow light signaled another beautiful sunrise. But with the beauty came the racket of the locusts searching for new victims. "I don't know if I can take five months of that noise."

"Look at this," Yitzhak said, pulling up the latest report from the 144,000 witnesses. Like Mr. Stein, they were reaching remote tribal groups that understood the message in their own language. Those people were becoming tribulation saints and spreading the message even more.

"I can't wait for Mr. Stein to get back and tell his story," Lionel said.

"That may take months," Yitzhak said. "Transportation is at a standstill."

Tsion wrote that one day the world system would require a mark on every person to buy and sell. Once a person took the mark offered by the Global Community, it would seal the fate of that person for all time, just as the mark of the believer sealed the person as a child of God forever.

> I beg of you not to look upon God as mean when we see the intense suffering of the bite victims. This is all part of his master design to turn people to him so he can demonstrate his love. The Scriptures tell us God is ready to pardon, gracious and merciful, slow to anger, and abundant in kindness. How it must pain him to have to resort to such measures to reach those he loves!
>
> It hurts us to see that even those who do receive Christ as a result of this ultimate attention-getter still suffer for the entire five months prescribed in biblical prophecy. And yet I believe we are called to see this as a picture of the sad fact that sin and rebellion have their consequences. There are scars. If a victim receives Christ, God has redeemed him, and he stands perfect in heaven's sight. But the effects of sin linger.
>
> Oh, dear ones, it thrills my heart to get reports from all over the globe that there are likely more Christ

followers now than were raptured. Even nations known for only a tiny Christian impact in the past are seeing great numbers come to salvation.

Of course we see that evil is also on the rise. The Scriptures tell us that those who remain rebellious even in light of this awful plague simply love themselves and their sin too much. Much as the world system tries to downplay it, our society has seen catastrophic rises in drug abuse, sexual immorality, murder, theft, demon worship, and idolatry.

Be of good cheer even in the midst of chaos and plague, loved ones. We know from the Bible that the evil demon king of the abyss is living up to his name—Abaddon in Hebrew and Apollyon in Greek, which means Destroyer—in leading the demon locusts on the rampage. But we as the sealed followers of the Lord God need not fear. For as it is written: "He who is in you is greater than he who is in the world. . . . We are of God. He who knows God hears us; he who is not of God does not hear us. By this we know the spirit of truth and the spirit of error."

Always test my teaching against the Bible. Read it every day. New believers—and none of us are old, are we?—learn the value of the discipline of daily reading and study. When we see the ugly creatures that have invaded the earth, it becomes obvious that we too must go to war.

Yitzhak turned the computer screen toward him and read the next paragraphs aloud. Through trembling lips he read:

46

"Finally, my brethren, with the apostle Paul I urge you to 'be strong in the Lord and in the power of His might. Put on the whole armor of God, that you may be able to stand against the wiles of the devil. For we do not wrestle against flesh and blood, but against principalities, against powers, against the rulers of the darkness of this age, against spiritual hosts of wickedness in the heavenly places.

"'Therefore take up the whole armor of God, that you may be able to withstand in the evil day, and having done all, to stand. Stand therefore, having girded your waist with truth, having put on the breastplate of righteousness, and having shod your feet with the preparation of the gospel of peace; above all, taking the shield of faith with which you will be able to quench all the fiery darts of the wicked one.

"'And take the helmet of salvation, and the sword of the Spirit, which is the word of God; praying always with all prayer and supplication in the Spirit, being watchful to this end with all perseverance and supplication for all the saints—and for me, that utterance may be given to me, that I may open my mouth boldly to make known the mystery of the gospel.'

"Until next we interact through this miracle of technology the Lord has used to build a mighty church against all odds, I remain your servant and his, Tsion Ben-Judah."

"Pray with me," Yitzhak said, bowing his head. "Lord God, I ask your protection on my young friend and his companions. Give them strength to follow your will. Show them the way to go and give them peace."

Lionel went back to his room and thought about what Tsion had written. Though the demons were terrifying and the world was in chaos, God was in control and would be victorious.

The sun peeked over the horizon and sunshine streamed through the window as Lionel put his head on the pillow and fell asleep.

It had been a long, exhausting day for Vicki. On normal nights the kids would stay up late talking or searching the Internet for the latest news. On this night they went to their rooms quietly and fell into bed.

Vicki jolted awake. Something moved. A locust landed on the covers of her bed. "Apollyon!" the creature said.

Vicki kicked at the covers and the locust flew away. She shuddered and thought about what had happened that day. Earlier, Conrad had played a game with Charlie and Darrion, seeing who could hit the most locusts with a baseball bat. Each took turns swatting at the beasts. Conrad made up rules as he went along. The kids were awarded singles, doubles, and home runs, depending on how far the locusts were hit and how long they were unable to fly.

Charlie hit two locusts with one swing, and the kids cheered. Darrion timed a swing perfectly and hit one locust into another. One locust screamed, "Apollyon" just as Conrad whacked it past the tree line. "No," Conrad said, "Apolly-going-going-gone!"

Lenore shook her head and took Tolan inside.

Shelly said the game was gruesome. "You're playing with demons!"

"Maybe we're saving somebody some pain," Conrad said. "If we keep these busy, they can't sting somebody else."

"It's just not right," Shelly said.

"We're just having a little fun," Darrion said.

"Can't you do something?" Shelly said to Vicki.

Vicki shrugged as Shelly went back inside. She finally asked them to stop when Conrad put duct tape on a locust's wing and watched it fly in a circle.

"Where do you think these things will go when they're finished stinging people?" Conrad said.

Now Vicki thought about the question as she lay awake. Maybe they would go back into the hole where the meteor hit. Perhaps they would disappear when God was through with them.

Someone moaned and footsteps sounded on the floor above her. Vicki climbed the stairs. Melinda was alone in the upstairs bedroom, half asleep but still writhing in pain. Janie's bed was empty. A door closed downstairs. Vicki walked quietly to the kitchen and tried the door to the basement. Suddenly, two locusts shot past her screaming, "Apollyon!"

Vicki jumped back and took a deep breath. She wondered when things would get back to normal. But what was *normal* now? People vanishing, earthquakes, meteors, freezing temperatures, and now flying demons. Nothing was like it used to be.

Something spilled in the kitchen and Vicki found Janie kneeling, picking up pills and stuffing them into her mouth.

"No!" Vicki said, grabbing the jar away from her.

"Give it back," Janie said. "I want to take all of them and get this over with."

Vicki shook her head. "It doesn't matter how many you take, you won't die."

Janie slumped to the floor and cried. Vicki put an arm around her, but the girl pushed her away.

"How long will you run from the truth?" Vicki said. "We tried to warn you and you wouldn't believe us."

Janie moaned and reached for more pills. Vicki dragged her from the pantry and closed the door.

"If I believe like you guys, will it take away the pain?" Janie said.

"No. Once you've been stung, you've just got to ride it out. And it might get worse."

"Worse!?!"

"You still have the chance to believe," Vicki said. "God will forgive you."

"I helped that woman and her baby. I put my life on the line for them. What more do I need to do?"

"You still think that doing good things will make you OK with God. That's not how it works."

"I've tried my best," Janie said.

"No. You didn't listen to a thing we've told you about how to connect with God. You've tried to be a good person and do good things so they'd outweigh the dumb stuff you've done."

"What dumb stuff?"

"The drugs and the lying," Vicki said. "You almost got yourself killed back at the detention center because nobody trusted you."

"Wasn't my fault," Janie whined.

"When are you going to take responsibility for your life? You're the one who's gotten yourself into this mess. Don't blame anyone else."

Janie grabbed her stomach and rolled on the floor. "How can you be so cruel, preaching to me when I'm in so much pain?"

"Because this is the first time you're listening. Maybe getting stung by that locust will be worth it if you finally realize—"

"Nothing is worth this much pain," Janie said. "You don't know what it feels like."

"You're right, I don't. But the pain you're feeling now is nothing compared to the pain of being separated from God forever. Multiply what you're feeling right now by about a million and—"

"Don't try to scare me."

"I'm telling you the truth!" Vicki yelled. She wondered if she had awakened anyone in the house. She paused, then heard Tolan cry in another room. A few minutes later he stopped and apparently went back to sleep.

Vicki looked closely at Janie and was scared. The girl's eyes were hollow and her lips chapped. Her face was white as a sheet.

"If God would do this to me," Janie said, "I don't want to *connect* with him. He doesn't care."

"That's not true," Vicki said. She grabbed a Bible. "God could have wiped out everybody who didn't believe in him. Instead, he's being patient with us."

"How do you figure that?"

Vicki turned to Second Peter. "This was written a long time before the disappearances, but it's still true. It says, 'He does not want anyone to perish, so he is giving more time for everyone to repent.' A little later it says, 'The Lord is waiting so that people have time to be saved.'"

Janie rolled her eyes. "God is stinging us and putting us through earthquakes because he cares? I say that's a weird way of showing it."

"Don't you see?" Vicki said. "This is your only hope."

But no matter how Vicki tried to explain God's love, Janie wouldn't listen. She stood and hobbled toward the stairs. "If you can find anything in there about how to kill yourself, let me know."

Vicki made sure Janie made it to bed before she went to her own room. Melinda awoke a few minutes later and screamed for some medicine to help with the pain.

It's going to be a long five months, Vicki thought.

6

THE NEXT day, Vicki heard a truck and rushed outside. The paralyzing fear that the GC would show up and bust them was gone, but anytime the kids heard a strange noise they knew it could be trouble. She stayed behind a tree and watched.

Vicki couldn't place the driver and the other passenger, but she knew Mark's smile. He jumped out and introduced Carl. Vicki noticed Carl had the mark of the believer.

"And you're not going to believe who I ran into," Mark said. A burly man walked out from behind the truck.

"Pete!" Vicki screamed.

Pete hugged Vicki and the others, then turned to the schoolhouse. "Some place."

"Works for us," Vicki said. "Come inside and catch us up on everything—"

Pete shook his head. "Work first—talk later."

The kids pitched in and unloaded the truck. This was the biggest shipment Z had sent them. They filled the shed and the storage area near the kitchen and moved to the basement. They even lined the underground tunnel with canned food, making sure there was room to get by in case they needed a quick escape.

Pete heard the moans and cries of Melinda and Janie upstairs. Vicki explained the situation and introduced Lenore and Tolan.

The truck was nearly empty when Pete suggested they take a break for lunch. He told the kids what had happened on his trip south. Vicki thought it incredible how God had prepared Pete to give the gospel message to people around the country. Each truck stop was a new opportunity.

While the others ate, Conrad asked Mark and Vicki to join him in the study room. "I know Carl's supposed to be a believer, but isn't it kind of dangerous bringing him here?"

"*Supposed* to be?" Mark said.

"I'm not trying to be difficult," Conrad said. "I just want to be careful."

Mark held up a hand. "I wrestled with the question a long time before I brought him. He's OK."

"I don't like it," Conrad said. "Even if his mark is real, he's still GC. If those guys track him here . . ."

"You were GC before we took you in," Mark said. "Why shouldn't—"

"Want to inspect my mark?" someone said behind them. "Go ahead."

Vicki turned. Carl stood in the doorway. "I don't blame you for being suspicious. Here. See if you can rub it off."

Conrad shook his head. "It's OK. I didn't mean anything—"

"Sure you did," Carl said, walking closer. "What we're doing is dangerous. If the GC find me, I'm dead meat and you guys would be next."

"Which is exactly what I'm saying," Conrad said. "I know how the GC operate. They could easily drag the truth out of any of us if they caught us."

"That's why I don't think I should go back there," Carl said. "There are just too many ways for the GC to—"

"We can talk about the future later," Mark said. "The point is, you're one of us now and you're here."

Carl looked at Vicki. "I want to learn as much as I can as fast as I can."

Vicki nodded. "We'll help you."

Lionel was still asleep when Judd awoke. Judd spent the day watching news reports of the locust attack and reading Tsion Ben-Judah's Web site. He couldn't wait to hear what had happened to Mr. Stein. He imagined the man riding through dangerous territory and giving the gospel in languages he had never even heard of before.

Judd wrote an e-mail about his travels and what he had seen in Africa. He sent it to Tsion Ben-Judah and the kids back at the schoolhouse.

Sam joined Judd and read over his shoulder. When he

finished, Sam said, "I've made up my mind. I'm going to see my father."

Judd turned his chair around.

"Don't try to talk me out of it."

Judd scratched his beard. He hadn't shaved in a few days and was surprised at the extra growth. He had tried growing a beard when he was a sophomore without much success. A few of his friends had laughed and made fun of him, but some of the girls thought he looked cute.

"I don't want to talk you out of it," Judd said to Sam. "I think you should go."

"Really?"

Judd nodded. "If your dad hasn't been stung yet, he will be soon. That may give you a chance to talk with him."

"Shouldn't I try to get to him before he's stung? He can't become a believer afterward, can he?"

"From what I read, it's still possible to become a believer after you're stung—it just won't take away the pain."

Sam sat in thought. Finally he said, "There's a woman who lives next door to our house. She watches the neighborhood like a hawk but stays inside all the time. Maybe she'll know."

Judd took some change from his pocket and handed it to Sam. "Find a pay phone a few blocks from here and call. We'll help you get to him."

"Thanks, Judd." Sam smiled, grabbed the change, and ran out the door.

When Lionel finally awoke, Judd told him the plan.

"You think Mr. Goldberg will be in any mood to talk?" Lionel said.

"For Sam's sake, I hope he's already been stung. That way Sam can talk to his dad and not worry about his dad taking him home."

"I need to talk to you about the deputy commander," Lionel said.

Judd gritted his teeth. "What about him?"

"It seemed like you enjoyed sending that locust after him back at Jamal's apartment. Am I reading it wrong?"

Judd looked away. "I was on the phone when that guy killed Taylor and Hasina. And then he lied—"

"I'm just as ticked off about what he did as you," Lionel interrupted. "Woodruff is a GC scumbag. But you looked like you were doing more than saving Jamal and his family. It looked like you were trying to get even."

"Well, I didn't," Judd said. "The only way to get even with that guy would be to kill him."

"What? You've considered that?"

Judd shook his head. "I haven't told anybody this, but I've thought about it a lot. When I heard what Woodruff did, I made a promise to Taylor and Hasina. If I ever had the chance, I'd try to get that guy back. It wasn't until I heard Woodruff's voice without seeing his face that it all came together."

Lionel ran a hand through his hair. "I don't believe this."

"Maybe I'm wrong for thinking this way," Judd said, "but maybe I'm right. A lot of believers might be spared if he's taken out."

"And what about the 'vengeance is mine says the Lord' stuff? Don't you see? This is the same thing you stopped Taylor Graham from doing when he wanted to shoot Nicolae at the stadium. You're going to get yourself and a lot of other believers in trouble if you try to kill him. And you're going to have to answer to God."

"What do you mean?"

"Ever heard of 'Thou shalt not kill'? I think it's still in effect."

Sam ran in, out of breath. "I talked with her. . . . She said there were droves of locusts around our house. . . ."

"Slow down," Judd said. As Sam caught his breath, Judd explained to Lionel about Sam's neighbor.

Sam continued. "She said that last night a GC ambulance showed up with guys in these weird outfits. They were covered from head to toe with protective gear. They carried my father out and took him to the hospital."

"He's been stung," Judd said.

"Yes," Sam said, "but that's not all. I called the GC hospital and finally talked with a nurse. She wasn't going to help, but I said I was his son. He's on the third floor recuperating from the sting." Sam's eyes widened. "And get this. Deputy Commander Woodruff is in the bed right next to him!"

Judd looked at Lionel. "We'll talk about this later," Judd said.

While the others continued unloading the truck, Vicki and Shelly took Carl into the computer room to begin his training. Lenore peeked in and asked if she could join them while Tolan took a nap. Vicki nodded and Shelly grabbed another chair.

"We'll break this down into three different segments," Vicki began. "First is basic Christian beliefs. You'll need an overview of what the Bible teaches. Second, we'll talk about the prophecies of the Bible and what's coming, so you'll have an idea what to expect. And third, we'll talk about how to share your faith with other people."

Carl nodded. Shelly gave him a notebook and he wrote furiously, trying to take down every word.

Vicki began with an overview of the Bible. God had created everything by simply speaking it into existence. He created Adam, then Eve, and had a close relationship with them. Then the people sinned. Since God is holy, he was forced to send the man and the woman away from his presence.

"God's plan all along was to send a Savior, someone who could help restore the relationship between God and people," Vicki said. "That's predicted as early as Genesis 3. Throughout the Old Testament, the coming Savior is predicted."

Vicki slowly worked her way through the heroes of the Bible: Noah, Joseph, Moses, David, Daniel, and many of the prophets. She showed Carl passages that pointed to the coming Messiah. She pointed out Isaiah 9: "For a child is born to us, a son is given to us. And the government will rest on his shoulders. These will be his royal titles: Wonderful Counselor, Mighty God, Everlasting Father, Prince of Peace. His ever expanding, peaceful government will never end. He will rule forever with fairness and justice from the throne of his ancestor David."

"Do you know who that's talking about?" Vicki said.

"It sounds like a baby," Carl said, "but then it sounds like God."

Vicki nodded. "It's talking about Jesus. Though he was a man, he's also God. Everyone, every person who has ever lived and every angel ever created, will one day confess that Jesus is Lord." Vicki turned a few pages and showed Carl verses from Isaiah 53.

"Read it out loud," Vicki said.

Carl read, "'He was despised and rejected—a man of sorrows, acquainted with bitterest grief. We turned our backs on him and looked the other way when he went by. He was despised, and we did not care.

"'Yet it was our weaknesses he carried; it was our sorrows that weighed him down. And we thought his troubles were a punishment from God for his own sins! But he was wounded and crushed for our sins. He was beaten that we might have peace. He was whipped, and we were healed! All of us have strayed away like sheep. We have left God's paths to follow our own. Yet the Lord laid on him the guilt and sins of us all.

"'He was oppressed and treated harshly, yet he never said a word. He was led as a lamb to the slaughter. And as a sheep is silent before the shearers, he did not open his mouth. From prison and trial they led him away to his death. But who among the people realized that he was dying for their sins—that he was suffering their punishment? He had done no wrong, and he never deceived anyone. But he was buried like a criminal.'"

Carl looked up. "Whoever this is, it doesn't sound too good for him."

"Throughout the centuries," Vicki said, "most Jewish people thought these two different passages described two people. But now some realize this is the same person you read about earlier. Jesus was both the one who suffered and the Prince of Peace."

Vicki turned to other verses about the sacrifices God required his people to make for their sins. Then she took Carl to the Gospels and showed how clearly Jesus had fulfilled all of the prophecies about the coming Savior. Jesus was killed, buried, and rose again.

"It's all coming together for me," Carl said. "What John told me on the ship and what Mark said made me believe that Jesus was the only way. Now I understand it so much better."

"And there's a whole lot more," Vicki said. She showed Carl verses that clearly taught about the nature of God. He was one spirit, but three persons, Father, Son, and Holy Spirit. She pointed out the depths of God's mercy and love for people, but also that God was holy and required perfection.

"That's why Jesus had to die in our place," Vicki said. "He was the perfect sacrifice for our sins. When we believe in Jesus, God no longer sees all the bad stuff we do. He looks at us and sees the perfection of Jesus."

"Awesome!" Carl said.

Vicki wanted to take a break for dinner but Carl wouldn't let her. "Keep going," he said.

Carl switched hands while taking notes. When his right hand got tired, he switched to his left. "I can use either of them."

Other kids moved in and out of the room while Vicki taught. Pete sat in the corner with Charlie. Conrad and Mark were in another room in a heated conversation.

By nightfall Vicki was again exhausted. She had completed a third of what she thought Carl needed to know. Carl rubbed his eyes and went to the kitchen for something to eat.

"Looks like your student's pretty excited," Pete said.

Vicki shook her head. "He has a lot more energy than I do."

"How long before you think he's ready?"

"Ready for what?" Vicki said.

"To go back to the GC," Pete said.

"Is that why he's so eager?" Vicki said.

Pete smiled. "I think he's eager because he's hungry for the message and he's got a pretty teacher."

Vicki blushed.

"I finally convinced him that we need somebody inside the GC here in the States," Pete said.

"I'm not putting him in that position," Vicki said.

Pete nodded. "And now I'm going to convince you of something."

"Me?" Vicki said.

Pete nodded. "I want you to go south with us."

7

VICKI sat up. She had thought about traveling in the last few days, but she wasn't sure why. Why go anywhere when the kids could reach millions through the Internet?

"You have a gift," Pete said. "The way you explained the Bible to Carl was incredible. You could do that for others."

Mark and Conrad ran into the room. "We just hooked up with Tsion Ben-Judah," Conrad said. "As soon as we get our Web site up, he'll link his site with ours."

"Fantastic," Darrion said.

Vicki pulled Mark aside. "Why were you two arguing?"

"We had a little disagreement about what to call it and what the icon should look like," Mark said. "We'll work it out."

Pete explained his idea to Mark and Conrad. "If Vicki and one or two others come along, you could really encourage some believers."

"What if they're underground?" Mark said.

"That's where Carl comes in," Pete said. "We let the GC ferret out the believers and before they can arrest them, we tip the believers off and give some teaching."

"Won't the GC figure out there's somebody working on the inside?" Conrad said.

"Maybe," Pete said. "Carl will have to be careful."

Vicki chewed on the idea. "How would we buy food or supplies while we're on the road?" Vicki said.

Pete handed her a heavy envelope. "Almost forgot. Z told me to give you this."

Vicki opened it and stared at a stack of bills. She didn't have to count it to know there was enough to last several trips.

"Z said it came from the sale of those coins," Pete said. "He was real happy to pass this on to you. The money from the treasure you guys discovered will probably help believers for years."

Pete paused. "So what do you say, Vicki? Will you go?"

Judd figured the best route to the hospital for the following day. Lionel and Sam researched locust stings. Using household items they came up with a mixture to put on that looked just like a real sting.

Jamal asked Judd about the plan. Judd explained Sam's concern for his father but didn't mention Deputy Commander Woodruff.

"I'm behind you," Jamal said. "If you need a vehicle, you can use mine."

Nada stayed to herself. Judd had seen her at meals, but they hadn't talked. Judd knew they needed to talk, but now wasn't the time.

Early in the morning, before they left, Judd found an e-mail from Vicki. She brought him up to date on all the changes at the schoolhouse. She asked about Mr. Stein. Then Vicki asked Judd about Pete's proposed trip. Judd's first reaction was to tell Vicki to play it safe. She was finally in a place where the GC couldn't find her.

Instead, Judd put himself in Vicki's shoes. What would he do in the same situation? Judd selected Vicki's last sentence and hit the reply button.

> <I really value your opinion about this.
> Love, Vicki>

> Vick,
> I only have one thing to say about the trip. Go for it! I wish I were there to go with you. Sounds like God has prepared you to help the people you'll meet.
>   Lionel and I will try to get back soon. Whenever that is, know that we're praying for you and wish you the very best. Be as careful as you can about the GC and as bold as you can about the gospel.
>   Love,
>   Judd

By the time Vicki received Judd's e-mail, she was completing her teaching with Carl. He had soaked up the basics of the faith and prophecy the first two days. During the third segment, Vicki brought in several others and had them tell their stories. Shelly, Mark, Conrad, and Lenore told of their experiences. Each story showed a different aspect of sharing your faith.

When Darrion stood, a hush fell over the room. "My story's a lot like yours," she said to Carl. "I had someone who was willing to put his life on the line for me.

"Ryan Daley was in the wrong place and got caught by some guys who wanted to hurt my dad. But Ryan told me the truth. I didn't want to hear it. I even told him to shut up a couple of times. But he showed what it means to be a true believer. He risked me being mad at him and those other guys trying to kill him just to give me the message."

Vicki looked through tears around the room. All the kids who knew Ryan were crying. The others were silent.

"How did he finally get through to you?" Carl said.

"I thought God was a force in the universe," Darrion said. "I'd meditate and try to work myself into a spiritual state. That was empty. Ryan said God was a person, and when he prayed, he prayed to somebody who cares. That's part of what turned me around and got me thinking that Ryan was right."

"Where's Ryan now?" Carl asked.

Vicki cleared her throat. "The earthquake. He was caught inside a house. He died at a hospital, and we buried him near the church where we first heard the truth."

"Sounds like a brave guy," Carl said. "Was he older than you?"

Vicki bit her lip. "He was the youngest of us. But in some ways, he was a lot older."

Phoenix came to Vicki and nuzzled her hand, almost as if he understood they were talking about his friend.

Judd drove Lionel and Sam to the GC hospital where Mr. Goldberg was being treated. Lionel spoke quietly to Judd. "What about Woodruff? Have you thought more about taking revenge?"

Judd nodded. "I've thought it over. I was wrong to think about taking the guy out. I won't try anything up there."

"Good," Lionel said. He turned to Sam. "How are we going to get clearance to go into your father's room?"

"I have a card that says I'm a family member of a GC employee," Sam said. "If that doesn't work, we'll sneak up."

Judd parked in front of the hospital, and the kids put on their act. They moaned and writhed in pain like others who had been stung. GC guards in protective masks and bulky gear guarded the entrance.

"One of us should wait with the car in case we need to make a getaway," Judd said.

"We'll draw straws," Lionel said, tearing two strips of paper. "Shortest goes inside."

Judd drew the shortest. Lionel grabbed him and whispered, "Any trouble and you're out of there."

Judd and Sam limped toward the entrance. The Global Community had wired an electric shield that zapped any locusts that tried to enter. When Sam spoke with the first guard, Judd couldn't hear the man's muffled response.

"Say again?" Sam said, moaning a little.

"Visitors go to the side entrance," the guard yelled.

The side entrance was a series of doors the GC had rigged to keep the locusts out. Sam and Judd slipped through easily and approached the front desk. A man lifted his visor to look at Sam's ID. He waved Sam through and Judd followed.

"Just a minute," the guard said to Judd. "Who are you?"

"He's my brother," Sam said. "Doesn't have an ID card with him."

The guard waved them on, and Sam pressed the elevator button for the third floor.

"Pretty smooth," Judd said.

"I didn't lie," Sam said. "You're my brother in Christ, and you don't have a GC ID card with you."

The elevator dinged on the third floor.

"Follow me," Sam said, "and act like you know where you're going."

Judd put his head down and walked briskly behind Sam. He glanced at the nurses' station, but they all seemed busy with charts or monitors.

"Three more rooms and we're there," Sam whispered.

"Stop!" someone shouted behind them.

Judd froze. Sam turned and meekly said, "I'm here to see—"

"This is a restricted area," the nurse said. She walked quickly toward them.

Judd stared straight ahead. Sam handed his ID to the woman and said, "It's my father. He's in that room down there. Please let me see him."

"If you two were stung, how are you walking?" the nurse said.

Judd let out a moan and grabbed his neck.

"They were light stings, ma'am," Sam said. "Tiny locusts."

The nurse lowered her voice. "You don't fool me. I know who you are. I see the mark on your forehead."

Judd turned as the nurse pushed up her hat and revealed the mark of the true believer. He sighed.

"I don't know what you're doing here," she said, "but I'd suggest you turn around and get out as quickly as you can. Who are you here to see?"

Sam told her. The nurse shook her head. "This floor is filled with top brass from the GC. Do what you have to and leave. If you get in trouble, I won't be much help."

Sam nodded and limped down the hallway. Judd followed him into his father's room. The shades were drawn. A curtain surrounded the first bed. Inside, some-one moaned in pain.

Judd walked to the head of Mr. Goldberg's bed and stayed in the shadows as Sam approached. Sam took a cool cloth and placed it on the man's forehead. Mr. Goldberg opened his mouth and groaned in agony.

"I bring you greetings from someone who loves you," Sam whispered.

Mr. Goldberg panted. He opened bloodshot eyes and struggled to see. "Who . . . are you?"

Sam knelt by the bed, clearly in anguish. "I'm so sorry this happened, Father."

"Samuel," Mr. Goldberg gasped. He sat up a little and took Sam's face in his hands.

"How do you feel?" Sam said.

He laid his head on the pillow. "They've given me so much morphine I can hardly believe I'm awake. But it doesn't do a thing for the pain." Mr. Goldberg looked at Sam's neck. "They got you?"

Sam hesitated. "No. I put this on to make people think I had been stung. Father, God has spared those who believe in him from this plague."

"You're lying," Mr. Goldberg moaned.

Sam peeled the fake sting from his neck and rubbed away the red coloring. "See? I'm not hurt. I'm telling the truth."

"You chose to leave," Mr. Goldberg said. "Let me die."

"You won't die. This pain will continue for five months, and you'll want to die, but you won't be able to."

"And that is evidence of the love of God?"

Sam drew closer. "Why can't you see I'm telling the truth? Ask God to forgive you."

"I'm already in such pain," Mr. Goldberg choked. "Why must you make it worse?"

"The Bible says if you confess with your mouth that Jesus is Lord and believe in your heart that God raised him from the dead, you will be saved."

"And doing that will take the pain away?"

"No, but it will bring you into God's family and bring us back together."

Mr. Goldberg grabbed Sam's shirt and pulled him close. There was foam at the corners of his mouth and he spit as he talked. "You are one of *them* now. The next time I see you, I will have you arrested."

Sam's lip quivered. "I pray for you every day, Father."

"Get out!" Mr. Goldberg yelled.

Someone grabbed the curtain around the other bed and flung it open. Deputy Commander Woodruff glared at Sam, then glanced at Judd. "You!" he muttered.

Judd kept his back to the wall and slid toward the door. Woodruff reached for something and knocked a metal tray to the floor. He hit a red button, and Judd heard an alarm at the nurses' station.

"Father?" Sam said.

"We have to go," Judd said. "Now!"

8

JUDD and Sam burst into the hallway and narrowly missed a nurse who was rushing to help. "What's going on?" she said.

"Those guys are in trouble," Judd said. "Lots of pain!"

Others rushed to the room. Woodruff screamed, "Get them!"

The nurse who had the mark of the believer stood at the end of the hall. "Don't take the elevators. Go up a floor and you'll find a walkway that leads to the parking garage. Take the stairs to the ground floor."

"Thanks," Judd said.

"God help you," the nurse said, "and don't come back."

As Judd and Sam reached the next floor, GC guards were on their way up. Judd opened the fourth-floor door and quietly moved inside. He located the walkway to the garage and ran down the hall.

A radio crackled behind them, and a voice came over speakers above their heads. "Security code blue. Security code blue. Secure all exits."

They were ten feet from the entrance to the garage when an electronic signal locked the doors. Judd pushed the handle with all his might, but it wouldn't budge.

"We're trapped!" Sam said.

Judd retreated a few steps and noticed an open door. He and Sam ducked inside as two security guards raced onto the floor.

"Use your passkey to check the garage," one man said. "I'll search the rest of the floor."

Judd and Sam knelt behind a large bin of some sort. The light was off in the room, but the door stayed open enough for them to see. When Judd's eyes adjusted to the dimness, he realized they were in the laundry room. Sheets and towels were stacked in neat piles on shelves. The hampers were full of dirty linen.

Judd glanced around the room and spotted what he was looking for. He closed the door quietly, locked it, and turned on the light.

"We have to work fast," Judd said. "Tie some sheets together as tightly as you can."

"What for?" Sam said.

"Just hurry!"

Lionel sat outside the hospital listening for more news about the locusts. Jamal's car had a shortwave radio, and Lionel tuned in reports from around the world. One station played a recording of a reporter in London who was standing on the roof of a building as the locusts descended. The man described the swirling cloud perfectly. Then, with the beat of locust wings growing louder, the reporter realized this was not a weather phenomenon but an attack by beings he had never seen before.

"They're coming now," the man said in his heavy accent, "flying beasts that look like they might be from some horror film. You can hear their wings and a weird chant of some sort."

The soundman for the reporter dropped his equipment and ran, only to be attacked and stung. His cries mingled with the wails of the reporter who also dropped his microphone.

The chilling report brought back the moment Lionel had first seen the locusts. As he flipped to another frequency, he noticed guards talking on radios and scurrying to the visitor entrance.

Lionel flipped off the radio and muttered, "This doesn't look good."

He pulled the car close to the building, parked behind a Dumpster, and got out. Locusts buzzed near closed windows. He walked close and heard the security alarm. *Judd and Sam must be in trouble*, Lionel thought.

He tried the visitor entrance but it was locked. A guard inside waved him away. Lionel nodded and walked around the corner. He saw a delivery truck parked near a service entrance. Lionel recognized the logo. It was a laundry truck.

The back of the truck was open, but there was no one inside. Lionel guessed it had been there since the locust attack. Lionel noticed a ring of keys on the ground.

Somebody was in a hurry to get out of here, Lionel thought. He picked up the keys and climbed onto the loading dock. Two doors. A huge one that rolled like a garage door and another smaller one to the side. Lionel fumbled with the keys. If he could find the right key, he might be able to help his friends.

Judd and Sam had tied several sheets together when the guard from the parking garage returned. "There's no one in there."

"We have the place locked down," the other man said. "We'll find them."

The guard tried the door to the closet. Judd dived behind the hamper.

"This is locked; they couldn't have gotten in here," the guard said.

When the two walked away, Judd tied the end of the last sheet around Sam's waist. "You're going for a little ride."

"Out the window?" Sam said.

Judd shook his head and walked to a small metal door on the wall. "Down here."

"The laundry chute!" Sam said. "Perfect."

"I'll lower you slowly and you can tell me what you find," Judd said. "Tug it once if things are clear. Tug twice if you want me to pull you up."

"Got it," Sam said. He climbed inside the chute and tried to walk on the metal tunnel. His footsteps echoed.

Judd shook his head again. "Don't walk. I'll lower you."

Judd hoped the sheets would be long enough. He lowered Sam inches at a time, making sure the knots they had tied didn't come loose.

"There's a curve at the bottom," Sam whispered from below. "I can't see anything down here, but I don't hear anything either."

Footsteps in the hall. Keys jangling. Someone said, "What's this door?"

"It's the fourth-floor laundry," a woman said. "We usually keep it unlocked because—"

Sam slipped and banged against the side of the chute.

"Did you hear that?" the man outside said. "Open this door. Now!"

"Let go!" Judd said to Sam.

Sam untied the sheet from his waist and slid out of sight with a thump. Judd quickly tied the end of the sheet to the handle on the chute door and climbed inside. The door closed and it was pitch-dark. Judd slid down, holding the sheets to steady himself. The door to the room burst open. Moments later he felt something tugging. Light from above. A man stuck his head inside. "He's going down the laundry chute!"

The click of a knife. Ripping. The guard was cutting the sheet on the handle. Judd fell and hit the curve in the chute with a terrific crash. Still holding on to the sheet, he flew into a huge hamper and landed in a soft pile of linens. Sam held out a hand. "We don't have much time."

A radio crackled. "They're in the first-floor laundry room," a man said.

"Good," another said. "Those doors are on lockdown. We've got them."

"Deputy Commander Woodruff wants them upstairs when we catch them!"

Judd and Sam raced through piles of laundry. Sam stopped at an empty bin and put one leg inside.

"They'll find us if we try to hide," Judd said. "We have to get outside."

Suddenly, a door swung open and light streamed into the room. Sam turned to run but Judd grabbed his arm. "Lionel!"

"Come on!" Lionel shouted.

A few locusts flew inside the open door as the boys raced out. Lionel closed the door and locked it behind him. Seconds later the kids heard voices and pounding on the door.

Judd jumped in the driver's seat and started the car. Lionel and Sam were barely inside when Judd floored it and squealed past the Dumpster. In his rearview mirror, Judd saw several GC officers in protective gear run into the street.

After he caught his breath, Lionel said, "What happened up there?"

Sam shook his head. "My father would not listen. He's so closed to the truth."

"But he would have let us go," Judd said. "It was Woodruff who sounded the alarm."

Sam stared out the window. "That may be the last time I ever see my father."

———————————————

Moving to the schoolhouse had been Vicki's idea, so the thought of leaving wasn't easy. Putting it in the hands of others was painful, but she felt it was the right thing to do.

Carl had soaked up the teaching faster than anyone. At the end of each session he peppered her with questions, asking her to clarify certain points.

"If a person rejects the message, what do I do?" Carl said. "Do I just move on to somebody else?"

"Think about what John did for you," Vicki said. "He didn't give up just because you rejected it the first time."

"What about inside the GC compound? They need to hear the message, too, but it'll be risky to talk."

Mark stepped forward. "Each of us has a different role. One person might need to be bold with everyone they meet. Another, like you, has to be careful. We're all working together to see that as many people as possible hear the message."

After each session, Lenore had stayed up late working in the computer room. Vicki asked what she was doing, but Lenore said, "It's a surprise."

When Vicki felt she had covered everything and Carl had no more questions, the kids packed and gathered in the kitchen. They all agreed to pray for Carl every day and ask God to give him safety as he worked from inside the Global Community.

Mark agreed to stay and take over the underground-online.com Web site. With Darrion's help, the kids hoped millions from around the world would read the questions and answers they posted in the next few weeks.

Conrad, Shelly, and Vicki would accompany Pete on his trip south. Their mission was to warn the various underground groups of believers who were being targeted by the Global Community.

Lenore volunteered to oversee the schoolhouse. With Charlie's help, she would care for Janie and Melinda, make sure the kids had meals, and keep an eye on her baby, Tolan.

Vicki agreed to keep the others informed with e-mails every few days. They set up an emergency alert system for Carl in case the GC caught onto him. Mark also developed a program that would turn their e-mails into a code that only the kids could read.

Carl pulled out a tiny computer and checked information on GC flights. Since the locust attack, all GC aircraft had been grounded. He sent a message to his superiors and told them he was returning to the base in the next few days.

"I have to make a run back through here every few weeks," Pete said. "I'll make sure these guys get back here as soon as possible."

Lenore approached Vicki with a wrapped package, tears in her eyes. "I made a little something for you."

"You didn't have to do that," Vicki said.

"I can't thank you enough for what you've done for Tolan and me. I'm sure we'd both be dead. And we wouldn't have known anything about God's love."

Vicki began unwrapping the package but Lenore put a hand on her arm. "Wait until you get on the road."

Vicki excused herself and ran upstairs. She wanted to say good-bye to Janie and Melinda, but both of them seemed not to notice her.

When she turned to leave, Janie gasped, "Where are you going?"

"Taking a little trip," Vicki said. "We have to find some people down south."

Janie tried to sit up. She clutched her stomach and fell back. "Bring us some medicine or something for the pain!"

"Try to eat," Vicki said. "You're both going to get skinny if you don't."

Pete pulled out and drove the truck cautiously along the country road. Vicki opened Lenore's package and found a notebook. She opened it and read: *I took short-hand in college too. I think I got just about everything in here. May God use you mightily in the coming days. Love, Lenore.*

Inside Vicki found her complete sessions with Carl. Every word, all three days, printed perfectly. *So that's what she was working on,* Vicki thought.

9

VICKI couldn't believe the room in the truck. Pete drove, Carl rode in the passenger seat, and Vicki, Shelly, and Conrad sat behind them in the sleeper. The truck had a satellite hookup for phone and video, an onboard computer, and a citizens band radio. Pete showed Vicki how to access the Internet through the satellite, and the kids surfed the Net as the truck rolled through Illinois and Indiana on its way south.

The interstates were a disaster in some places and fine in others. In the more populated areas, GC crews had repaired roads. Other areas hadn't been as hard hit by the earthquake. But nearly every overpass in Indiana had collapsed. Pete would take each exit and return to the highway on the other side of the collapsed bridge.

The road was nearly deserted. Other than a few large trucks and an occasional car, they were alone. "We're going to make good time," Pete said.

The kids picked up satellite reports from GC news sources. Other countries had suffered the same fate as the state of Illinois. Streets were deserted. People suffered. In South Africa, a news van passed a row of houses, and a high-powered microphone picked up the howls and sobs from inside. A doctor interviewed in China, who had the mark of the believer, showed beds filled with people who had tried to kill themselves. They drove cars into concrete walls, drank poison, cut their wrists, sat in garages with cars running, leaped into deep water, even jumped from high buildings in attempts to take their own lives. Though some of the patients' bodies were torn and bleeding, not one of them had died.

Vicki turned away from the monitor and watched the passing towns. In Kentucky, horses ran by the road.

"Earthquake destroyed a lot of fences," Pete said. "The farmers almost had them repaired when the locusts came. Now the horses are running wild."

Night fell and Vicki felt the familiar pop in her ears as they climbed the Smoky Mountains. A few years earlier she had traveled with her family in a small RV her father had borrowed from a friend. Her dad wanted to take the family to Orlando to a theme park, but the vehicle had broken down in Georgia. They spent the entire vacation in a little hotel about fifty miles from the ocean, waiting for the RV to be fixed.

As she drifted off to sleep in the truck, Vicki recalled how much she had complained about that trip. Her mom and dad weren't Christians at the time and they both drank a lot of beer. The pool at the hotel was the size of a postage stamp, there was no cable TV, and the air conditioner only cooled the room to eighty degrees.

"This is worse than staying home in our trailer!" Vicki had yelled one night. "You said we'd see the ocean."

"I said a lotta things," Vicki's father said, "but this is outta my control."

Then the screaming had begun. The family next door called the manager and the manager called the police. Vicki wound up running out of the hotel and walking a lonely road most of the night. She hated being poor. She hated her parents for messing up their lives. And she hated being stuck in a hot hotel room with her little sister, Jeanni. To make matters worse, Jeanni was having a great time.

The police didn't arrest anyone that night, and the RV was fixed a few days later, but her parents had used all their vacation money on the hotel. They canceled the rest of the trip.

"Please let us go by the ocean," Vicki had pleaded as they started their long drive home. What Vicki's father did next shocked her. It still surprised her, just thinking about it. He pulled the RV to the side of the road, backed up, and turned around.

"You kids are gonna get your feet in the Atlantic if it's the last thing I do," he said.

Jeanni had screamed with delight when they saw the water. It was the first time she had seen anything bigger than Lake Michigan. They parked and Vicki took off her shoes and ran to the shoreline, digging her toes in the wet sand. She picked up a few shells and stuffed them in her pocket.

She looked back and saw her mother and father at the RV, shouting at each other. Vicki walked into the water. She wanted to keep going, just walk until the water was over her head.

"What are you doing?" her father screamed, standing by the shore. "Get back here!"

Vicki waded back, a wave toppling her when she turned. Her dad grabbed her arm as she went under and pulled her up, her hair wet with the salty water. Then he smiled.

It had been such a long time since Vicki had remembered her father's smile. The events since the disappearances had kept her so busy she didn't think much about the past. But now, with the rumble of the diesel engine and the shaking of the truck cab, she let herself go back. She remembered little things like her dad's stale-beer breath, the brand of cigarettes he smoked, and little Jeanni's screams as Vicki chased her around the house. She remembered the laundry her mother used to hang on a line by the trailer. Seeing one of her shirts or a pair of pants flapping in the breeze had always embarrassed Vicki.

But there had been moments, even before her mom believed in Christ, when they sat at the kitchen table and talked. Vicki's mom had shared some of her dreams that would never come true. Vicki tried to listen and say helpful things, but sooner or later another fight would start, and her mother would grab a bottle and Vicki would slam her bedroom door.

"Do you want something to eat?" Vicki heard someone say.

86

"Mom?" Vicki mumbled. She opened her eyes and saw Shelly. They were sitting in front of a truck stop.

"I'm not your mother," Shelly laughed. "Come on. Sun's coming up. We're in North Carolina. You've been sleeping all night."

The truck stop was almost empty. There was no one healthy enough to work in the diner, so Pete picked out some packaged food and paid for the fuel.

"How much longer?" Vicki said as they sat in a grimy booth at the back of the restaurant.

"We'd be about eight hours away under normal conditions," Pete said. "With the damage from the earthquake and the tidal wave after the meteor, we'll be lucky to get there by nightfall."

While Pete rested in the passenger seat, Carl got behind the wheel. He looked scared of all the gears at first, then seemed to get used to them. Locusts skittered among the trees as they drove through the mountains. Carl slowed as locusts flew toward the windshield. Once they saw everyone's mark, the locusts flew away.

By late afternoon Pete awoke and took the wheel as they crossed the South Carolina border. Ruins of destroyed homes littered the roadside. Tiny shacks with signs advertising shrimp and crabs had sprung up. Then the scenery changed. Through the palmetto trees, Vicki saw the expanse of water she had dreamed about.

"This whole area was devastated by the wave," Carl said. "Changed everything."

"How did the GC keep their military buildings?" Conrad said.

"Most of them were destroyed," Carl said. "Had to be rebuilt from the ground up. A few made it through."

Pete opened his window and an ocean breeze blew through the cab. Vicki closed her eyes. She could almost hear the water lapping at the shoreline.

"Can we stop and get out?" Vicki said.

Pete turned and eyed her.

"It's been so long since I've been in salt water. It'll just be for a minute."

Pete smiled and pulled to the side of the road. A sandy path led through what had been a small park. A crooked teeter-totter and monkey bars were all that remained.

"Enjoy yourself," Pete said. "We'll stay here for the night."

Vicki, Shelly, and Conrad took off their shoes and jogged down the path. They stretched their legs and raced to the edge of the water. Vicki closed her eyes and breathed deeply. She could almost hear her family from years ago. When she looked at the horizon, the sun dipped below the salt marshes and sea oats. The tidal wave had changed what people had built, but it couldn't take away the natural beauty God had created. The sky turned a purplish orange as the sun faded.

Carl came running onto the beach and kicked water at the others. "Pete says dinner's about ready. And good news. We're pretty close to the location where the group I was telling you about is supposed to meet. Thought we'd head over that way a little later and see if we can find anybody."

Pete boiled shrimp and made sandwiches for everyone. Vicki didn't know how to peel the shell off the
shrimp, so Carl showed her. Soon the kids were full.

"What's this place called?" Vicki said.

"We're near Beaufort," Carl said. "We'll drive down
by the river and you can see some of the old mansions.
A few of them are still standing."

"What about the believers?" Shelly said. "You think
they meet somewhere near here?"

Carl pulled out a map of the area with a red circle
around a nearby town. "The report we had said they met
in an old Christian radio station near Port Royal."

Pete helped Carl pull motorcycles from the back of
the truck. "I'm bushed. Going to get some shut-eye. You
kids be careful."

Carl and Vicki rode ahead of Conrad and Shelly.
They found Main Street in Beaufort, and though much
of it had been washed away, Vicki could tell how beautiful it once was. Mansions dating back to the Civil War
had somehow survived the massive onslaught of water
after the meteor. A few shops remained but were darkened.

Carl checked his map again and rode farther south.
Spanish moss hung from live oak trees that lined the
road. The radio station was small. Pine needles and
branches covered the driveway. When the motorcycles
stopped, Vicki heard insects singing their evening song.
A light flickered inside the building, then went out.
Something scurried in the leaves.

"What was that?" Shelly said.

"Probably an egret or a heron," Carl said. "Most of the deer and the foxes were killed by the wave."

A short-necked bird with red eyes darted overhead. Vicki screamed and jumped back.

"It's just a night heron," Carl said. "It's OK."

Carl walked up the concrete steps and tried the door. It was locked. He knocked softly. Conrad went around the side of the building to look in a window. When no one answered Carl's knock, he called out, "We've come to help you. Let us in."

Conrad shuffled around the corner, his hand behind his back. Behind him was a burly young man. He had sandy hair and arms like tree limbs. He held Conrad's arm with one hand and had a knife in the other.

"Throw down your guns and anything else you got," the boy said, "or this guy's history."

The kids put up their hands. "We don't have any weapons with us," Carl said.

"I know that uniform. You're GC."

Vicki stepped forward. The boy's face was shaded from the moonlight. "Are you a believer?" she said.

"Tom, get a flashlight out here now!" the boy shouted.

Another boy, shorter but just as athletic, opened the door. He shone a light on Carl's forehead and on the rest of the group. The teen holding Conrad let go. "Didn't know we'd have other believers visiting or we'd have cooked you guys some dinner."

"Let me apologize for my brother," the shorter one said. "I'm Tom Gowin. This is Luke. Come in."

The kids shook hands and entered the tiny building.

Seven other kids stood in a circle around an old radio transmitter. Vicki loved their accent and was excited to have found other believers.

"We came to warn you," Carl said. "The Global Community knows about this group and has a good idea where—"

"We know," Tom said. "They came here just before the big bugs did."

"They took some of our supplies and dumped the rest in front," Luke said. "I think they were gonna torch the place."

"What happened?" Vicki said.

"Didn't have the chance," Tom said. "Sky opened up and poured some of God's little demons on their heads. Those GC went flyin' outta here. Don't think they'll be back anytime soon."

"They'll be back," Carl said. He explained what he knew about the GC plan to locate and capture believers. "They're targeting people who are spreading the message."

"People like Dr. Ben-Judah," Tom said.

"Right," Vicki said. "But Tsion is safe. The Trib Force won't let—"

"You talk like you know him," Tom said.

"We do," Vicki said, and from the beginning she explained how the kids had been left behind and eventually met the famous rabbi from Israel.

"I can't believe you actually know him," one of the other kids said.

"We read his Web site before the tidal wave hit," Tom

said. "Haven't been able to get the computer working since."

"How did you survive the wave?" Conrad said.

"Long story," Tom said. "Had to go inland a couple hundred miles and when we came back . . . well, you can see what happened."

Luke stepped forward. "Can you tell us what's going on with the Tribulation Force? We want to be a part of it, but there's so much we don't know."

Carl looked at Vicki and smiled. "Where's your note-book?"

10

AFTER Judd and the others arrived at Yitzhak's house, they hid the car and spent a few days keeping out of sight. As Tsion Ben-Judah had predicted, people were busy avoiding the locusts or were hurting from their stings.

Jamal was concerned for the kids' safety, but he didn't seem as peeved as before. Sam was dejected about his father.

"Your dad could have kicked you out when he recognized you," Judd said. "It was Woodruff who caused the problem."

"God can still get through to your dad," Lionel said. "Just because he was stung doesn't mean there's no hope."

Late one afternoon Judd climbed to Yitzhak's attic to spend some time alone. He took Yitzhak's laptop and logged on to Tsion's Web site. Tsion included many of the stories of the 144,000 witnesses who had gone to remote places. He searched for Mr. Stein's name but couldn't find it.

Judd clicked on theunderground-online.com icon and was surprised to see how much material was already on the Web. He recognized many of the questions and answers. He and Mr. Stein had worked on them a few weeks earlier. Just looking at the material made him long for home and his friends. He wondered if Vicki had gone on the trip and what was happening at the schoolhouse.

He jotted a quick note to Mark and asked for an update, then checked his own e-mail. He found hundreds of messages from kids who wanted answers. He composed a reply and told everyone to check out Tsion's Web site and theunderground-online.com.

As Judd went through rows of messages, one caught his eye. It was from Pavel, his friend in New Babylon. Judd hadn't talked with him in a long time. Pavel's father was a worker with the Global Community, and Judd had been thrilled when the boy had responded to the message of the gospel.

Judd opened the message. It read: *I know where you are. Please e-mail me as quickly as you can. I have some wonderful news. Better yet, let's talk by computer link. Pavel.*

Judd set up the laptop's camera and sent a message to Pavel. As he waited, he heard a noise on the stairs. It was Nada.

"Am I disturbing you?"

"Not at all," Judd said. He looked around for a chair.

"I'll sit on the floor with you," Nada said.

Judd explained who Pavel was and that he lived in New Babylon. "Perhaps he knew my brother?" Nada said, scooting closer. She sighed. "Judd, I want to talk about what happened back at my house. My mother says I should move on, but I can't pretend I don't have feelings."

Judd stared at the computer as Nada continued. "I've seen how much you care for your friends. You're willing to risk your life. You've done the same for me. You don't know how hard it was at home, being cooped up, hiding, and taking people in. Then you came. The talks we had were wonderful. I feel like I've known you all my life."

"I enjoyed talking too," Judd said. "We have a lot in common, with our faith and wanting to work against the GC."

Nada grew quiet. Finally she said, "I don't know if I should tell you this. I have prayed about it and I think God wants me to . . ."

"Go ahead," Judd said.

"I think you're running."

Judd laughed. "Yeah, we're all running from the GC."

"No, I mean on the inside. I see it in your eyes. You've told me bits and pieces about your life, and it seems you're always on the move. Always flying here or moving around with your friends."

"We've had to stay on the run from the GC—"

"I'm not explaining it well," Nada said.

Judd looked at the floor and nodded. "If you'd have known me before, you wouldn't have liked me. I guess there's still a part of me that's restless."

"I'm wondering if you could ever . . . if before the Lord's return you could be interested . . . in someone like me?"

Judd looked into Nada's eyes. She glanced down but

Judd touched her chin and lifted it. "I told you I care a great deal about you. But there are things you don't know. Things even I don't understand."

Judd scooted closer. "God put us together for a reason. I don't know why. Maybe he wants us to . . . to get more serious. Or maybe he just wants us to stay friends."

"I'm twenty and I know that we have almost five years before Jesus will return. I want us to be more than friends during those years."

Judd nodded. "I understand. I just need some time."

Nada turned away. "That means I'll never hear from you again. You'll go off on some—"

"Stop," Judd said. "It means I need some time. That's all."

Nada stood to leave. A message popped up on Judd's computer. It was Pavel. "Stay," Judd said. "I want you to meet him."

Pavel pushed his wheelchair close to the computer. His voice seemed weak. "Is it really you, Judd?"

Judd introduced Nada and briefly told Pavel what had happened to them since coming to Israel. Pavel couldn't believe all of Judd's travels. "I found out you were in Israel from some of your friends back in the States."

"What's the exciting news?" Judd said.

"My father has become a tribulation saint!" Pavel said, beaming.

"What happened?" Judd said.

"It's a long story. But reading Tsion Ben-Judah's Web site was an important part of him coming to the truth."

"Did he pray before the locusts came?" Judd said.

"Yes, but as you know, he works for the Global Community and nearly everyone has been stung there. He has had to fake a locust sting in order to not appear suspicious. We also have a safeguard on our e-mail and computer transmissions. He met a believer named David who also works for the Global Community. David helped my father set up this system so it could not be traced."

"What's the word about Nicolae and the ten rulers?" Judd said.

"They're keeping everything a huge secret," Pavel said. "Carpathia and his right-hand man, Leon Fortunato, are in an underground shelter for protection."

"The locusts wouldn't bite Nicolae," Judd said.

"Why not?"

"Too afraid they'd be poisoned."

Pavel laughed, then coughed. His face seemed pale but when Judd mentioned it, Pavel shook his head and continued. "The ten kings and even Peter the Second have been stung. They're suffering terribly."

"With every judgment, Nicolae has turned it into something good for himself," Judd said. "I don't see that happening with the locusts."

"He will try," Pavel said. "My father says Nicolae is preparing a televised message for the entire world. He will say the stories of poisonous bites are exaggerated."

Judd laughed. "With everyone suffering? He can't possibly—"

"To convince people, he will conduct his speech with a locust sitting on his shoulder."

"What?!?"

"My father says Nicolae wants to convince people these things can be tamed like pets. But don't believe it. The locust was created with trick photography. Make sure you watch the telecast."

"What a liar," Judd said. "With all the suffering, he's playing games."

"He's not the only crafty one," Pavel said, scooting closer to the camera. "Have you heard about the Christian literature that is flooding the globe?"

Judd nodded. "Lionel told me they helped pack some of it for delivery."

"Nicolae Carpathia has sent his pilots to deliver food and supplies to some of the rulers where people are suffering most. What he doesn't know is that his very plane is carrying shipments of the rabbi's studies in different languages."

"Incredible," Judd said.

"That is the other exciting news."

"You want us to help pack more pamphlets?" Judd said.

"It's not that. It's better. Have you read how Tsion believes this is the time for believers to travel?"

"Sure," Judd said.

"I want you to come here."

"To New Babylon?" Judd said. "How?"

"The pilot of Carpathia's plane, who is also faking a locust sting, is picking up a shipment from Israel in a few days. My father talked with him and explained your situation. The way is clear for you to fly with him and stay at my house. You could possibly get a transport back to the States or anywhere you wish."

Judd could hardly catch his breath. He had seen pictures and videos of the city Nicolae had built, but he never dreamed he would have the chance to see it in person. Before he could answer, Nada quickly stood and walked out of the attic. Judd called for her but she didn't turn around.

"Is something wrong?" Pavel said.

Judd shook his head. "We just had a disagreement."

"I assume you'll want to think about the offer," Pavel said.

"Do I have to come alone?" Judd said. "I have two other friends who want to make it back to the States as well."

Pavel adjusted his glasses. "I will speak with my father and get back to you at midnight."

Vicki retrieved her notebook and was ready to meet with the kids from South Carolina the next day. Pete took Carl to hook up with the GC and finish his run to Florida.

Pete told Vicki and the others where and when to meet him. "Give me three days and then we'll head north."

Carl thanked the kids for their help and made sure they had access to a computer. "After I get back to the GC, I'll be in touch. Look for my e-mail."

Vicki, Conrad, and Shelly kept the motorcycles and

rode behind Luke and Tom's pickup through the low-lands. The smell of saltwater plants was refreshing. They hid the truck and cycles deep in a thicket. Vicki knew she wouldn't be able to find the spot again without Luke and Tom's help.

"What were you guys doing at the station last night?" Vicki said.

"We'd been waiting all day to see who showed up," Tom said. "We put the word out that anyone interested in getting serious about being a part of the Trib Force should be there."

"How'd you know we'd show up?" Shelly said.

"We didn't," Tom said, "but Luke had a dream last night. He was sittin' in a classroom, studying the Bible like nobody's business. I thought he'd had too much shrimp sauce, but he swore it was a message from God."

Luke helped the kids into a small boat. He pushed off and paddled into the middle of the marsh and started the engine.

Vicki turned to ask a question but Luke stopped her. "Just wait. You'll see."

Luke took them through a maze of creeks and small rivers. He knew each sandbar and shallow stream. Twenty minutes later the river widened, and it felt like they were headed to the ocean. Luke pulled the boat up to what looked like a tangle of scrub oak and some old logs.

"Who's there?" someone said from behind a tree.

"It's Luke and Tom and some friends," Luke said.

Vicki stepped out of the boat onto dry ground. What had looked like something to avoid from a distance was actually an island with a cabin stocked with food, drinking water, and even a solar-powered computer.

Several people came out of the cabin to greet the kids. Most were teenagers, but a few were a little older. Some, like Luke and Tom, had the mark of the true believer. Others didn't but for some reason hadn't been stung by the locusts.

Everyone crowded around the cabin. Vicki asked questions and discovered most of the kids had lost one or both parents in the disappearances.

"My daddy was a shrimp boat captain," one boy said. "I'd work on the boat all day long when I wasn't in school. The summer before, he tried to convince me to come to his church. He used to drink and cuss a lot, but since he started going there he'd quit doing both.

"He convinced me to go out with him one night, said he had a new plan. I didn't want to go, but he kept after me. He talked about God the whole way and I said I wasn't interested.

"Now, when he was fishing, he always tinkered with something. Nets. The motor. But when we got way out and set anchor, I didn't hear anything. Nothing but the waves lapping at the side of the boat."

"What did you do?" Vicki said.

"I went back to find him, and all that was there were his clothes and his gear. It was the spookiest thing ever. I didn't know if he'd fallen overboard or maybe jumped for some reason. I looked for maybe a half hour before I called a Mayday, but by then things were going crazy. Wasn't too long later that I hooked up with Tom and Luke and they explained stuff to me that made sense."

"Still doesn't make sense to me," said a girl who didn't have the mark.

"That's why these guys are here," Tom said.

Vicki opened her notebook and looked at Shelly and Conrad. She took a deep breath. "All that's happened— from the disappearances to the earthquake, the tidal wave to the locusts—has happened because God wants to get your attention."

11

FOR THE next three days, Vicki showed the kids from South Carolina what following God was all about. Shelly and Conrad told their stories and talked with the kids one-on-one.

By the end of the three days, everyone on the island had the mark of the believer. Conrad helped Tom fix their computer and work on the small generator that powered it. Vicki encouraged the kids to read Tsion Ben-Judah's Web site and theunderground-online.com and keep looking for what was coming next.

Luke and Tom took Vicki and the others to meet Pete. As they waited, Luke said, "A lot of what you said we knew, but we didn't know how to tell others. It was a big help watching you explain it."

Vicki promised she would have Lenore put her notes on theunderground-online.com Web site. Pete's truck rumbled in the distance.

"Where are you guys headed next?" Tom said.

"Wherever God takes us," Conrad said.

Lionel listened to Judd explain Pavel's plan. At first, Lionel couldn't believe Judd was serious. But the more Judd told him, the more sense it made. The pilot might be able to get them back to the States or know a different way.

"Pavel's supposed to get in touch in a few minutes," Judd said, "but there's something else I need to talk about."

"I hope this is not about Nada," Lionel said. When Judd nodded, Lionel said, "Are you crazy? Haven't you learned anything? Jamal's going to—"

"I don't think he's ticked off at me anymore. I think he understands this is between his daughter and me."

"What did she say this time?" Lionel said.

Judd explained the conversation. When he said Nada thought he was restless, Lionel screamed, "I don't believe this! Why are you having the conversation? When she came up here you should have—"

"Fine," Judd said, throwing his arms in the air. "I thought I could talk to you. I thought you could help me work through this."

Lionel took a deep breath and walked to the attic window. "OK, I'm sorry. You're right." He turned back to Judd. "What's keeping you from just telling her that you like her, but you're not interested in anything long-term?"

Judd stared at the computer.

"Why don't you just tell her that you don't feel the same way she does and leave it at that?"

Judd looked up. His eyes were red. "Because it's not true."

"What?"

"My problem isn't telling her I'm not interested. If that were true I could do it. The problem is, I *am* interested."

Lionel sat down hard. He felt light-headed. "Whoa, I didn't expect that."

"Neither did I," Judd said. "I've always thought we'd go back to the States, but this evening it occurred to me that I could stay and work from Israel."

"Man, you've been here way too long," Lionel said. "Sorry, I didn't mean that."

"So, what do you think?"

Before Lionel could answer, the computer beeped and Pavel stared into the monitor. Judd hit a few keys and they were linked.

"I have good news," Pavel said. "My father talked with the pilot and he says he can bring the three of you. But no more than that. I have aliases for all of you. Mac will bring your IDs.

"He will pick you up at Jerusalem Airport as the pamphlets are being loaded. Listen for your names over the loudspeaker and Mac will tell you where to go."

Judd said good-bye to Pavel.

Lionel said, "How can you commit to going to New Babylon when you don't know what you're going to do about Nada?"

"I think we should go see Pavel no matter what," Judd said.

"Nada will think you're running again."

"Maybe," Judd said, "or this might work to confirm what we're both feeling."

Vicki sat in the passenger seat and explained to Pete what had happened. He was excited to hear about the new believers in South Carolina and how much help the kids had been.

"Luke and Tom said they're moving their head-quarters to the secret island," Vicki said.

"I'm glad you guys got to them before something bad happened," Pete said.

While Shelly and Conrad looked for the latest news on the satellite, Vicki asked about Carl. Pete frowned. "I've been waiting for an e-mail from him. He said as soon as it was safe he'd get in touch and I haven't heard a thing."

Pete had such a load of food and supplies the kids could barely get the motorcycles in the trailer. "Where are we going with all this stuff?" Conrad said.

"Z said there's a group in North Carolina with a storage facility—"

"Hey, hey, I think we have something here," Shelly interrupted. "A message from Carl."

Vicki looked back over her shoulder.

"Read it," Pete said.

"It's all garbled," Shelly said.

"It's code," Conrad said. "We have to run it through the program."

Shelly pasted the text into another document and ran the code-breaking program. "OK, here it is," Shelly said. *"Sorry it's taken so long to write. I ran into some trouble explaining how I got back and why I hadn't been stung. The GC is major paranoid about the locusts. About 80 percent of the Peacekeepers have been infected. They're trying to keep the other 20 percent healthy and protected with their weird gear.*

"My commander asked about the group in Illinois and I told him it was a dead end. I said the people up there were dealing with the locusts just like everyone else. They pressed me about Mark—they knew he was John's cousin—and I said the two were as different as night and day."

"That's true," Vicki said.

"I told him the God stuff doesn't run in the blood like the locust stings, and he seemed to buy it."

"I'd been praying Carl would be able to think on his feet," Pete said.

"Listen to this," Shelly said. *"The GC are taking the remaining troops that haven't been stung and they're moving them out to several test areas. They're going back to South Carolina. Tell our friends there to stay low the next couple of weeks."*

"We'd better e-mail Luke and Tom," Vicki said.

Shelly kept reading. *"There are two other hot spots the GC have targeted. One is Johnson City, Tennessee. Don't ask why— they must have reports that the believers there are really strong."*

Pete punched in the coordinates for Johnson City on

his computer. "We could be there by tomorrow morning if we push it."

"The other place is Baltimore. I found a memo from the guy who's head of the Enigma Babylon One World Faith there. He's been complaining that a lot of his followers have left. They're reading Tsion Ben-Judah's Web site and some are meeting in a nearby warehouse. All three places—South Carolina, Tennessee, and Maryland—are supposed to get hit Sunday morning."

"That's tomorrow morning," Shelly said.

"Those people probably have no idea the GC are onto them," Vicki said. "What about Baltimore?"

"We'll have to go to Tennessee and let someone else figure that out," Pete said.

"There's more," Shelly said. *"I don't have any names in Johnson City, but the believer in Baltimore they're targeting is Chris Traickin. Used to be a senator or congressman before the GC took over. They think he's telling people about God to get them to start a new government. All three of these hits are supposed to be splashed on the news. They want to make these believers an example so it'll discourage others from following Tsion's teaching."*

"There's got to be a way to get in touch with that Traickin guy," Vicki said.

"I don't understand how the GC can even try this with the locusts still buzzing around," Conrad said. "Write Carl and ask about this suit they're using. Is there any way a locust could get inside?"

"And see if he can get us information on Traickin," Vicki said.

Shelly typed the questions in code and sent them
to Carl at GC headquarters. "I'm going to send all this
to Mark back at the schoolhouse," Shelly said. "He might
be able to find out something from there."

"Good idea," Vicki said.

Pete went as fast as the big truck could go over the
crumbling roads. Vicki knew they were racing against
time and the GC.

The next morning, Judd asked Nada to go for a walk
with him.

She frowned. "I thought you were staying out of
sight."

"A short walk in the back," Judd said. "Please."

Sam rushed up to Judd. "Lionel just told me about
the trip. Thanks for including me."

Judd nodded and excused himself. Nada stared at
Judd as they walked into Yitzhak's backyard. A patch of
grass led to a rock wall. Up the incline was a waterfall
that snaked its way to a tiny pond at the bottom with
multicolored fish swimming beneath lily pads. The water
trickled down the rocks.

"You've made up your mind," Nada said. "You're
running again."

"Hear me out," Judd said as he lifted her up onto the
wall so they could speak face-to-face. "After we talked last
night, I realized something. I've known that I care about
you a lot, but I didn't know how much until I talked with
Lionel.

"I've only been a believer a couple years. My goals are a lot different than they used to be. Now I want to learn as much as I can about God and tell people about him. And I want to make it to the Glorious Appearing, when Christ comes back again.

"In the back of my mind, I've always thought it would be nice to share the pain and the sadness and the few glimpses of joy we get with someone else."

"What are you saying?" Nada said.

"I can see myself staying here."

"What?"

"I never thought I could get used to living outside the States. But living in Israel with your family feels . . . OK. It's good. I could stay, if that's what God wants."

Nada leaned forward. Judd stood on the grass and was at eye level with her. "I want to use this trip to confirm what I feel about you."

"Which is what?"

"I . . . I really like you. Being around you, talking, sharing our faith. I think I might be . . ."

"Will you just say it?" Nada said.

"I might be falling in love. Whoa, that was stupid, wasn't it?"

Nada jumped down and hugged Judd. "It wasn't stupid. It was the most wonderful thing I've ever heard." She pulled away and said, "But I'm afraid this trip will change your mind, or maybe you'll head back to the States and I'll never see you again."

"I wouldn't do that," Judd said.

"We have to make the most of every moment we

110

have together," Nada said. "We don't know what will happen next."

"I agree," Judd said, "and I'm hoping to accomplish two things. I want to confirm my feelings for you and take advantage of the freedom we have while the locusts are loose."

Nada stepped back. "And if I said I didn't want you to go?"

"I have to," Judd said. "Something tells me this will be good for all of us. Maybe I'll get Sam and Lionel a way back home."

"I know I can't talk you out of it," Nada said.

"If things go the way I plan . . . oh no."

"What is it?"

"I'll have to talk with your father—that's how it works, right?"

Nada blushed and smiled. Judd took both her hands in his. "You're going to have to teach me about your culture. You know, what happens when you're dating or engaged."

Nada laughed. "You'll catch on quickly."

Judd leaned close and kissed Nada's cheek.

"I love you," she whispered.

Saturday evening Vicki checked their e-mail and found a response from Tom Gowin in South Carolina. Tom thanked them for alerting them to the GC activity and said they would pass the word. Mark had also written saying that he had traced the name *Chris Traickin* to an apartment near Baltimore. Mark had tried the phone number repeatedly, but there was no answer and no answering machine.

Good work, Vicki wrote. *Keep trying.*

The truck rolled into the night. "How far are we from Johnson City?" Vicki said.

"We just passed Asheville," Pete said. "We could be there in an hour or two, depending on the roads. Question now is, what are you going to do once you get there?"

"Pray," Vicki said. "Pray hard."

12

VICKI and the others hit the outskirts of Johnson City, Tennessee, as the sun peeked over the mountain range. Vicki had seen trees and mountains like this in movies, but she'd never seen them this close.

"Just got another e-mail from Mark," Shelly said from the sleeper. "He found somebody who knows Traickin and left a message."

"All we can do is pray Mark gets through to him in time," Pete said.

Pete rolled into a truck stop for a quick refuel, and the kids split up to see if they could find any information about the believers in town. The restaurant was nearly empty. Vicki grabbed a stool close to an older man who sat hunched over a cup of coffee. He had long hair that hung past his eyes. Vicki leaned over to reach for a packet of sugar and tried to see his forehead, but the man didn't look at her.

"Nice morning," Vicki said.

The man sipped coffee and grunted, his hands shaking.

"You guys got those locusts around here too. We've seen them everywhere."

The man turned to Vicki and rolled up his sleeve. At the top of a tattoo of an eagle was a huge red welt. The man gritted his teeth in pain. His eyes were bloodshot, and it looked like he had been up several nights in a row.

"I'm sorry," Vicki said.

The old man turned back to his coffee, and the cook stepped from the kitchen. He wore a soiled apron and a chef's hat. He studied Vicki carefully and said, "What can I get you?"

"A cup of coffee would be great," Vicki said.

As the cook poured the coffee, Vicki said, "You haven't been stung?"

The cook shook his head.

"Why not?"

"Lucky, I guess. Why do you ask?"

Vicki leaned over the counter. "Can you pull that hat back a little?"

The cook smiled. He tipped his hat and revealed the mark of the believer. "How about something to eat? It's on the house."

Vicki moved to the end of the counter, out of earshot of the old man. "I'm looking for a group of believers that meets somewhere in town. Can you help me?"

The cook squinted and pointed toward Vicki's face. "No offense but can I make sure that's real?"

Vicki nodded and the man ran a finger across her forehead. "OK," he said, reaching out his hand. "Name's Roger Cornwell."

Vicki introduced herself and asked about the believers again.

"It's funny—about a half hour ago these two unmarked vans pulled up. Tinted windows. My boss stays inside his glass booth over there. I'm the one who goes outside since he thinks locusts don't sting people who work in the kitchen." Roger snickered.

"The people in the van were believers?" Vicki said.

Roger shook his head. "Don't think so. The driver talked to me through this little speaker mounted by the windshield. Told me to fill up the vans and slid some money through a slot by the door handle. I started to clean the windshield and get a look inside, but the guy told me not to bother. I did see a stack of guns near the side door."

"There were two vans?"

Roger nodded. "And locusts were buzzing around the things like bees to a hive."

"They were GC," Vicki said.

"That's what I thought," Roger said, "but I couldn't figure out why they were way out here. We don't have any militia—"

"It's not about the militia," Vicki said. She explained what they had learned about the GC plan.

Roger nodded and looked at his watch. "The GC must know where we meet. It's a bowling alley on the other side of town. People might already be there praying."

"Can you contact anyone and call the meeting off?" Vicki said.

Roger scowled. "We're talking hundreds of people. Some have e-mail, but mostly we pass along information at the weekly service."

"What about a phone?"

"Phone lines are down out there."

Roger scribbled directions on a napkin. Vicki grabbed it and ran to the truck.

The departure time for Judd, Lionel, and Sam was changed to late afternoon in Israel. Yitzhak drove the boys to the airport and prayed for them. Judd was surprised that Nada hadn't come, but she said she didn't like good-byes and would see Judd when he returned.

The names Pavel gave them were called over the loudspeaker, and Captain Mac McCullum met the boys in a VIP room. He was all business until the door closed and they were alone. Mac shook their hands warmly and told them what to expect once they boarded the plane.

"Our space is a little limited with all the materials we're carrying," Mac said. "The cargo hold is full, so we're putting some of the boxes of pamphlets in the main cabin."

Judd led the way onto the tarmac when the time came to board. He had never seen a plane outfitted with so much leather.

The last of the materials were being loaded as Judd

and the others were seated. "I'll call you to the cockpit once we're in the air."

The takeoff was flawless, and as Mac said, he called the boys into the cockpit after the plane reached its flying altitude. Judd and Lionel were full of questions.

Mac explained that he had taken over flying the plane from Rayford Steele. "Ray knew it was only a matter of time before the potentate had him killed. He decided to bolt during the Meeting of the Witnesses, then came back and flew Tsion and Chloe home."

"What about Buck?" Judd said.

"He's still stuck in Israel," Mac said. "And it's a shame. He needs to get home to his wife."

"That's right," Lionel said. "Chloe's having a baby soon."

"It's still a few months out, but we're working on a plan that'll get him back in time for the delivery."

"How are you getting us into the country without anyone being suspicious?" Sam said.

"Pavel's dad worked it out," Mac said. "He'll pick you up and drive you to his place. I'm off to deliver some more of the potentate's pamphlets."

Mac laughed. It was wonderful to hear someone laugh again. "I'd like to see old Nicolae's face when he finds out what his personal plane was used for."

"They know the stuff is getting out there, right?" Lionel said.

Mac nodded. "Leon and Peter the Second are furious about all the stuff that's flooding the globe. Those of us who are believers are really in a tight spot. There have been executions already."

"What?" Lionel said.

"A couple of Peter Mathews's staff mentioned something Peter thought was private. They were killed the same day. Carpathia sent Peter a note of congratulations."

Judd shook his head. "No telling what they'd do if they found out you're a believer."

"Exactly," Mac said, "and it might be soon that I have to reveal myself."

"What do you mean?" Lionel said.

"Leon doesn't think we need religion anymore since we have Nicolae to worship. He wants to pass a law that people have to bow when they come into Nicolae's presence."

"That's crazy," Lionel said.

"Just shows what kind of trouble we're in," Mac said.

"Which is why I don't understand why you'd take this kind of chance with us," Judd said.

"I argued with Pavel's father about this little joyride," Mac said, "but this one goes all the way to the top. Some people heard about his son and the condition he's in. They OK'd it so I couldn't say no."

"What condition?" Judd said.

"You didn't hear?" Mac said. "Pavel is . . . well, let's just say the disease that put him in that wheelchair is winning."

"He's going to die?" Judd said.

"I'm sorry you had to hear it from me," Mac said. "I thought you knew."

Vicki told Pete and the others what she had learned. Pete punched in the location of the meeting place and shook his head. "We're about forty-five minutes away if we take my rig."

"Roger showed us a back way," Vicki said.

"I'll get a bike," Conrad said.

Pete ran inside the truck stop and returned with Roger. Conrad rolled a motorcycle down the ramp and gassed up.

"You stick with Pete and help him navigate," Vicki said to Shelly. "We'll see who gets there first."

Vicki grabbed the directions and hopped on the back of the motorcycle with Conrad. Pete and Roger unhooked the trailer.

"What's he doing?" Vicki shouted.

"Maybe he can get there faster without that big load," Conrad said.

Vicki pointed the way as Conrad weaved through back roads. As Vicki suspected, they passed few cars. Some were parked in ditches along the main highways. Vicki guessed these were people who had been driving when the locusts attacked.

"It should be on the other side of this mountain," Conrad said as he turned onto a dirt road that seemed to go straight up.

Vicki held on tightly as they climbed the rutted road, bouncing their way to the top. The only thing more frightening than going up was coming down. Conrad rode the brakes, but it felt like Vicki's stomach was doing flip-flops.

When they neared the bottom, Conrad slowed and turned off the engine. They coasted the rest of the way and came to a stop near a paved road.

Vicki stood on the backseat and craned her neck. She saw the long, white building with a bowling pin on the front.

"Hide!" Conrad whispered. "We've got company."

Conrad pushed the cycle behind some bushes. Two white vans slowly passed and moved toward the bowling alley.

"They're going the wrong way," Vicki said.

The vans drove about a half mile and parked overlooking the bowling alley. "They're probably going to wait until everyone's inside, then spring their little trap," Conrad said.

Vicki and Conrad walked closer to the vans, making sure they kept out of sight. Locusts swarmed around the windows. Every few minutes the drivers activated a spray that sent the locusts scattering. Moments later, the locusts were back, trying to get inside.

From this spot above the valley, the GC could see every car and person who walked inside. Fifty cars lined the parking lot and more were coming every minute.

"How are they going to get all those people into custody?" Vicki said. "There's no way these two vans can hold them."

"Maybe they're bringing in buses once they bust them," Conrad said. "Or maybe they don't plan to take them into custody at all."

"What do you mean?"

Conrad looked at Vicki. "Maybe there won't be believers left alive after they're through."

Vicki shuddered. "That guy at the truck stop said he saw a stack of guns inside the vans."

120

"Come on," Conrad said, "let's cut across the field."

Vicki nodded and they made their way down the hillside.

Judd reeled at the news that his friend was going to die. *Why didn't Pavel tell me?*

Mac's information about the Global Community brought Judd back to the conversation.

"That's why those of us who are believers have to stay together and look out for each other," Mac said. "Carpathia and Leon are plotting against Mathews. I've heard the whole thing and it's ugly. It's just like Tsion said in one of his e-mails. This is not just a war between good and evil. It's also a war between evil and evil."

Lionel asked Mac how he became a believer and Mac quickly told the story. Rayford Steele had been there shortly after he had prayed.

"We're heading for some dark clouds up ahead," Mac said. "Maybe you guys had better head to the back and buckle up. We'll talk after we get through this."

Lionel opened the cockpit door and gasped. "I don't believe it. Judd, you'd better come see this."

Vicki and Conrad rushed inside and saw people sitting in chairs and even in the bowling lanes. One by one they took turns praying over the sound system. A man came up to Vicki and looked at her forehead.

"If you're a believer, you're welcome," the man

whispered, "but the meeting won't begin for another hour. We spend this time—"

"You have to get out of here," Conrad said. "The GC are onto you."

"What?"

Conrad pulled the man inside what used to be a bar. He pointed out the window. "Two vans are filled with Global Community guards. They were sent here to arrest you, or worse."

The man smiled. "Even if there were GC guards up there, the locusts would take care of them."

"They have special suits to keep the locusts out," Vicki said.

The man checked their marks again and said, "You kids aren't from around here, are you?"

Vicki sighed. "Illinois. But we're wasting time. Who's in charge?"

The man stiffened. "Listen, I know you mean well, and as I said, you're more than welcome—"

Vicki ran for the front of the building. A woman was at the microphone in the middle of her prayer. She stopped when Vicki jumped over the front desk.

"Amen," Vicki said. She looked out over the audience. People were streaming through the front door. "I'm sorry to interrupt, but you have to listen."

Vicki's heart beat furiously. "A friend of ours told us to warn you. There are two vans filled with GC guards on the hill. They're waiting—"

"That's enough!" the man with Conrad said, grabbing the microphone.

"Let her talk," another man said, stepping forward. He looked at Vicki and Conrad and asked their names. Vicki told him, then explained what Carl had told them.

People hurried for the doors. The man put a hand in the air and said, "Hold on. If those are GC, we can't leave all at once."

"What do we do, Pastor?" a young man yelled from one of the lanes.

Others echoed, "Yeah, what do we do?"

"First we're going to pray for those people in Maryland. Then we're going to ask the Lord to show us exactly what we should do."

Judd pushed Lionel aside and walked into the cabin of the airplane. A box of pamphlets was open, and a few pieces of paper littered the floor. Someone knelt to pick them up.

Judd's heart sank.

"Hi, Judd!" Nada said.

Vicki wiped away a tear as the pastor finished his prayer. A few more people entered the bowling alley and asked what was going on. The pastor asked everyone to sit.

"I don't think we have time to wait," Conrad said.

The pastor nodded. "We need to do something fast. That's true. But if we—"

The alley fell silent. Vicki shuddered at the sound outside. Rumbling. Air brakes. The noise shook the building.

"They're here," Vicki said.

13

VICKI Byrne heard rumbling outside the bowling alley and desperately wanted to make a break for the motorcycle. But she couldn't run. At least a hundred people inside needed her help.

She and Conrad had seen Global Community guards nearby. Demon locusts buzzed around the specially equipped vans. The guards inside wore protective clothing.

People whimpered and cried as the pastor tried to calm them. "No matter what happens, we trust in the Lord!"

Conrad ran to the front of the building. "I don't see anything in the parking lot!"

"They must be around back!" someone shouted.

Vicki took the microphone and explained what the kids had heard from Carl Meninger, their friend working as a Global Community Peacekeeper. "The GC has discovered where believers are meeting. They want to make examples of us and a group in Maryland."

"Are they going to kill us?" a woman said.

"We don't know," Vicki said, "but we have to get out of here."

Someone banged on a metal door in the back.

Conrad shouted, "The white vans are still on the hill."

"Then who's at the door?" Vicki said.

Someone shouted and pounded on the door again. Vicki thought she recognized the voice.

———————————

Judd Thompson Jr. couldn't believe his eyes. Lionel Washington and Sam Goldberg stood by an empty box in the airplane. Beside it stood his friend Nada.

"How did you get here?" Judd said.

Nada stared at him. "Aren't you happy to see me?"

Judd glanced at Lionel and Sam. "Of course, but—"

"I stowed away in a box of pamphlets," Nada said. "I wanted to be with you when you meet your friend in New Babylon." Nada explained how she emptied a box of pamphlets and marked it "Main Cabin."

The plane dipped and lightning flashed. The pilot, Mac McCullum, spoke through the intercom. "Better buckle up and hang on."

Nada sat by Judd. "You look angry."

"I'm not! I'm just concerned. You've put us in a bad situation."

126

"How?"

"This is Nicolae Carpathia's plane. We were only cleared for three people in New Babylon. When four of us get off, we could be in trouble. Or we could put Mac in a tight spot."

Judd explained what Mac had said about Judd's friend Pavel. Their visit had been cleared because "it's his last wish that I visit him."

"Pavel is dying?" Nada said.

Judd nodded.

"What's going to happen when we get there?"

The plane dropped suddenly and Judd felt his stomach surge.

"Sorry about that," Mac said on the intercom. "This is a rough one. Stay in your seats."

"I have to talk with you," Judd said.

Mac came on the intercom. "Wait till we get out of these clouds, Judd."

Judd looked at Nada. Could Mac hear everything they were saying? Could he also hear Nicolae Carpathia when he was on the plane?

"I'll let you know when it's safe," Mac said.

Lightning flashed again. Nada whispered something.

"What did you say?" Judd said.

Nada turned. Her eyes were red. "There's another reason I had to come with you."

"What?" Judd said.

Nada put a hand to her forehead. "I can't go home. I'm running away."

Vicki ran to the back door. Conrad and the pastor told her to stop, but she ignored them. The door wouldn't open.

"What are you doing?" Conrad shouted.

"Hang on!" Vicki said, finally opening the door.

Sunshine poured in and Vicki saw her friend Shelly. Behind her was Pete's huge truck and trailer. Pete ran to meet them.

"The GC are on the hill behind us," Vicki said.

"I saw 'em when I drove in," Pete said. "How many people you got in here?"

Vicki showed him, then started to introduce the pastor. Pete cut her off. "No time to chat. That guy back at the gas station, Roger, told me on the radio that there's a couple of huge transport vehicles headed our way."

"They're going to arrest us?" the pastor said.

"Not if I can help it," Pete said. "I'll back the truck up as close as I can to the door and you get the people in a single file. If we work fast, we can get everybody in without them knowing what's going on."

Conrad raced up. "The vans are pulling out. Coming our way."

"Nada!" Judd said. "You can't run away from your family!"

"To be with you," Nada said, "I have to."

"Wait. Back up. Start from the beginning."

Nada took a deep breath. "I told my mother you and I were getting more serious. She was excited for me. She likes you a lot. But . . ."

"Your father?"

Nada looked away. "She said he likes you as a person but doesn't think we should go further with our relationship."

Judd frowned. "He's entitled to his opinion."

"But he said if you return to Israel, we can't be together. I was afraid I'd never see you again."

Judd pulled Nada's head to his shoulder and brushed her hair with a hand. "You should call your folks and tell them—"

"No!" Nada said, jerking away. "They'll make me come back."

"They'll blame me," Judd said. "Neither of us wants that."

Nada stared at Judd. "You're scared of him! You care more about what my father thinks than you do about me."

Judd shook his head. "I just want to do this the right way. Your dad changed his mind once about me. When he sees how much I care about you, he'll change it again."

"You don't know my father," she said. "He can be so stubborn."

Judd smiled. "A family trait?"

Nada opened her mouth wide and punched Judd in the shoulder.

Vicki helped people onto the truck. Pete told them to move to the front and sit in tight rows. Some panicked and pushed their way inside.

"Where are you taking us?" an older man said.

"Away from the GC," Pete said.

Locusts buzzed at the back door but apparently flew away when they realized the occupants were believers.

Conrad returned. "Can't see the vans. Probably take them five minutes to get past the ridge."

Vicki nodded. As people hurried past she said, "Stay calm." She noticed a woman with a small electronic device. "What's that?"

"I record the meetings," the woman said. "I play it for people who can't get here."

"Can I have it?" Vicki said.

"But—"

"Trust me," Vicki said.

The woman handed over the recording and Vicki raced to the office and put it into the machine. A man's voice came through the speakers. "Before we get started, we want to let anyone who wants lead us in prayer."

"Perfect," Vicki said. She turned up the speakers full blast and found the switch for speakers outside the bowling alley.

When she reached the back door, Pete was closing the truck. "Let's get out of here."

Once the plane made it through the storm, Judd headed to the cockpit.

"How were you able to hear us?" Judd said.

Mac stared at him. "Can't tell you. Let's just say the conversations back there are relayed to the rest of the Tribulation Force."

Judd explained the situation with Nada.

"The GC let you come because of Pavel's condition," Mac said. "Carpathia has no idea the cargo hold is jammed with Ben-Judah's studies in different languages. An extra person is gonna raise a red flag."

"Why do they have to know?"

"Cargo's one thing," Mac said. "Human beings are another. If the guards notice Nada, we could be in trouble."

Judd scratched his head.

Mac said, "What kind of ID does she have?"

Judd went back and got it from Nada, then showed it to Mac. "Her brother was with the GC in New Babylon. Killed in the earthquake."

"You serious?" Mac said.

"He was a Peacekeeper in Carpathia's main complex."

Mac flipped a few switches and pulled out his cell phone. "What was her brother's name?"

Judd told him and returned to his seat.

A few minutes later, Mac called Judd and Nada forward. "I got through to one of my superiors, one of the few who hasn't been stung yet. I told him I'd located a family member of a deceased GC worker who wanted to pay her respects. They're putting you up in the main complex. Who knows, you might even get to meet Carpathia himself."

Vicki sat next to Pete as he pulled the truck out of the parking lot.

"So far so good," he said as they chugged onto the road back to town.

"What about all the cars in the parking lot?" Vicki said.

"I bet the GC will hang around and wait for people to come back."

"And then nab them," Vicki said. "Guess we just lost our motorcycle."

Pete gave a low whistle. "Up ahead."

Coming around a curve in the distance were the two vans, colored lights swirling on top. Between them was a huge bus with the Global Community insignia on the side.

"Stay calm," Pete said.

The first van passed going far over the speed limit. The wind from the bus nearly drove Pete off the road. The second van slowed and blocked the truck.

"Let me handle this," Pete said.

"I should warn the others," Vicki said. "Some of us could get away."

Pete put a hand on her shoulder.

A GC Peacekeeper stepped out of the van and was swarmed by locusts. The man slapped them away from his white protective suit and motioned for Pete to roll down his window.

Pete didn't seem nervous. "What can I do for you?"

"You just came from that bowling alley back there."

"Me and my little sister got sidetracked. Had to turn around."

"Where you headed?"

"Got a delivery in town," Pete said. "Hope we make it before the load goes bad."

The man moved back, swatting at locusts. "What kind of load—"

"Sure was a wacky bunch back there," Vicki interrupted. Pete gave her a look.

"What do you mean?" the man said.

"I heard all this preaching and hollering," Vicki said. "You need to put those people away before they hurt somebody."

The Peacekeeper looked toward the bowling alley. Vicki noticed through her outside mirror that the other van and the bus had reached the parking lot. Several officers in protective gear pointed guns toward the building.

A radio squawked from the other van. "They're here! We need backup!"

The Peacekeeper rushed back to his van and sped away.

"Good work," Pete said.

"Thanks," Vicki said. "Wonder how long it'll take them to figure out it's not a real meeting?"

"Hopefully long enough to get these people to safety."

Pete took the curves at full speed and Vicki wondered how those in the back were holding on.

"Up there!" Vicki shouted, pointing. The ramp to the highway rose in the distance. She jumped in her seat. "We've made it!"

Pete put up a hand and shook his head. A siren wailed behind them. Vicki's heart sank as she checked the mirror.

14

"FLOOR IT!" Vicki shouted.

Pete shook his head. "No way. They'll know we're up to something." He pulled to the side of the road and bowed his head. "Lord, protect us." The siren wailed behind them. "And please do it fast. Amen."

Pete opened the door and jumped down. Vicki followed close. The GC van skidded to a stop in the middle of the road and a man shouted, "Stop where you are, hands in the air!"

They both put their hands over their heads. "Something wrong?" Pete shouted.

A Peacekeeper stepped out, surrounded by locusts. He smacked at them with his gun and pointed at Vicki. "On the ground! Hands on your head."

Vicki sat in the road. The Peacekeeper trained the gun on Pete.

"What did we do?" Pete said.

Vicki studied the guard's protective white suit. On his back was an oxygen generator. A series of heavy-duty zippers connected the boots with the rest of the suit. The helmet was made of shiny plastic and latched into the collar. Locusts pinged off the face shield and swarmed near the man's legs. "Apollyon!" they screamed, but they couldn't get through.

"We counted more than a hundred people going into that bowling alley," the Peacekeeper said.

"Bowling can take your mind off your problems," Pete said.

The Peacekeeper didn't smile. "Now the place is empty. A tape was playing."

"That's what I heard?" Vicki said.

"Shut up! Open the truck!" The Peacekeeper waved toward the van and the other man, short and round, got out. The suit made him look like a snowman. He pointed his gun at Pete. A small red dot appeared on Pete's chest.

At the back of the man's protective gear Vicki noticed a zipper at the bottom of the heel. Pete frowned and walked to the trailer.

"Open it now!"

Pete unlatched the door and grabbed the handle. Just as he was about to swing it open, Vicki reached and quickly unzipped Snowman's heel. A locust immediately moved into the hole and began chewing at the inner lining, a thin layer of plastic.

Vicki scooted left and unzipped the other Peace-keeper's suit. Several locusts moved in, their hideous voices screaming.

136

Pete opened both doors, revealing the huddled mass of believers. Conrad and Shelly, near the door, squinted at the light.

An alarm sounded in Snowman's helmet. He cursed as air hissed from his leg. "Oxygen breach!"

"Your leg!" the other yelled.

The man screamed, dropped his gun, and fell in a heap.

The other Peacekeeper ran toward him as an alarm sounded in his suit. He stopped and swatted at the locusts boring through the plastic at his heel. Before he could zip his suit, he straightened, threw his arms into the air, and let out a terrifying scream. He pitched forward and smashed face first onto the pavement. Locusts swarmed.

Pete ran to the GC van, grabbed the keys, and threw them over an embankment. Vicki did the same with the guns.

"Let's get out of here," Pete said, taking something from the van.

"What about them?" Vicki said. One guard writhed, the other lay still, unconscious.

"It's already too late for them," Pete said.

Judd told Lionel and Sam what was going on as the plane neared New Babylon. At Mac's suggestion, Nada took his cell phone and called her parents in Israel.

Judd returned to the cockpit. He guessed Mac was about fifty. Mac said he was twice divorced, no kids. He had flown commercial and military planes.

"How did you become a member of the Tribulation Force?" Judd said.

"It's a long story, but briefly, I was flying with a guy who had become a believer after his wife and son disappeared. He told me his story and I believed. When I went to tell him, I saw the mark on his forehead. That was some morning."

"Where were you when the earthquake hit?"

"Right on top of Carpathia's building," Mac said. "Makes me sick to think about it. The guy actually kicked people away from the helicopter so he could save his own skin."

"So Nada's brother didn't have a chance," Judd said.

"The only ones with a prayer were the people on the roof. If her brother was inside or nearby, he was probably killed instantly. Leon Fortunato says he himself was killed in the collapse."

"Yeah, he says Carpathia raised him from the dead."

Mac snickered. "I say Leon's as big a liar as Nicolae."

He pointed out New Babylon on the horizon and a strange feeling came over Judd. It was as if they were entering a place of evil. Judd had heard and read so much about the gleaming buildings and streets second to none. After the earthquake, Nicolae Carpathia had made rebuilding the city his top priority.

As the plane neared the city, Judd was impressed by the sparkle of glass in the sunshine. Beautiful buildings rose out of the sand, each a monument celebrating the reign of Nicolae Carpathia.

Judd went back to his seat. Nada was wiping her eyes.

138

"What happened?" Judd said.

Nada laid her head on his shoulder. "They were frantic trying to find me. Yitzhak and my father had just gotten back from looking in the streets."

"What did you tell them?"

"That I didn't mean to cause trouble. I just wanted to be with you. I told my mother I was going to visit the place where Kasim died."

"Let me guess. It didn't help."

"No. And my father was so angry he could hardly talk. I told him I loved him and would see him soon. He called me an impulsive teenager." She imitated her father's voice, " 'We don't have time to play love games. A wrong move could cost our lives.' "

Nada's father was right. She was impulsive. But that appealed to Judd.

Mac landed and escorted the kids through a private entrance for GC employees. He explained that the believers working behind the scenes for the Global Community had faked locust stings.

"Are there many believers here?" Lionel said.

"Not many," Mac said, "but we're finding new ones who read Tsion Ben-Judah's Web site. We have a guy who knows computers. There's another pilot. And we hope many more new believers before we have to get out of here."

"Why wouldn't you stay?" Lionel said.

"Sooner or later Carpathia will make everybody take some form of ID right on their skin. You'll have to have it to buy or sell or move around." .

Mac told Nada to be careful. "If anyone finds out you're a believer, they'll report you in a second."

"Just keep quiet and let them go to hell?" Nada said.

Mac scratched his neck. "If you were my kids, I'd say the same thing."

Judd and the others nodded.

"How do we get back home?" Nada said.

Mac shrugged. "I doubt you'll be able to fly commercial. Let Judd work that out with this Pavel and his dad."

Mac led them through the nearly deserted airport. The locusts had hit the GC hard. An older man checked the kids' identification. Mac explained who they were, and the man eyed them carefully, then waved them through.

Vicki held on as Pete drove as fast as possible to the highway. She kept watching for the white GC vans.

Pete pulled out a tiny radio and flipped it on. "I got it from the van."

The radio squawked message after message to the downed Peacekeepers. Finally, another crew reported the mishap.

"They'll come after us now," Pete said.

He took an exit and barreled into the gas station where he had switched trailers. Pete raced inside. Vicki opened the trailer and the people tumbled out, looking dazed and disoriented.

"We thought we were goners," Shelly said.

A call came over the radio. "We're almost to the highway. They couldn't have gotten far."

Pete returned with Roger Cornwell and yelled for everyone to be quiet. "They're on their way, so we have to hide. I'm taking the truck back to the highway—"

"No!" Vicki shouted.

"It's the only way," Pete said. "Roger says there's a cave about a half a mile back in the trees behind the station."

"We know where it is," a teenage boy shouted.

"Good," Pete said. "Lead the way."

"But, Pete," Vicki pleaded.

"Trust me," Pete said. "I'll be all right."

Vicki ran with the others into the woods. She stopped at the tree line and watched Pete drive away. "Protect him," she prayed.

New Babylon gleamed in the sunlight. Mac drove near all the sights the kids had seen on television and pointed out significant buildings and landmarks. The streets were nearly deserted. Locusts were out in full force, waiting to sting anyone without the mark of the believer.

When they came to Nicolae Carpathia's office complex, Mac slowed. He told them the structure had been built on the same site as the old building that had collapsed during the great earthquake.

"This is where my brother worked," Nada said, her voice trembling.

"You'll stay in the apartment complex over there," Mac said.

"What about us?" Lionel said.

Mac stopped and opened the door for Nada. "You guys are down a few more blocks."

Judd hugged Nada. "Be careful," he said. "I want us back in Israel in one piece."

Nada smiled. "You're the one I'm worried about."

Out of the corner of his eye, Judd saw Lionel shake his head.

15

MARK Eisman struggled with his role at the schoolhouse. He wanted to follow the latest news and work on their Web site, theunderground-online.com, but with Vicki, Conrad, and Shelly gone, and no chance of Judd or Lionel returning soon, his job was holding everything together.

Lenore Barker was a big help with the daily chores, but she had to look after her baby, Tolan. Melinda and Janie, who had been stung by locusts, suffered great pain. They wailed and moaned from their room upstairs.

Mark put Darrion Stahley in charge of following the travels of Vicki and the others. She had kept in contact with the kids through South Carolina, but something went wrong as they neared Tennessee. Darrion hadn't heard anything more from them. She also monitored what was going on in Baltimore with another crackdown on believers. She kept track of incoming e-mail and watched for news from Carl Meninger at the GC outpost in Florida.

But Mark was baffled by Charlie. He was the only unbeliever who hadn't been stung. Lenore and Darrion met with Mark after dinner to talk.

"I don't know what to think," Darrion said. "If he were disabled in some way he would have been taken in the Rapture, right?"

"There must be some way to explain it," Mark said.

Lenore shook her head. "If it hadn't been for you guys, I wouldn't have escaped those things."

"Let me throw something out," Mark said. "The locusts didn't sting Tolan because he's a baby. Even though he doesn't have the mark on his forehead, God must have put some kind of protection around him."

"Okay," Darrion said.

"What if there's some kind of protection from God around Charlie?"

"But he's had every chance in the world," Darrion said. "From what Vicki said, he wants to be part of the club. He's still trying to do things to earn the mark."

Mark nodded. "But maybe he's so close that . . ." He noticed someone at the kitchen door.

"I've been trying to figure it out myself," Charlie said, walking inside. He sat slowly, a strange look on his face. "I know I deserve to get stung just like those two girls, but I didn't."

"Charlie, you've heard what Vicki and the rest of us have said about God," Darrion said. "You know the truth, right?"

"I know that if I want to get a thing on my head, I have to pray that prayer."

"Is that why you prayed?" Mark said.

Charlie looked away. "Vicki was nice to me. I wanted to be one of you guys. Nobody's ever liked me because I'm kind of weird. And I know God doesn't like me."

"Wait," Mark said, "the whole point is that God loves you. He cares about you."

"He likes you if you do good things," Charlie argued.

Mark moved closer. "We were just wondering if maybe God protected you because he knew you were close to really understanding and accepting his love."

Charlie wrinkled his brow. "Why would he do that?"

"God loved you enough to die for you," Darrion said. "Protecting you from those locusts is nothing compared to that."

Charlie closed his eyes.

Mark looked at Darrion and Lenore and whispered, "Pray."

Judd said good-bye to Mac and thanked him. "We'd never have made it here without you."

"Be careful," Mac said, "these buildings have ears. Call me if you need anything."

The kids made their way through a series of doors designed to keep the locusts out. They found the elevators and Judd punched the right floor number. The building had an atrium with exotic flowers, plants, and a huge waterfall. The only thing missing was people. Judd figured they were either cocooned in their rooms or recuperating from their stings.

"I wouldn't mind living like this," Sam said.

"I'd rather live in a tent than work for Nicolae Carpathia," Lionel said.

Judd put a finger to his lips. "Remember what Mac said about this place having ears?"

The three got off the elevator and looked for Pavel's apartment. A door opened and a man in uniform stepped out, a hat pulled low across his face. "What are you doing out without proper protection?"

"We're looking for a friend," Judd said. "His name is Pavel."

The man smiled and took off his hat. Judd sighed when he saw the mark of the true believer on his forehead.

"You must be Judd," the man said, extending his hand. "I'm Pavel's father, Anton Rudja."

Judd introduced Lionel and Sam and they went inside. "Why didn't Pavel tell me about his illness?" Judd said.

"You weren't supposed to know," Mr. Rudja said. "Pavel has the idea that he is going to be healed."

"What's wrong with him?" Lionel said.

Mr. Rudja whispered, "The doctors aren't sure. The disease weakens his muscles and bone structure. There are other diseases like it, but nothing quite like what he's going through."

"Is he able to see us?" Judd said.

Mr. Rudja smiled. "When he can speak, it is all he talks about. He has to stay in bed almost all day now."

146

Mr. Rudja explained how he had gained clearance from the Global Community for them to come to New Babylon. "My superior knows about Pavel and I told him he wanted his friend from the North American States to visit. Since he may not have much time . . ." Mr. Rudja looked away and shook his head. "I'm sorry. I promised him I would not be emotional about this."

"We understand," Judd said.

Lionel and Sam waited in the living room while Judd met with Pavel. The shades were drawn and the room was dark. Judd let his eyes focus and recognized the pictures on the wall and the furniture in the room. This was what he had seen every time Pavel hooked up with him via computer.

The boy slept, his head propped up with pillows. A piece of medical equipment stood like a soldier by the bed. It beeped every few seconds and lights blinked. Judd took the boy's hand. No response. He knelt by the bed, still holding Pavel's hand, and prayed.

"God, I thank you that you brought Pavel to yourself and that you used him to help his father know the truth. Please heal him and make him well. In Jesus' name. Amen."

Pavel squeezed Judd's hand weakly and smiled. "You made it."

"Why didn't you tell me how sick you are?" Judd said.

"Would it have changed anything?" Pavel said. "You are my friend. I knew you would come."

"You're right," Judd said.

"I have good news," Pavel said. "God is healing me."

Vicki ran behind the others thinking about the danger Pete was in. The GC would surely catch him. What then? Would they throw him in prison?

The pastor of the group worked his way back and helped Vicki. "Watch your step as we go up the side of the mountain."

The dirt path wound through trees and seemed to go straight up. People huffed and puffed as they climbed over rocks. Vicki was the last to make it to the top. The mouth of the cave could fit two people; then the passage opened into a huge cavern. Burnt wood lay in piles throughout the cave.

"This was our meeting place after the earthquake," the pastor said. "The bowling alley was more convenient for everyone so we moved there."

Shelly rushed back to Vicki, trembling. "I told them I didn't like caves. Last time I was in one of these—"

Vicki put a hand on Shelly's shoulder. "I know, the snakes. You're going to be okay."

The pastor called people together and prayed for Pete. Another prayed for Roger at the gas station.

Conrad whispered to Vicki, "The kid who led us up here says everybody's desperate for more teaching."

Vicki frowned. "There's no way I'm going to get up in front of all these people."

"You did it in South Carolina," Shelly said.

"But there weren't that many," Vicki said.

"I told the pastor what you know," Conrad said.

"You what?"

Before Conrad could respond the pastor said, "You all know how new to this I am. Well, we have someone with us who wants to encourage us." He motioned to Vicki. Vicki looked around the crowded cave.

"Come on, girl," someone said.

People clapped and the pastor called for quiet. "We don't need to make the GC's job any easier." He turned to Vicki. "The floor's yours, young lady."

Mark tried to talk with Charlie, but the boy ran from the schoolhouse.

"You want me to go get him?" Darrion said.

Lenore said, "I think that boy is starting to understand. Leave him alone."

An hour later, Mark found Charlie on the hillside near the grave of the other Morale Monitor, Felicia. His eyes were red. "I drank some of that poison water but I didn't die. That bug thing flew near me but turned around and stung Melinda. Why?"

"I don't know," Mark said, "but I think it has something to do with God loving you."

"What do you mean?"

"God wants you to be his child. He cares what happens to you."

"I want to be his son," Charlie said. "Before, I just wanted to be one of you guys."

"In the Gospel of John it says that if you believe in him and accept him, he gives you the right to become a child of God."

149

"That's what I've been trying to do," Charlie said. "I've tried really hard to do what's right so God and you guys would accept me."

Mark got down on one knee. "That's where you've made the mistake. You don't do anything to get God to accept you. If you believe you've done bad things and ask God to forgive you, he'll come into your life and change you."

Charlie opened his eyes wide. "So he'll help me do things the way he wants me to do them?"

"Yes."

"You're saying if I want to be a child of God, I don't have to do good stuff, I just believe that Jesus is God and ask him to change me?"

Mark nodded. "You want me to pray with you?"

Charlie shook his head. "No, I want to do this myself." He closed his eyes. "God, I think I understand. Thank you for protecting me from those bugs and that poison water. I don't just want that thing on my forehead. I want to be your kid.

"Forgive me for the bad stuff I've done. I believe you died for me and I believe you came alive again like Vicki said. Help me to do what you want me to do from now on. Amen."

Mark smiled. Charlie looked around the hillside and took a deep breath. He turned to Mark. "I see it! On your forehead! It looks like a cross, doesn't it?"

Charlie ran to the schoolhouse and found Lenore, then Darrion. Mark couldn't wait to talk with Vicki and tell her the news.

150

Vicki felt nervous as she spoke, but the more she saw how eager people were, the more she relaxed. She explained how she had become a believer and what Pastor Bruce Barnes had taught her. "He showed us the truth of the Bible and he lived it in front of us. He even adopted me before he died."

Vicki paused to compose herself. A few people whispered prayers. "I studied the Bible on my own and with friends, but I figured no one could ever take the place of Bruce. But not long after we lost Pastor Barnes, I met Tsion Ben-Judah."

Someone gasped. "You actually met him?"

Vicki nodded. "And the things I learned from reading his messages and hearing him speak have changed my life. This gathering here is evidence that what he's saying is true. We're in the midst of a great soul harvest when millions will come to know God personally."

A young man raised a hand. "What's going to happen next?"

Vicki took a deep breath. She didn't want to scare the people, but she knew the truth wouldn't be easy to take.

16

JUDD introduced Lionel and Sam to Pavel.

Pavel was interested in Sam's situation. "I know what it's like to have a father who doesn't believe. Don't give up."

The conversation turned to Nicolae Carpathia. Pavel glanced at a clock and said, "The television transmission I told you about is supposed to begin in about twenty minutes."

"Where is Carpathia?" Lionel said.

"From what I've heard, he and his righthand man, Leon Fortunato, are holed up in an underground bunker that keeps out the locusts."

"Any idea how many top GC people have been stung?" Sam said.

"The ten kings, or rulers as Nicolae calls them, have all been stung. So has Peter the Second."

"Serves him right," Judd muttered.

"The GC news would never report this, but my father said two of Peter the Second's staff were executed before the locusts came."

Lionel gasped. "Executed? What happened?"

"They repeated something they heard in Peter's office. Peter said the information was private and had them shot."

Lionel shook his head. "Just what you want in a religious leader."

"This will really make you sick," Pavel said. "Nicolae sent Peter a note of congratulations."

Judd sighed. "What do you expect from the most evil man on the planet?"

"The word's out that Christian literature is everywhere," Pavel said, "but no one knows how it's being transported."

"For Mac's sake, let's hope it stays that way," Judd said.

"My father also said that there's talk of requiring everyone to worship Nicolae. I hope I never live to see that. . . ." Pavel paused, realizing what he had just said.

"Come on," Judd said, "let's watch old Nicolae make a fool of himself."

The kids gathered around to watch the live broadcast. Television producers had tried to spruce up the fallout shelter, putting up backdrops and arranging furniture. Nicolae appeared to be sitting in his office, the skyline of New Babylon behind him. But there was something strange about his voice.

"Sounds boomy," Lionel said, "like he's broadcasting from my basement."

"Ladies and gentlemen of the Global Community, I bring you greetings from the greatest city on the face of the earth, New Babylon."

Nicolae turned as if he were looking out the window. As Carpathia continued, a locust flew onto his shoulder and landed. Judd moved closer to the TV to get a better look.

Nicolae gave several statistics about the positive things that had happened since he had taken over the world system. He assured viewers he was in control. Suddenly he stopped, as if he had just seen the locust on his shoulder. The locust leaned toward Nicolae's ear.

Nicolae smiled. "Yes, I know we have heard reports about poisonous bites coming from these harmless creatures. While there may be some truth to those rumors, rest assured they are exaggerated."

"It's a trick," Judd said. "That locust isn't real; it's computer generated."

Nicolae turned to the locust. "Do you think a cute little fellow like this would harm anyone? Of course not. I urge all the followers of the Global Community to put aside fear. While these beings are new to our world, there is no reason to panic or hide."

"And he's saying this from an underground bunker," Lionel said.

"In order to ease fears about the world economy," Nicolae continued, "I am personally taking charge of global commerce."

"What does that mean?" Sam said.

Pavel coughed and lay back on a pillow. "It means he can pay off his ten kings and keep them loyal."

Carpathia put up a hand to pet the locust. The camera zoomed in on his face. Judd thought of people around the world who were falling for this trick. They had believed Nicolae wanted peace. They completely trusted the Global Community to fix their problems and take care of them. They were even buying the Global Community's religion, which taught that everyone could have their own beliefs, except those who really wanted to know the God of the Bible.

"We must not let a few bugs steal our commitment to our new world," Nicolae continued. "There will be those who will say this is a sign from the heavens. We are bad people who need to be punished.

"I ask you, what kind of god would punish people for trying to do the best they can? We have survived many disasters. It is time to put aside this silly talk and move ahead.

"We hold our own destiny in our hands. Our plans of peace and rebuilding will continue. We will unite. I have plans for good for all citizens, and I will not rest until they become a reality."

The camera pulled back, showing the locust snuggling up to Carpathia's neck. "Now does this look like any kind of judgment from an angry God? We must not allow anyone, especially those who claim to speak for God, to take away our dream of unity and peace."

A telephone number and a Web site address flashed on the screen. "If you suspect someone you know may be working against the Global Community, please call this number or contact the Web site you see on your screen.

"And if you suspect someone you know follows the teachings of Rabbi Tsion Ben-Judah, contact us immediately. Even now we are working on ways to rehabilitate those who see the Global Community as a threat."

The scene faded to black and Nicolae's voice echoed. "Do not let your hearts be troubled, my friends. Trust in me."

Vicki couldn't stop thinking about Pete. If the Peacekeepers had caught him, they would try to get information. That meant she might never see Pete alive again. She looked out over the faces of her audience.

"Do you need to take a break?" the pastor said.

Vicki nodded. The pastor handed her a bottle of water and showed her a place to sit. "What you're saying is exactly what we need to hear," the man said. "I'm not a real pastor. I just know more than the others. They all voted me the leader." He extended a hand. "I'm Greg Sowers."

"How did you figure out the truth?" Vicki said.

"I read Tsion's Web site," Greg said, "and I remember a lot from when I was a kid. My parents took me to church every time the doors were open. I won ribbons and buttons, knew all the verses. Memory stuff was easy for me. I could look at a verse once and say it right back to my Sunday school teacher."

"So how'd you get left behind if you knew all of that?" Vicki said.

"Knowing verses about God doesn't make you a

believer in him," Greg said. "I fooled a lot of people. I'd live one way at school and with my friends, then clean up my act on Sundays and Wednesday nights. I even married the preacher's daughter."

"You're kidding," Vicki said.

Greg shook his head. "I used to sit with her dad and talk about the Bible till late at night. I could really talk about God, but I didn't know him."

"How did your wife find out you weren't a true Christian?"

"She never did," Greg said. "I was such a good liar. I'd come home late without an excuse and blame her for being suspicious."

"The truth never sank in?" Vicki said.

Greg put his head against the wall of the cave. "I sat through so many services. I even took notes. But it didn't mean anything until that morning."

"The morning after the disappearances?"

Greg nodded. "I told my wife I had to work overtime, but I was really out partying with some friends. I slipped into bed before sunrise and woke up late. Her nightclothes were in the bed beside me, but I didn't think anything was wrong. Then I heard the news and realized she was gone."

"That's when you prayed?" Vicki said.

Greg shook his head. "I was mad at God. Cussed him out. Then I came to my senses. I didn't have a choice. It was either ask God to forgive me or wind up following the devil's guy." Greg pointed to his forehead. "You can see what I chose."

"I'm glad you did," Vicki said.

"Now will you tell us what's next?" Greg said.

Vicki sighed. "I can, but it's not going to be easy."

Judd and the others talked about Nicolae's message. "For all their talk of tolerance, it sounds like they want to wipe out any resistance to the GC," Judd said.

Pavel nodded. "Exactly. And if they can turn citizens into GC bloodhounds to sniff out believers, what hope do we have?"

"We have this hope," Judd said. "No matter how many times Nicolae quotes the Bible as if he made it up, in the end, God wins."

Lionel held up a hand and pointed to the television. "Something's going on in Maryland. Turn up the sound."

The report showed someone under a huge cover being shoved into a GC Peacekeeper cruiser. Pavel turned up the sound.

". . . has been identified as former senator from Maryland, Chris Traickin," the news anchor said. "Traickin is suspected of subversion against the Global Community, running a religious organization that worked directly against Nicolae Carpathia and the Global Community.

"Peacekeepers equipped in special protective gear conducted the raid on Traickin's apartment and a nearby meeting place filled to capacity with followers of Rabbi Tsion Ben-Judah. It's not yet known how many others were arrested."

"I wonder how much more of that we're going to see," Judd said.

"Too much," Pavel said.

Someone handed Vicki a Bible and she read from Revelation 9. " 'Then locusts came from the smoke and descended on the earth, and they were given power to sting like scorpions. They were told not to hurt the grass or plants or trees but to attack all the people who did not have the seal of God on their foreheads. They were told not to kill them but to torture them for five months with agony like the pain of scorpion stings. In those days people will seek death but will not find it.' "

Vicki looked up. "We know this has been going on for some time. People are still being stung and a lot of them have tried to kill themselves but can't.

"Everything that's been predicted in Revelation has been right on schedule. The locusts are part of the fifth Trumpet Judgment. Now comes the sixth."

Vicki paused. People scooted closer to make sure they could hear. "I don't exactly know how it's going to work, and I don't think Dr. Ben-Judah does either, but there's going to be an army of 200 million mounted troops let loose on the earth."

"You mean people on horses," a boy said, "or could these be military machines?"

"I guess they could be machines of some sort," Vicki said, "but if the locusts were real, my guess is that these are too, only bigger."

"What do the horsemen do?" someone said.

"That's the awful part. Dr. Ben-Judah has said that only one-fourth of the people left behind at the Rapture will survive until the Glorious Appearing. But this judgment is worse than anything we've seen so far. This army is going to kill a third of everybody still left on earth."

"A third?" a woman said, trembling.

Vicki nodded. "And the Bible makes it clear that most of the people who come out of this alive will continue to reject God. They'll keep on doing the evil things they've been doing."

Greg Sowers stood. "You've heard me talk about the harvest of souls that God wants to bring during this time. Well, that time is almost up. If you have loved ones or friends who are still alive, you need to get the message to them quickly."

Conrad ran into the cave out of breath. He bent over, grabbed his side, and gasped, "Somebody's coming up the trail!"

17

VICKI pulled Conrad aside and whispered, "Do you think it's the GC?"

"I couldn't tell," Conrad said, trying to catch his breath. "I heard them and ran up here."

Groups of believers gathered to pray. A shadow appeared at the entrance to the cave. It was Roger Cornwell from the gas station. He dropped a heavy sack as Vicki rushed to him and asked about Pete.

"The GC flew past in those vans a few minutes after Pete left," Roger said. "I don't think he could have outrun them."

"Where would they take him?" Conrad said.

Greg Sowers stepped forward. "I hope you're not thinking of trying to free your friend. You'll get in trouble. Besides, we don't know if he's been caught."

"What do we do?" Vicki said.

"Wait here," Roger said. "The GC will come back and question me. I'll let you know what I find out."

Roger left as the sun was going down. Vicki, Shelly, and Conrad huddled in a corner of the cave.

"Wonder if those people in Maryland are okay?" Conrad said.

"We did all we could," Shelly said.

Vicki shook her head. "All our stuff was with Pete. If the GC get our computer, they could find out about the Young Trib Force."

"Pete's been through this before," Conrad said. "He'll be okay."

"I should have stayed with him," Vicki said.

Shelly changed the subject. "These people were sure hungry to hear what you said."

"They're starved for information," Vicki said. "Now they know what's coming."

Two teenagers tried to start a fire, but Greg made them put it out. "No fires! The GC will see the smoke."

Someone opened the sack Roger had left and found cheese, crackers, and fruit. They all ate hungrily.

"I don't know about you," Vicki said, "but I'm going to find Pete as soon as it gets dark."

"The less time I spend in one of these caves, the better," Shelly said.

"I'm in too," Conrad said.

———————————

Mark followed the news about the former senator from Maryland and was sad to see how many believers had been arrested. Mark had left a phone message at Traickin's apartment, but it hadn't helped. As he scanned articles he found on the Internet, he knew something was wrong.

After Lenore put Tolan down for the night, Mark gathered all the believers together. "If the GC had found believers in Tennessee, it would probably be all over the news," Mark said.

"What do you think they'll do with the Traickin guy?" Darrion said.

Mark flipped through some news files on the computer and shook his head. "Something's not right with that story. Before the disappearances, this guy was constantly in the news. He was against President Fitzhugh about the military. They caught him with campaign money and somehow he wiggled out of it. Then the disappearances happened and Carpathia came to power."

"What did Traickin say about that?" Darrion said.

"He supported Nicolae at the start," Mark said, "but look at this." Mark turned the screen so everyone could see the story.

Traickin Urges a Return to God

While politicians and citizens alike have fallen in love with the Secretary General of the United Nations, Nicolae Carpathia, Senator Chris Traickin has fallen in love with God.

No stranger to controversy and scandal, Traickin says he believes America and the world may be following an evil man.

"We have the Pied Piper from Romania here," Traickin said in an interview from his home in Maryland. "This guy is not a friend of God-fearing Americans."

"Well, he was sure right about that," Darrion said.

"Now look at this," Mark said, clicking on another news story. "A week before that story ran, Traickin had a meeting with Carpathia. Then, after World War III breaks out, his name shows up in connection with the militia uprising."

"So the guy who fought Fitzhugh about the military winds up being part of the militia?" Darrion said.

"Yeah, and you know what happened to the militia," Mark said.

"It got toasted by GC troops," Darrion said.

"Right," Mark said. "A few months later, Traickin shows up in another story that says he reads Tsion Ben-Judah every day and he's looking for people who want to stand up against the Global Community."

"I don't get it," Darrion said.

Charlie sat forward. "You think this guy is working for Carpathia?"

"Bingo," Mark said. "Buck Williams talked about Nicolae's mind-control tricks. What if he got to Traickin?"

"You mean he ratted on the militia and now he's working against believers?" Darrion said.

"Right," Mark said.

"How do you know you're right?" Lenore said.

"Does the way Traickin talks sound like any believers

you know?" Mark said. "I think this guy was setting a trap and he succeeded."

"Then why did the GC take him off in handcuffs?" Lenore said.

"It's part of the act," Mark said.

Lenore sighed. "I don't know whether I ought to be praying for that guy or praying against him."

Charlie stood and walked toward the stairs. "Do you guys smell that?"

"What?" Mark said.

Something dripped from the ceiling. Charlie touched a drop and sniffed it. "Gasoline!"

Mark looked at Darrion and the others. "Janie and Melinda!"

Mark took the stairs three at a time and burst into Janie's room. The girl turned a gas can in her hands. She threw it but Mark ducked. Melinda lay on her bed, dazed. The room smelled like a gas station.

"What are you doing?" Mark shouted.

Janie opened a box of matches. "I'm going to end this, and there's nothing you can do to stop me!"

Judd awoke early the next morning to the phone ringing. Mr. Rudja said, "It's for you."

Judd staggered to the phone. It was Nada. "I thought Mac made it clear we shouldn't—"

"I have to see you," Nada said. "It's urgent."

"My friend is dying," Judd said. "I can't just run out on him."

"Please," Nada said. "I can't talk on the phone. There's a park a few blocks from you. Meet me there in a half hour."

Vicki tried to sleep but couldn't. Greg Sowers found her. "We could sure use someone like you around here if you thought you could stay."

"I have to find out what happened to Pete," Vicki said, "then we need to get back to Illinois."

"I understand," Greg said, "but I want you to know we'll make a place for you and your friends to stay for as long as you'd like."

After dark, Vicki, Conrad, and Shelly slipped out, one by one, and met near a grove of pine trees on the hillside. The sky was overcast and the wind had picked up.

"Wish we had a flashlight," Shelly said after she tripped and nearly fell.

"Stay close to me," Conrad said. "I know the way."

When they made it to the bottom, Conrad led them through a field toward the gas station. The kids saw the hazy glare of lights in the distance.

They slipped through the tall grass and hid in the shadows of the station. Conrad peeked around the corner, then quickly returned. "One of those GC vans is in front."

A few minutes later the van pulled away and the kids rushed into the station. Roger Cornwell sat behind a cash register staring out the window.

"Did they catch Pete?" Vicki said.

Roger turned and glared at them. "Where are the other believers?"

"Still at the cave," Vicki said. "What about Pete?"

Roger looked away.

"Tell us!" Shelly said.

"Pete's dead," Roger said. "The truck plunged into a ravine."

"But—"

"It caught fire," Roger said. "No one could have survived that. The GC think all those believers died too. Pete bought us some time. They'll be back in the morning to inspect the wreckage, so we have to get those people out of the cave tonight."

Vicki sat down hard. They had lost one of their best friends. How would they get back home? And when the GC discovered an empty trailer, what would happen then?

"I'll go with you," Conrad said to Roger. He put a hand on Vicki's shoulder. "You and Shelly stay here."

Vicki nodded. She felt numb. It was going to be a long night.

Mark couldn't believe how thin Janie and Melinda had become in such a short time. The kids had given them meals but the girls didn't eat much. "You're out of your mind!" Mark yelled. "You want this whole place to go up?"

"Yeah," Janie said, "I'm going to prove you wrong. I *can* kill myself."

"You won't," Mark said, taking a step closer.

"You want to go up with us?" Janie said, holding a match next to the box.

"Okay," Mark said, backing away. "Let me get everybody out of the house first. The baby's asleep downstairs."

"Okay," Janie said, pulling the match away, "but you'd better not try anything."

Mark yelled for everyone to get out. Lenore ran for Tolan. When Mark was sure everyone was outside he turned to Janie. "I know you think this is the answer to your troubles, but I've been reading reports of people jumping off tall buildings, cutting their wrists, everything you can imagine. Not one of them has died, and you won't either."

"Have any of them tried to burn themselves?" Janie said.

Mark shook his head. "No, but—"

"I don't care whether it works or not," Janie said. "I want the pain to stop!"

"That's what I'm telling you," Mark said. "The pain of the locust sting isn't going away, no matter what you do. If you try this, you'll burn yourself and the school."

"That's what you care about, isn't it?" Janie said. "Your precious hideout."

"No," Mark said. He noticed Melinda shaking uncontrollably. "At least let her out before you do this."

Janie looked at Melinda. "You want to go? Then get out of here."

"Maybe Mark's right," Melinda said, standing. "This might just make things worse for us."

As Melinda passed Janie, Mark darted behind her and

170

lunged at the matches. Janie jerked away and Mark fell to the floor.

"Not fast enough, are you?" Janie said, holding the matches over her head. "Now you're going up with me."

As she struck the match, Charlie bolted through the door and tossed a bucket of water on Janie, dousing the matches. Janie screamed and cursed at him, then tried in vain to strike another match.

Mark wrestled Janie to the floor and dragged her down the stairs. They would need to keep a tight watch on her in the future.

Vicki and Shelly huddled behind a counter in the truck stop. They were glad Roger had locked the front door and turned out most of the lights.

"I can't believe Pete's really gone," Vicki said. She looked at the phone on the counter. "We have to call and tell the others."

Vicki reached for the phone. Someone moved at the front door and Vicki hit the floor. She pointed toward the door and Shelly peeked over the counter. "I don't see anything."

Vicki grabbed Shelly and pulled her down just as a GC radio squawked.

18

VICKI'S heart beat wildly. She expected a storm of GC Peacekeepers breaking into the station. Instead, someone pecked lightly on the front window.

"What in the world?" Vicki muttered, peeking around the cash register. A big man stood near the door.

"Pete!" Vicki screamed. She rushed to the door and unlocked it. "We thought you were dead!"

Pete hugged Vicki and Shelly. "They're going to have to try a lot harder than that to kill old Pete."

"What happened?" Shelly said.

"I knew those GC would be right behind me and I remembered a ravine just up the road. No guardrail or anything. I slowed down until I saw the vans in my mirrors. I wanted to draw them away from the gas station until you guys could get to the hills."

"It worked," Vicki said, "but how did you get out?"

"I put it in neutral and let the thing go," Pete said,

showing them his scratched-up arms. "Jumped out on the
passenger side and rolled into a thicket.

"The GC were all over the place, scurrying around,
dodging the locusts, and trying to see the truck. Fortunately it caught fire and—"

Pete was cut off by a transmission on the tiny radio he
had taken from one of the Peacekeepers. "We'll head back
to the gas station and set up a lookout there," a man said.

"Where's Roger?" Pete said.

"He went to get everybody out of the cave," Vicki said.

"He can't bring them back here," Pete said. "We have
to stop them."

———————————

Judd tried to leave Pavel's apartment quietly, but Mr.
Rudja stopped him. "Where are you going?"

"I have to meet a friend at the park," Judd said.

"Sit," Mr. Rudja said. The man poured a cup of coffee
and leaned against the kitchen counter. "My son does not
have much longer to live. The doctors are amazed he has
held out this long."

"I'm really sorry about—"

The man held up a hand. "I realize you took a great
risk coming here, but we also have taken a great risk
bringing you. One slip, one mistake could mean being
found out by the Global Community."

"I understand," Judd said. "I looked in on Pavel. He's
resting."

"Who is it you're meeting?"

"A girl."

The man smiled. "Ah, even in the middle of the end of the world our hearts can be stirred. . . ."

Judd chuckled nervously. "I guess, sir."

"The park is a ten-minute walk," he said, pointing out the window. "If you're not back in an hour, I'll send someone—"

"I'll be back," Judd said.

The streets were nearly deserted. Every road seemed to sparkle. Glass buildings reflected the sunlight.

The park looked like Judd's idea of the Garden of Eden. There were immense trees imported from various countries. Vines, ivy, and moss hung from branches and grew on rock walls. Ponds were stocked with exotic fish from every part of the world. Colored gravel filled a jogging path that passed a lush, green field. He spotted Nada at a bench and ran to greet her.

Nada stood and hugged Judd, then gave him a kiss on the cheek. "Thank you for coming. I didn't know what to do."

Judd sat. "What's up?"

"I was questioned by a woman from the Global Community as soon as I went inside. She wanted to know why I hadn't been stung, why my family hadn't responded to the letter the potentate sent about my brother's death, all kinds of things."

"What did you tell her?"

"I was creative," Nada said with a smile, "but it's the girl I'm rooming with that has me stumped. She's loyal to Carpathia, but she's asking questions about God."

"Might be a trap."

"Her name is Kweesa Darjonelle," Nada said. "She knew my brother. I think they dated. He told her things that made her think he wasn't completely loyal to the GC."

Judd sat up. "You mean, he may have been a believer?"

"I don't know. Before he died, Kasim told me Carpathia wasn't all he said he was. I never even thought he might have believed."

"What did this Kweesa want to know?"

"She kept probing, asking what my brother was like at home, what my parents believed about Carpathia. That made me nervous."

"It should," Judd said.

"Then she handed me this." Nada pulled out a tiny computer from her handbag. "Kasim left it at her apartment the night before the earthquake."

Judd opened the computer.

"It doesn't work," Nada said. "Kweesa said there's something wrong with the power supply."

"There may be a clue in here," Judd said. "Why hasn't Kweesa been stung?"

"She hasn't gone out of her building. There's an underground tunnel from her apartment to her office."

"The GC are smarter than we think."

"She asked me this morning if I knew anything about Tsion Ben-Judah," Nada said.

"What did you tell her?"

"I didn't know what to say. I kept thinking maybe this is someone I need to tell the truth to. She seems sincere."

"But if they link you to me, and me to Pavel and his dad . . ." Judd looked around. He couldn't expose Pavel and his father.

"I wasn't followed," Nada said. She took a breath. "I think I'm going to tell her the truth."

"I admire your faith," Judd said, "but don't talk yet. Wait and see what else she asks."

Judd glanced at a nearby building and saw two GC Peacekeepers with binoculars. One pressed his hand to an earpiece.

"Gotta go," Judd said. "I'll look this computer over and get back with you soon."

"Wait!" Nada said, but Judd was already on the jogging path, heading back to Pavel's apartment.

Vicki tried to keep up with Pete as they ran through the night. They found Roger leading a group down the hill. When Roger saw Pete, he nearly fainted. Pete told him the news and said, "You have to get back there."

"What are you going to do?" Roger said.

"Our truck's gone. We'll have to hide until we can find some new wheels."

An older woman stepped forward. "I have a pretty big house with a barn behind it. I can take at least half of you all in."

Several others chimed in and volunteered to keep people who lived too far away to walk home.

"As soon as I locate another truck," Roger said, "I'll get in touch with you."

"Good," Pete said.

Vicki and a few others followed the woman through a valley and up another ridge. "My place is just on the other side of this mountain," the woman said.

The sun was almost up when they arrived, and Vicki was exhausted.

About twenty people crowded into the woman's kitchen as she started breakfast and assigned rooms. Conrad went to the barn with a few teenage boys. Vicki and Shelly said they were too tired to eat and made their way to a musty, downstairs room with bunk beds. Vicki sneezed and pulled the covers over her head. Finally, she fell asleep.

The gasoline smell was so strong that Mark and the others at the schoolhouse were forced to sleep outside. Charlie kept an eye on Janie and Melinda.

The next morning the kids got to work hosing down the upstairs room. The kids voted to put Janie and Melinda downstairs where they wouldn't be able to harm themselves or anyone else.

Darrion helped Charlie and Lenore study the Bible. The kids prayed for Vicki, Judd, and the others and asked God to protect them from the Global Community. Charlie prayed, "Please bring Vicki back so she can see I've finally understood what you did for me."

Over the next few days, Judd watched Pavel's health grow worse. The boy had trouble breathing and could hardly sit up. Judd tried to start the computer Nada had given him but couldn't. Pavel asked to look at it. His skin was pale and his fingers thin as he turned the machine over.

"Looks like the solar panel," Pavel said. "It's not getting power." He showed Judd where to hook up a regular power supply. Within a few minutes the computer was working.

As Judd inspected different files, he noticed the daily entries of Nada's brother. "This is almost like a diary," Judd said. He read a few entries to Pavel.

" 'I've been assigned duty at the potentate's headquarters tomorrow,' " the boy wrote in an early entry. " 'I finally get to see things up close.*' "

Judd was puzzled. "I wonder what that asterisk means. There's a bunch of them throughout the entries."

"Let me see," Pavel said. He raised his head and clicked through the file. "There are notes embedded in the text. Something he doesn't want anyone to see." He fiddled with the tiny keyboard and a screen popped up. "It's asking for a password. Four letters."

"What could be in those secret files?" Judd said.

Pavel shook his head and typed several words, then letters and numbers. He tried combinations using letters from the words *Global Community*, but each time the computer denied access.

"Sometimes people will use their own initials or birthdays or names of people they're close to," Pavel said. "Makes it easy to remember. What's this guy's name?"

"Kasim," Judd said. "I don't know his middle name."

Pavel typed more words but came up with nothing.

179

"Wait," Judd said, "his sister is Nada. Try that."

Pavel typed in her name and the computer whirred. "Bingo!"

The document revealed nearly one hundred pages of single-spaced notes Kasim had written. Pavel scrolled down and Judd read over his shoulder.

"Nada came to the training camp today and embarrassed me," Kasim wrote. "She's just as committed to her beliefs as I am to Nicolae Carpathia. I hope she'll see that she's wrong about him."

"Can you find anything else about Nada in there?" Judd said.

Pavel did a word search and came up with several more sections with Nada's name. "Here, read it to me."

Judd took the computer. " 'Talked with Nada today about the facilities here. There is so much luxury and wealth. My room is like a palace compared to back home. Why can't my family see the truth?' "

Judd skipped to the last few pages of notes. " 'I talked with Nada tonight about seeing Leon Fortunato in the hallway of the building. It's exciting anytime I see someone famous, but I can't tell Nada what's really going on in my heart.' "

Judd scrolled up and found passages that talked about Kasim's feelings for Kweesa. Kasim mentioned another friend named Dan. " 'Dan seems to know what's going to happen before it does. He thinks there's a big earthquake coming sometime soon. I've asked how he knows all this and he's been pretty cagey.' "

The next entry talked about Dan wanting to meet with Kasim after they finished work the next day.

"What happened with that?" Pavel said.

Judd scrolled down and found the answer. " 'It was like talking to my family,' " Kasim wrote. " 'Dan believes everything they do. I tried talking some sense into him, but he wouldn't budge. He gave me a Bible but I refused. I don't know what to do. He's working for the potentate but is totally against him. I am betraying what I believe by not exposing him, but I haven't exposed my family either. What should I do?' "

Pavel put his head back. "I'd like to hear more, but I'm so tired."

"It's okay," Judd said. "Rest. I'll tell you how it ends when you wake up."

Vicki awoke sneezing and red eyed. She wandered upstairs around midday and found an old computer. She tried to check e-mail but couldn't.

The woman who owned the house came into the kitchen. "I don't know anything about that thing. It's my son's. He ran off a few days before the locusts came and I haven't heard from him since."

"Is he a believer?" Vicki said.

The woman wiped sweat from her face with a paper towel. "I tried to talk with him time and again. As far as I know, he's not one of us."

Vicki kept working with the computer as she listened to the woman's story. She had gone to church since she was a girl and had taken her children as well. "I always heard that going to church doesn't make you a Christian any more than walking into a garage makes you a car. I guess they were right."

Pete came into the room. "That computer's no good. I tried to get a message to the co-op but I couldn't get through. It's something with the phone lines."

"Then there's no way to get in touch with Carl or Mark," Vicki said, "or those people in Maryland."

Pete shook his head. "Local radio reported they arrested a bunch of people, including that former senator."

Vicki plopped into a chair. "The GC is getting tighter, and we're stuck."

"Yeah, we're stuck," Pete said, "but on the positive side, you've got a lot of people to teach. That pastor came by about an hour ago and asked if you'd talk to people tonight."

"If we meet, we might get caught," Vicki said.

Pete smiled. "When has that ever stopped us?"

19

JUDD stayed with Pavel while doctors monitored the boy's condition from remote computers. It was clear that Pavel was getting worse. While Judd waited, he read page after page of Kasim's diary. Kasim mentioned Kweesa often and wrote about missing his family in Israel as well. *Nada's parents would love to see the files*, Judd thought.

The most interesting sections detailed the turmoil Kasim experienced when he wrote about Dan. "The more I see of the Global Community and the way they treat people," Kasim wrote, "the more confused I get. They talk about tolerance, then threaten people if they visit the Ben-Judah Web site.

"I saw pictures of the two aides Peter had executed. This guy is supposed to be the head of the one world religion. If that's the kind of religion the GC wants us to follow, I can't do it.

"Every day I think about what my family believes. If

they're right, I'm working for the devil. But how could that be? Nicolae Carpathia is doing so many good things."

Kasim went back and forth with his arguments. On one page he listed the positives of both belief systems.

Global Community	My Parents' Beliefs
Nicolae Carpathia is god.	God is supreme.
Every religion has a bit of truth.	There is only one way to God.
Religion is a set of rules to follow.	You can know God personally.
Plagues are bad.	Plagues are to get our attention.
Morality is up to each person.	Truth is based on what God says.

"I want to believe what the Global Community stands for," Kasim wrote, "but something tells me my parents are right."

Judd found the entry for the night before the earthquake and read it over and over. He checked Pavel's condition and phoned Nada. "I need to see you right away."

Vicki met with members of the Johnson City underground church in the musty basement. Shelly and Conrad helped her move a mountain of canning jars and dusty boxes to make room.

About twenty people crammed into the tight space. Some sat on the floor. Others brought chairs. These people were hungry for any kind of teaching.

Vicki went over the same information she had taught Carl Meninger when he was at the schoolhouse. She referred to the notes Lenore had typed for her, but as she went over the Scriptures, she found herself relying less on notes. Things Tsion Ben-Judah had said or written came back to her, and the people were amazed such a young woman could teach so well.

Pete slipped in after the meeting and reported the latest from Roger. "As far as we can tell, the GC are gone."

"Why would they leave?" Vicki said.

"They came to the station and made a big show about pulling out," Pete said. "I guess they looked at the truck and were satisfied."

"They didn't find any bodies," Conrad said. "I'll bet they're hiding somewhere waiting for the believers to come back for their cars."

"We'll stay here another day to make sure," Pete said. "I've got a line on another truck we can use. Our supplies from Florida are still in the parking lot of the gas station."

Vicki tried to sleep, but the dust and mildew were too much for her. After dark, she found Shelly and they walked to the backyard. They found two rickety chairs and sat near an outdoor fireplace. Vicki breathed in the cool, mountain air. An owl hooted in the distance.

"Until I met Judd," Vicki said, "I'd never lived in anything bigger than a trailer." She looked at the tree-lined mountainside and sighed. "All this space is incredible."

Shelly suggested they get some covers and try sleeping outside. Suddenly, someone cried in the distance.

"What was that?" Shelly said.

"I don't know," Vicki said, "but it didn't sound like an animal. It sounded human."

Crickets chirped and frogs croaked from a nearby pond. Vicki finally turned to go inside and heard the cry again.

Shelly pointed. "It's coming from up there."

Vicki headed up the hill. Shelly protested but finally tagged along. The two quietly made their way in the moonlight. They cautiously walked around a small pond and followed a narrow creek bed. The trees were thick and several times Vicki had to retrace her steps and go around them.

Finally, they reached a clearing and climbed through a barbed-wire fence. In the distance, a small cabin was built into the side of the hill.

"I don't like this," Shelly said. "Let's go back."

A light flickered inside. "There's somebody in there," Vicki said. "Maybe they're hurt."

"And there might be a bear or something waiting to jump out at us!"

Vicki shook her head and climbed the side of a smooth rock to the top of the ridge. The cabin was made of small logs. The holes had been filled in with mud, but the glow of a lantern shone through.

Someone inside let out a piercing scream that echoed

through the valley. "Please," Shelly whispered, "let's get out of here."

"I have to see who's in there," Vicki said.

The door to the cabin burst open and someone stood in the shadows with a gun. "Who's out there?" the man shouted.

"It's okay," Vicki shouted back. "We're friends of the woman in the house at the bottom of the hill."

"You better come inside, or those stingin' bugs'll bite you."

Vicki took Shelly's hand and the two walked into the cabin. The man was thin with a scraggly beard. He wore a dirty baseball cap pulled low. The man's eyes were red and there were beer bottles strewn about the cabin. He motioned for them to sit by the fire that burned in a pit in the middle of the room.

"You were stung, weren't you?" Vicki said.

The man pulled a blanket over his shoulders. He leaned against the wall and propped his head against a log. "What are you doing at my mother's house?"

Judd slipped into the back pew of the Enigma Babylon One World Cathedral, not far from Pavel's apartment. The church was a monument to every religion except Judaism and Christianity. There were statues of gods and goddesses, pictures of people on their knees before pieces of wood and stone, and framed speeches of Nicolae Carpathia. Since the attack of locusts, all services had been canceled, but the building was open to anyone. Huge

stone archways stood a hundred feet above Judd's head.
Inscriptions were written on pillars throughout the sanctu-
ary. The first said, "One world, one faith." Another simply
said, "Tolerance." Still another read, "Strive for unity."

Each seat had its own interactive screen and headphones. He slipped the headphones on and watched a
recording of a recent service. As the "Veneration Leader"
sang and read "holy texts," Judd followed the words as
they flashed on the screen. He scrolled through the
service and found a message by Pontifex Maximus Peter
Mathews. Several times during the message people were
asked to give an opinion on a religious question by
touching the screen.

"How can a person find the true way to spirituality
and inner peace?" Pontifex Mathews said. "*(a)* by following a list of rules and regulations, *(b)* by following someone who says there is only one way to God, or *(c)* by
following your own beliefs and letting your heart be your
guide."

The audience had unanimously chosen "c." As he
scrolled through the rest of the message, Nada slipped in
beside him. "How is Pavel?" she whispered.

Judd frowned. "He's getting worse."

"Why did you want to meet here?" Nada said.

"I think we were being watched at the park." Judd
handed Nada a printout of some of the pages from
Kasim's hidden journal. "There may be a chance Kasim
became a believer before the earthquake."

Nada was obviously moved by the words of her
brother. She scanned the pages.

188

Judd finally took them from her and said, "There's only one person who could know whether your brother became a believer before he died. It's this guy, Dan."

"Maybe Kweesa knows him," Nada said.

"For all we know, he could have died in the earthquake, but we have to find out. If you can take home proof that your brother became a believer, your dad won't be so mad at you."

"I'll go right now," Nada said.

Nada rushed out and Judd continued scrolling through the sermon archives. The last recording was made the day of the locust attack. Judd clicked it and up popped the video of Pontifex Maximus Peter Mathews at the podium. He was in his full outfit, complete with the huge hat and long robes. Judd couldn't resist. He turned the sound up and put on the headphones.

"Some in our world have the mistaken notion that we are wrong," Peter said. "They believe in an angry, mean-spirited god who would punish people. I ask you, is this the kind of god you want?"

Peter waited as people locked in their responses. A number flashed on the screen and the man smiled. "One hundred percent of you agree that god is not like that."

Judd noticed a humming in the background. As it grew louder, he realized what was coming.

Peter threw his arms open wide. "God is here right now with you and me." He placed his hands over his heart. "God is in us! We are god!"

Someone screamed in the back of the church. Peter tried to calm the people, but off camera the droning of wings and shrill voices of locusts overtook the congregation.

Peter stepped from behind the podium and the camera panned the frantic crowd. The locusts attacked people at will, stinging them and sending them to the floor.

"Don't panic!" Peter screamed. The camera focused on him just as several locusts flew his way. He screamed and threw his hat at the beasts, cursing. He pulled his thick robes over his head and fell.

A locust found the exposed flesh of Peter's leg. Judd hadn't seen such a vivid picture of a person being stung before. The camera zoomed in as the beast threw its head back and bared its fangs. It sent the demonic venom deep into the bloodstream of the thrashing Pontifex Maximus. The camera swiveled wildly and the transmission went dead.

———————————

Vicki introduced herself and the man said his name was Omer. He had been bitten when the locusts had first come. He was in great pain, but it seemed to be getting a little better.

"My mother was on me every day about religion," he said. "I knew I had to get away or I'd go crazy. I went to stay with a friend and started drinking. His dad threw me out, so I bought some booze and came up here."

As Vicki's eyes grew accustomed to the dim light, she saw piles of bottles stacked around the room. "Does drinking make it less painful?"

190

Omer shook his head. "I can't even get drunk. I try but it doesn't have the same effect."

"What do you think of your mom's religion now?" Shelly said.

Omer frowned. "I just want to be left alone. Is that so much to ask?"

"Your mom is worried," Vicki said. "You should let her know where you are."

"She'd be up here with a bunch of you people trying to get me to change my mind."

Vicki sighed. She wanted to talk with Omer about God, but he wasn't ready. "Your mom says that's your computer in the kitchen. Are you any good with it?"

"It's about all I am good at," Omer said.

"I'm trying to get a message to some friends but I can't hook up," Vicki said. "Can you help?"

Omer scratched his beard. "If you don't tell anybody about me, I'll meet you at the back door tomorrow night."

Judd grew concerned when Nada didn't return. Had she asked Kweesa too many questions? Maybe the GC was onto her.

He found a phone and called the apartment. A woman answered on the third ring.

"Kweesa?" Judd said.

"You must be Judd," the woman said. "Nada told me you might call. Something terrible has happened."

"What's wrong?"

"Nada came a few minutes ago and asked a lot of questions about Kasim's friend Dan. I told her everything I knew, but I don't think I should have."

"Why?"

"Dan was arrested a few weeks ago," Kweesa said. "He's in a GC prison."

"Arrested for what?" Judd said.

"Subversion," Kweesa said. "I don't know what he did, but Nada is in real danger."

"Where is she?" Judd yelled.

"She's gone to the prison to see him!"

20

JUDD couldn't believe Nada had gone to a GC prison, but since Kweesa wasn't a believer, he tried to act calm. "Why are you upset with Nada?"

"First of all, she took my car keys and ran out," Kweesa said. "She's going to get stung. And second, if she does make it to the prison, this Dan guy is off-limits. He must have done something really bad and the guards might think she's mixed up with him."

"She's grieving her brother," Judd said. "She wants information. Won't they understand?"

Kweesa paused. "I don't think so."

"I'll try to stop her," Judd said. He asked directions to the prison and ran into the street to hail a cab, but there were none. When he reached Pavel's apartment, he found the elevators were out of service. Judd raced to the stairs.

Mr. Rudja put up a hand when Judd rushed into the room. "Quiet. The doctors are doing more tests on Pavel."

Judd caught his breath and quickly explained the situation. "Will the GC let her in to talk with him?"

Pavel's father groaned and shut his eyes. "Daniel Nieters is a restricted case. Only a few people know the charges against him."

"What did he do?" Judd said.

"He's a believer. He spoke with someone in Leon Fortunato's office about God and the person turned him in."

"Wouldn't the GC want to make an example of him in public?"

"Fortunately, Leon was embarrassed that a Judah-ite was working for them. I think he kept it quiet from the potentate for a while. They put Dan away and made the information classified."

"So there's no way they're going to let her talk to him," Judd said.

Mr. Rudja picked up the phone. "Dan is in isolation so he can't talk with anyone, but security will detain and question anyone who asks for him."

While Mr. Rudja talked on the phone, Judd checked on Pavel. Lionel and Sam sat quietly in the room as a doctor examined him from a remote location.

"Have you ever seen anything like that?" Lionel whispered as the probe scanned Pavel's body. "House calls without leaving the hospital."

Lionel and Sam joined Judd in the next room. Judd explained what he had discovered on Kasim's computer and where Nada had gone.

Lionel rolled his eyes. "More trouble. I thought Mac told her to play it safe."

"I can understand why she's excited," Sam said. "If I thought a relative of mine might have become a believer before he died, I'd want to know."

"Yeah," Lionel said, "but find out in heaven. Don't risk your life and everybody else's."

Pavel gave a cry and his father hurried into the room. As he passed, he handed Judd a set of car keys and said, "Wait here a moment."

"I'm going with you," Lionel said.

"Me too," Sam said.

Judd convinced Sam to stay and help. Mr. Rudja walked slowly out of the bedroom. He rubbed his face with both hands and sat heavily on the couch. "Take the car and go to the prison. I've explained to the warden how emotional the girl is and he's agreed to let her talk with Dan. They'll keep her in the waiting room until you get there."

"How'd you manage that?" Judd said.

"It was more an order than a request," Mr. Rudja said. "Tell her all conversations are recorded. Be extremely careful about what you say."

Judd nodded. "Is something else wrong?"

"It's Pavel. The report is not good. He might not be with us much longer."

Judd's heart sank. He wanted to know more, but Mr. Rudja pushed him toward the door. "Hurry to the prison and bring Nada back safely. I'll tell you about Pavel when you return."

Lionel agreed to ride with Judd and return Mr. Rudja's car. Judd was in a daze as they drove to the prison.

"I have to tell you," Lionel said, "I don't like the way this is working."

"I didn't ask Nada to come," Judd said.

"Didn't say you did. But you're encouraging her. She's talking about marriage."

"So?"

"It's crazy! You're not ready for that."

"Let's talk later," Judd said. "I have to get Nada out of there and try to get back to Pavel."

Lionel stared out the window.

"What?" Judd said.

"When you want to shut people down you always say you want to talk later."

A sign pointed the way to the prison. Judd expected an imposing building on the outskirts of town with razor wire and guards every ten feet. Instead, the building was stately, with a sprawling lawn surrounded by a stone wall. It wasn't until he pulled up to the entrance that he noticed the electronic sensors inside the compound.

Judd got out. "You'll be okay?"

"Yeah," Lionel said as he drove away.

Judd walked to the front gate and said his name into a speaker. A man told him to come to the parking garage and follow signs for building "B."

Judd walked through a series of secured doors. A guard met him and looked surprised that Judd hadn't been stung. The deputy warden shook hands with Judd and showed him to a waiting room where Nada sat alone. When she saw Judd, she stood and hugged him.

196

The deputy warden gave them a few instructions. "We'll call you when the prisoner is ready."

"I'm sorry I didn't come back for you," Nada said after the man left. "When I found out where Dan was, I—"

"It's all right," Judd said. "I understand."

Judd put his face close to Nada's ear and whispered, "Don't say anything you wouldn't want Nicolae Carpathia himself to hear. Mr. Rudja says we'll be monitored in every room. We have to be careful with Dan or we could all wind up in this place."

Nada stepped back, a look of horror on her face. "I've done it again, haven't I?"

Judd leaned close. "Play up your emotions. We've convinced them you're here to find out about your brother and that you're ticked at Dan for trying to lead him astray."

Nada immediately burst into tears. She put her head on Judd's chest and said, "Why did he have to die?"

Judd played along. "It's been a long time since the earthquake. You need to move on."

"Oh yeah? Did you have a family member die in the quake?"

"No."

"Then don't tell me to move on! I miss him. I want to know what happened. They never found his body!"

Nada collapsed into a chair and Judd sat beside her. "Good stuff," he whispered. "Keep it up."

"If they're listening to us, how are we going to talk to Dan?" Nada whispered.

"We just let him talk," Judd said.

The deputy warden returned and escorted them into a small room with a table and three chairs. There were two huge mirrors on each side of the room.

Moments later the door opened and a man in shackles shuffled in. He looked to be in his twenties and wore handcuffs around his wrists. His face was swollen and bruised. Though the man's face was discolored, Judd could still see the mark of the believer plainly on his forehead.

The man sat and leaned back in his chair. When he saw Judd and Nada's marks, he smiled. The guard left and closed the door.

"Who are you?" the man barked.

Judd leaned forward. "Are you Dan Nieters?"

"You know who I am—now what do you want?" Dan said.

Judd was glad Dan was speaking gruffly. He surely had no idea who they were and what they wanted, but if he kept this act up, they might make it out okay.

Nada leaned forward and shouted, "You knew my brother! Kasim!"

Dan caught his breath and shifted in his chair. "Yeah, I knew him. We worked security. He was in the Administration Building when it came down. I'm sorry for your loss."

Nada chose her words carefully. "My brother was devoted to the Global Community. You tried to take him away with your foolish ideas, didn't you?!"

Dan squirmed in his seat. He looked like he was searching for the right words.

"My family didn't get to say good-bye," Nada said. "Were you with him before he died?"

Dan stared at them. Finally, he said, "Jesus is Lord."

"Don't give us that!" Judd said.

"'God so loved the world that he gave his only Son. . . .'"

Someone moved in the next room. Dan glanced at a mirror. The door to the room burst open and a guard grabbed Dan and pulled him to his feet.

"I tell you the same thing the angel said to the women who came to the tomb!" Dan shouted. "Matthew 7:7!"

The guard pulled Dan from the room and slammed the door. Nada put her head on the table. A few moments later the door opened and the deputy warden joined them. He held up his hands in disgust. "I'm sorry you had to hear that. You can see what we have to deal with."

Nada sobbed. "Why did he speak that way? Why couldn't he tell me something?"

"This man is a religious zealot," the deputy warden said. "I knew he wouldn't cooperate, but I understand you had to try."

When they were in the car, Nada said, "What do you think Dan meant?"

Judd put a finger to his lips. He drove through the gate and a few minutes later pulled to the curb and stopped. Judd searched under the seats and throughout the car. "I want to make sure they didn't plant some kind of listening device. He was definitely trying to send us a message, but he knew we'd be in big trouble if we just talked."

"I don't get it," Nada said. "Was he saying Kasim became a believer?"

"I'm not sure," Judd said.

Judd took Nada to Pavel's apartment and told the others what had happened. Mr. Rudja had called the prison shortly after Judd and Nada left. "You did well. They don't suspect anything."

Judd repeated exactly what Dan had said.

Lionel grabbed a Bible and opened to the book of Matthew. "Let's assume he was trying to tell you something and the 'Jesus is Lord' was him getting the GC's attention off of you.

"The second part is from John 3:16," Lionel continued. "It's probably the most famous verse in the Bible."

"Do you think that means Kasim became a believer?" Nada said.

"It's a good guess," Judd said, "but maybe there's more."

"Yeah," Lionel said as he flipped pages, "the next part is about what the angel said to the women at the tomb."

Lionel searched passages in all four Gospels and concluded that Dan had to be talking about Luke 24. The kids gathered around and read the passage.

"But very early on Sunday morning the women came to the tomb, taking the spices they had prepared. They found that the stone covering the entrance had been rolled aside. So they went in, but they couldn't find the body of the Lord Jesus. They were puzzled, trying to think what could have happened to it. Suddenly, two men appeared to them, clothed in dazzling robes. The women were terrified and bowed low before them. Then the men asked, 'Why are you looking in a tomb for someone who is alive? He isn't here! He has risen from the dead!' "

Nada smiled. "That's it! Dan was telling us that though Kasim died in the earthquake, he's alive spiritually. He must have believed!"

"Maybe," Judd said, "but Dan could have come right out and said that and not endangered us."

"Maybe the answer is in the last verse Dan gave you," Lionel said. He opened the Bible to Matthew 7:7.

" 'Keep on asking, and you will be given what you ask for. Keep on looking, and you will find. Keep on knocking, and the door will be opened.' "

"I know he's telling us that Kasim became a believer!" Nada said.

An alarm rang in Pavel's room. Judd ran to the boy's side and found Mr. Rudja on his knees by the bed. Doctors in the monitor barked orders.

Pavel's face was ashen. His pulse was weak and erratic. Suddenly, the line went flat and the machine sounded a piercing beep.

"Do something!" Judd yelled.

21

WHILE Shelly kept watch for anyone moving around the house, Vicki met Omer at the back door. He looked around the kitchen nervously. "You sure my mom didn't put you up to this?"

Vicki shook her head and whispered, "I didn't tell her anything. Everybody's asleep except for our friend Pete. He's at the gas station."

Omer sat in front of the screen and entered a few codes.

"Where did you learn to type that fast?" Vicki said.

"Just because I'm from Tennessee doesn't mean I'm stupid," Omer said.

"I didn't mean it that way," Vicki said.

Omer winced in pain from the locust bite and pointed to the screen. "I put a block in here on the satellite phone."

"You have a satphone?" Vicki said.

"One of the toys I was into back when the disappearances happened," Omer said. He changed some codes and tried to dial. "Who are you trying to reach?" Omer said.

"Some friends in Illinois," Vicki said. "We haven't had contact with them since—"

The back door opened and Pete walked in, out of breath. Vicki introduced Omer, who stood to leave.

"Stay where you are," Pete said to Omer. He looked at Vicki and Shelly. "You'll be glad to know our new rig is lined up. We can head out tomorrow morning."

Omer continued working, determined to fix the problem. He grabbed a screwdriver and took the back off the computer. As he tinkered with the inside, Vicki saw someone out of the corner of her eye.

"O?"

Omer turned. "Mom."

The woman, in her bathrobe, hugged her son and wept. "I didn't know if I'd ever see you again."

Omer looked at the floor.

"It's okay," his mother said. "What's important is that you're back."

"I'm not staying."

The woman looked stunned. She glanced at Vicki and Shelly. "I must look a mess. Let me get you all something to eat."

"I'm not hungry," Omer said. "I'm just going to get this computer going for these girls; then I'm leaving."

Vicki and Shelly turned to leave.

"Don't go," Omer said. "I'm going to hook you up with your friends."

Judd and the others stayed outside Pavel's room as the doctors gave instructions to Mr. Rudja. Judd wanted to run for a doctor or get some medicine. All he could do was wait.

A few minutes later, Pavel's father walked slowly out of the room.

"Is he . . . ?" Judd said, but he couldn't finish the sentence.

"The doctors have him stabilized," Mr. Rudja said, "but he's unconscious."

Nada put a hand to her mouth. "Oh no!"

"He may come out of it," Mr. Rudja said, "or he could slip into a coma. They're sending a helicopter to take him to the hospital."

Judd felt guilty for not spending more time with Pavel. He had been so concerned about Nada and finding out about her brother that he hadn't been there for Pavel.

Mr. Rudja put a hand on Judd's shoulder. "Would you mind staying with him while I prepare for the transport?"

"Sure," Judd said.

The man paused. "You coming here has been a great gift to Pavel."

"I could have done more," Judd said.

Mr. Rudja shook his head. "You may still have a chance."

Late at night Mark watched for news coming from the Global Community about Johnson City, Tennessee. *No news is good news*, he thought. Several times Mark had written Vicki but there was no answer. He tried contacting Pete in the truck but got a recorded message.

Charlie joined Mark and the two scanned the latest news stories. Mark was amazed at how much Charlie had changed since understanding the message and becoming a true believer. He seemed more confident.

A bulletin from the East Coast GC headquarters in Baltimore popped up on the screen. A picture of Chris Traickin accompanied the flash. Underneath the photo was the word *Escaped.*

"Former Senator Chris Traickin, arrested for subversive activities with a group of religious rebels near Baltimore, attacked two Global Community Peacekeepers and escaped early today in a specially equipped GC van. The suspect is considered armed and dangerous.

"Officials say Traickin overpowered two Peacekeepers who were transporting him to a different holding facility.

"Anyone who sees Traickin is urged to avoid confrontation and phone Global Community officials immediately," the report said.

"Wow," Charlie said, "that's great!"

Mark frowned. "It's not right."

"What do you mean?" Charlie said. "He got away from the GC! That's good, isn't it?"

Mark turned to Charlie. "Think about it. He got loose this morning and they're reporting it now?"

"Maybe they just found out."

"If he'd really overpowered two Peacekeepers *and* stolen a van, it would have been all over the news as soon as it happened. Doesn't make sense."

"You think they let him loose? Why would they do that?"

Mark shook his head.

"Isn't there a chance that you're wrong?" Charlie said. "Maybe this guy is a true believer—"

"The whole Traickin thing stinks," Mark said. He turned back to the keyboard and quickly typed an e-mail. "Maybe Carl can find out what's going on."

Charlie sat back. He scrunched his eyebrows.

"What?" Mark said.

"I feel like we need to pray for Vicki."

While Omer worked on the computer, Vicki asked his mother to step into the next room. "I know this isn't really any of my business, but I think Omer just needs to be left alone for a while."

The woman turned. "How could you possibly know what's best for my boy?"

"He talked to us about what happened to him after the Rapture," Vicki said. "I think he's coming around to the truth."

"If he would have realized the truth sooner, he wouldn't have been stung by those locusts," the woman whispered.

"I know," Vicki said, "but if you keep after him, you're going to drive him away. I think deep down he knows what you're saying is true, but he has to accept it for himself. I'm afraid he's going to hide again."

"Where?" the woman said.

"I promised I wouldn't say," Vicki said.

The woman looked away. "I've heard him out there in the middle of the night. He must live like an animal." She turned to Vicki. "Do you know the story of that guy in the Old Testament who went crazy and lived out in the wild?"

Vicki shrugged. "Don't think I've read that one yet."

"He had a really long name. He wouldn't give God the credit he deserved, so God made him eat grass like a cow. He went crazy and I think that's what's happening now. God's trying to get my son's attention one more time. I just don't want him to miss it."

Vicki nodded. "He knows the truth. It's up to him."

The woman nodded and went back to the kitchen. Omer didn't look up from his work. His mother put a plate near the keyboard and leaned close. "You're welcome to stay here anytime you like. I'm praying for you, and I still love you."

With that, she kissed her son on the forehead and went back to her room. Omer didn't turn around until she had closed the door. He glanced at Vicki. "She does make a pretty mean ham sandwich. Just wish I felt hungry enough to enjoy it."

Vicki smiled. "Any progress?"

Omer took a bite of the sandwich. "Get some sleep. If I figure it out, I'll wake you."

Vicki thanked him and headed down the hall.

"And, Vicki," Omer said, "thanks."

Judd sat by Pavel's bed as Sam and Lionel helped get things ready for the helicopter flight. Judd picked up Pavel's lifeless hand and squeezed it. He hung his head and prayed silently for the boy.

God, I don't know why you would allow something like this to happen. I guess there are some things I'll never under-stand until I get to heaven. You must have some kind of purpose for putting Pavel through this. I pray you'd help the doctors figure out what to do. Help his dad . . .

Judd finished his prayer and turned to the computer. In Pavel's e-mail were scores of messages from people around the world who had written about the gospel. As Judd read further, it became clear. Pavel had led many people to the truth about God. Pavel had hardly any strength, but what he had he used for God.

Someone moved behind Judd. It was Pavel.

"Thought you could read my mail while I was out of it, huh?" Pavel said weakly.

"Let me get your father," Judd said. "The helicopter will be here soon."

"Wait," Pavel said. "I want to talk."

Pavel closed his eyes and motioned Judd closer. He spoke just above a whisper. "I dreamed last night that I saw my mother in heaven." The boy smiled. "We ran together and laughed." Pavel's eyes filled with tears. "Remember when I said God was going to heal me?"

Judd nodded.

"It's true. He's going to give me the ultimate healing. He's going to take me home."

"You're going to be okay," Judd said. "Just rest."

Pavel leaned forward. "The message from Dan. The sayings from the Bible."

"You heard us talking about that?"

"Sure, I heard everything. I just couldn't respond."

"What do you think it means?" Judd said.

"I think Dan was trying to tell you something more. Find out where Dan lives. Go there."

"That would almost be suicide, wouldn't it?"

"Perhaps," Pavel said, "but there is a reason Dan spoke in a riddle. Ask. Look. Knock."

Judd nodded. He noticed Mr. Rudja in the next room and called for him.

"There's one more thing," Pavel said. "God is going to heal me soon."

"Yeah," Judd said.

Pavel smiled as his father hugged him and whispered something to the boy. Judd slipped out of the room and left them alone. The helicopter came a few minutes later and carried him away.

Vicki and the others were ready to leave the next morning, but Omer was still working on the computer. His mother sipped coffee at the kitchen table.

"I thought I had it a few minutes ago," Omer said.

Vicki put a hand on his shoulder. "We're headed home. We'll get in touch with our friends on the way."

Omer looked up and winced in pain. "Once I get it in my head to fix something, I can't hardly stop."

Vicki typed a message to Mark and the others back at the schoolhouse. "If you do get through, send this to them."

Omer promised and walked them outside. He showed Pete a shortcut to the gas station through a wooded area. Omer turned to Vicki. "I've been thinking about all the stuff you told me about God."

"You mean the stuff I tried to tell you," Vicki said, smiling.

"Yeah. Well, maybe when I feel better I'll give it another shot."

"I hope you will," Vicki said, "but don't wait."

Omer nodded. "I'll keep trying to hook up with your friends."

Vicki looked back as they walked into the woods. Omer stood on the front porch, waving.

22

AT THE schoolhouse, Mark continued his work on the kids' Web site, theunderground-online.com. More and more young people wrote each day with questions and messages of encouragement. Mark took Tsion Ben-Judah's latest e-mails and helped kids understand them. Even adults who had written said they had been helped by the site.

Vicki hadn't checked in, but Mark hoped she was okay. He was excited to find a message from Tom and Luke Gowin in South Carolina. They thanked Vicki and the others for their teaching.

We all feel like we're better able to stay out of the GC's way and spread the message, Tom wrote.

Another message caught his eye. Mr. Stein wrote the kids from Africa. *God is doing wonderful things here. I can't wait to see you all in person so I can explain. As soon as I can travel to Israel or back home, I'll let you know.*

While he was reading, an urgent message came from Carl Meninger in Florida. Mark hooked up the video-conferencing feature and seconds later saw Carl. He was in his room at the GC compound in Florida. Carl looked tired.

"Everything okay?" Mark said.

"I worked all night and you're not going to believe what I found out," Carl said.

Carl explained that two GC Peacekeepers were stung by locusts in Tennessee. "The guys could hardly talk, but they said a red-haired girl and a big truck driver were responsible."

"Vicki and Pete!" Mark said.

"All the believers got away," Carl said.

"Are the Peacekeepers still looking for them?"

"I talked with one guy involved in Tennessee this morning. He said they're waiting for some kind of secret operation, but he doesn't know what it is. He told me they're going to get these people just like they did in Baltimore."

"I read about that," Mark said.

"Here's the weird part. You know that former senator you asked me about?"

"Traickin?" Mark said.

"Right. Well, it turns out the guy's a fake. Somehow he got hooked up with a group of believers and he got them arrested."

"How could he fake his mark and escape the locusts?"

"You got me," Carl said. "And one more thing—"

"Let me guess," Mark interrupted. "The story about him escaping is fake too."

"Right. And if there's one imposter working for the GC, there have to be others."

"Which means we have to warn people about the possibility of moles like Traickin," Mark said.

"Put it on your Web site and do everything you can to get the word out," Carl said. "As time goes on and the effect of the locust stings wear off, the GC will arrest anyone who sides with Dr. Ben-Judah."

"Which means you being inside the GC is even more important," Mark said, "and even more dangerous. Any other believers down there?"

"Haven't seen any," Carl said. "One day they'll ask me to bow down to Carpathia's picture or some statue and I'll have to get out. But for now, think of me as your eyes and ears inside the belly of the beast."

Vicki followed Pete and Shelly as they hiked through the woods. Conrad was last in line. He told Vicki what he had learned about the Tennessee believers.

"I'd say about nine out of ten people I talked with had gone to church before the disappearances," Conrad said. "Some of them were even regular attenders."

"Why didn't they believe?" Vicki said.

Conrad shrugged. "I guess you have to do more than just show up. God offers a gift, but you still have to receive it."

Conrad asked Vicki about Omer. Vicki explained how they had met and what had kept him from believing. "Some people are stubborn. Others have pet sins they

215

don't want to give up. But I think a lot of people have never seen anyone have a real relationship with God."

Pete stopped at the top of a knoll and asked the kids to be quiet. He pointed to a red truck hitched to a trailer. "That has all our supplies from Florida. I'm going to see if Roger will let us leave it here to feed the believers in Johnson City."

"You think the GC is still around?" Conrad said.

Pete nodded. "One of the kids rode to the bowling alley and said there's at least one van still there."

"I wish we could get our motorcycle back," Vicki said.

"If that's the biggest sacrifice we make, I'll be happy," Pete said.

Shelly said, "Why do you think they held back? They could have sent out search parties and questioned people."

"Roger said they stopped by his place a couple of times," Pete said. "But you're right; it doesn't make sense."

Pete led them to a back entrance of the gas station. As usual, only a handful of people were in the diner. Pete found Roger and discussed the food shipment. Roger said they would organize a group to come during the night and transfer the food to the cave and a few nearby houses.

"You're fueled up and ready to go," Roger said.

Vicki hugged the man and thanked him. "I hope we get back here again."

"Me too," Roger said. "You guys saved us. And everyone's said good things about your teaching. We can't thank you enough."

Roger handed Vicki a paper bag. "You'll find some goodies for your trip in the sack. God bless you."

Pete told the kids to stay inside while he unhooked the trailer. He pulled it close to the trail that led to the cave and parked.

As Vicki and the others said one last good-bye, Pete hurried inside. His face was pale.

"What is it?" Conrad said.

Pete pointed toward the highway. Exiting the ramp and heading straight for the gas station was a white GC van.

Judd urged Nada to phone her parents and explain what they had discovered about Kasim. Her mother and father were still upset with her but glad to hear the news.

Judd arranged to take Nada back to Kweesa's apartment but didn't tell her about Pavel's hunch. He didn't want to upset her.

Judd knew Lionel and Sam were not only upset about Pavel's condition, but also restless. Lionel had thrown out hints about going back to Illinois.

Judd and Nada made it through the tight security and anti-locust gauntlet at the apartment complex. Kweesa met them by the elevators and shook Judd's hand.

Kweesa was tall with long, braided hair. She spoke with a heavy African accent and wore her Global Community uniform. She took them to her apartment and asked about the meeting with Dan Nieters.

Nada told her about the prison. "It was actually pretty

disappointing. Dan started ranting and raving about God and they took him away."

Kweesa shook her head. "I've heard those people can act crazy. After all Nicolae Carpathia has done, to say he is anything but God is insanity, right?"

Judd bit his lip. "When the GC found out about Dan, did they go through his apartment?"

Kweesa nodded. "I think they searched it."

"Anything turn up?" Judd said.

"Not that I heard," Kweesa said. "Why?"

"Just a hunch," Judd said. "I figure a guy like that probably wouldn't work alone. Is his apartment still empty?"

"I'm not sure," Kweesa said. She went into another room to find a directory of GC personnel.

"What are you doing?" Nada whispered.

"Just covering the bases," Judd said. "I want to make sure we don't miss any clues."

Kweesa returned, flipping through the directory. "Here it is. He lived in this building, only three floors below me."

Vicki froze. They were so close to leaving and now this.

"Let's get out of here," Conrad said.

Pete shook his head. "They'll nab us for sure. Better play it cool."

The kids split up and sat in different booths in the diner. Pete hid in the office and let Roger answer the GC's questions. Instead of refueling, the van parked so it blocked the front door.

This doesn't look good, Vicki thought.

Locusts swarmed around the van. A man in white protective gear got out of the driver's side and carefully stepped inside the station.

Vicki sat at the last booth, her back to the door. The man squeezed through the door without letting any locusts in.

"What can I do for you?" Roger said from behind the counter.

The man spoke through a speaker inside the helmet. "Are there any GC Peacekeepers here?"

"Looks like you're the only one, pal," Roger said. "You and whoever's in that van out front."

"I'm alone," the man said. "I'm looking for somebody."

"Okay," Roger said. "Can't say I know everybody around here. Who are you looking for?"

"Followers of Tsion Ben-Judah," the Peacekeeper said. "I'm looking for believers in Jesus Christ."

Judd said good-bye to Nada and Kweesa and took the stairs three floors down. Dan's apartment was at the end of a hallway. He approached carefully, trying not to make noise.

Judd found the apartment and stood outside. Even if someone new lived there now, Dan might have left a clue about Kasim the GC had overlooked. A couple dressed in GC uniforms opened a door behind him.

The man looked at Judd. "Can I help you?"

"Somebody told me this was the place where Dan Nieters lived," Judd said.

"It was," the man said. "You a friend?"

"Don't know the guy," Judd said, "just heard he was one of those religious fanatics."

"Yeah," the man said, "a shame too. Dan was a hard worker. He could have done a lot of good if he hadn't been brainwashed."

"Does anybody live here now?" Judd said.

"Haven't assigned it yet." The man squinted at Judd. "How did you get in here?"

Judd cleared his throat. "I dropped off a friend upstairs. Just thought I'd stop and see where the crazy guy lived."

Judd was glad when the man and his wife turned to leave. *I'd better get out of here fast.* The woman glanced at him and Judd turned back to Dan's apartment. What he saw took his breath away. The peephole in the apartment was dark. When Judd turned, it was light again.

Someone's in Dan's apartment! Judd thought.

Vicki gasped. She glanced back just as the Peacekeeper unlatched his helmet. Oxygen hissed as it escaped the airtight suit.

"You're looking for those crazy people who think God's behind all that's happening?" Roger said.

The man nodded and took off his helmet. On his forehead was the mark of the true believer.

"I don't believe it!" Roger said. "You're one of us."

The man smiled. Pete came out from the office and called the others. The man in the white suit shook hands and hugged everyone. "I sure am glad to see some of my own kind."

"You don't know how glad we are to see you," Pete said, introducing himself. "We've been hiding out since those two Peacekeepers got stung."

"So you're the one who was driving the truck?" the man said.

"You bet," Pete said, putting an arm around Vicki. "Me and my little accomplice, Vicki."

The man smiled at Vicki and put out a hand. "Pleased to meet you, Vicki. I'm Chris Traickin."

23

"**YOU'RE** the former senator!" Vicki said. "We tried to warn you about the GC, but we got stuck here."

"I heard on the news that you escaped," Pete said. "How did you do it?"

Chris Traickin shook his head. "Everybody talks about the Global Community having the best and brightest, but I don't see it. Two Peacekeepers were transferring me and I knocked them both out. I changed into this outfit and took the van."

"How did you know to come here?" Conrad said.

"I heard the GC talking about a group of Ben-Judah followers in this area," Traickin said. "I listened to the radio and followed their signals. Finding you guys was just blind luck."

Conrad checked out the GC suit. "What happened to your friends in Baltimore?"

Traickin pursed his lips. "We were headed for a meeting. I stopped at my apartment and heard a phone message from someone saying I'd better get out of there."

"That was Mark!" Shelly said. "He's back in Illinois at the school—"

Conrad interrupted. "If you knew the GC was going to crack down, how did you get caught?"

"I rushed to the meeting to warn my friends," Traickin said. "Before I could get everybody out, the GC showed up in full force."

Traickin explained that the GC had separated him from the others when they recognized who he was. "They took me to a different jail to question me."

"What are you going to do now?" Pete said.

Traickin frowned. "Hadn't really planned anything more than finding some other believers and trying to stay away from the GC. I guess I'm on their most-wanted list now."

Conrad muttered something. While Pete and Roger talked more with Traickin, Vicki pulled Conrad aside. "What's the matter with you? Why are you being so cold?"

Conrad leaned close to Vicki and whispered, "Something's not right with this guy."

"Are you kidding?" Vicki said. "He's a hero."

"I don't know," Conrad said. "The way he got away from the GC, the fact that he has one of their vans and they haven't found him, the way he said luck brought him to us. How did he know Pete drove the truck?"

"He probably heard it on the radio," Vicki said. She couldn't believe Conrad was so suspicious of their new friend. "What about the mark on his forehead?"

Conrad shook his head. "I don't know."

Vicki rolled her eyes. "I don't believe this. If he's not one of us, why hasn't he been stung by a locust?"

"How long you think he's had that suit on?" Conrad said.

Vicki walked away. Conrad called after her but she joined the others.

"It's settled," Pete said.

"What's settled?" Vicki said.

Pete put his arm around Traickin. "We're taking our friend back with us to Illinois."

Judd met with Lionel and Sam when he returned to Pavel's apartment. They hadn't heard from Mr. Rudja about Pavel's condition.

Lionel shook his head when Judd told him about the mysterious person in Dan's apartment. "You're lucky you got out of there without being arrested."

"You think it was GC?" Judd said.

"Who else?" Lionel said. "They've probably planted somebody to watch the place."

Sam cleared his throat. "I know we're waiting on news from Pavel, but do you have any idea when we're leaving?"

Judd looked at Lionel.

"We've been talking," Lionel said. "I don't think it's

good for Sam to go back to Israel. I want to take him to the schoolhouse."

"That's a long way from home," Judd said to Sam.

"When I became a believer in Christ, my home changed," Sam said. "It's been wonderful being with other believers. I've studied and learned a lot from Lionel since we've been here. But the longer we stay, the more anxious I am to leave New Babylon."

"Me too," Lionel said. "I don't know what that means for you and Nada."

Judd put his head in his hands. He knew he had to make a decision soon. Would he start a new life with Nada or return to the States?

Before he could speak, the phone rang. It was Mr. Rudja at the hospital.

"How is he?" Judd said.

Pavel's father could hardly speak. At last he whispered, "My son is finally free of pain. He is with his mother now. And he is with God."

If Conrad hadn't told her his suspicions, Vicki would have been elated. Transporting Chris Traickin to Illinois and helping him escape the GC would encourage all believers. But Vicki couldn't get Conrad's words out of her mind. She stared at the mark on Traickin's forehead. Was it her imagination or was there something strange about it? And there seemed to be more locusts swarming around the windows of the gas station since he had arrived.

Vicki wanted to talk with Pete, but the more she

thought, the sillier she felt. What would she do, ask to inspect the former senator's mark? Open the door and ask him to run around outside without protective clothing?

Pete suggested they get rid of the GC van. Roger knew about an old barn a few miles into the hills where they could stash it. "Who knows, the thing might come in handy one of these days," Roger said.

While Roger drove the van away, Pete and the others waited.

Conrad whispered to Vicki, "I'm going to expose this guy."

Judd phoned Nada with the news of Pavel's death. She wept and asked to meet with him. "Kweesa isn't here, and I don't want to be alone."

"I understand," Judd said. He suggested they meet outside the GC building so Judd wouldn't have to go through security.

Lionel spoke up. "You think we should get out of here soon?"

"Mr Rudja can arrange for us to stay," Judd said. "Let's wait until after the funeral and figure out our next move."

Lionel hesitated.

"What?" Judd said.

"I've been checking possible flights," Lionel said. "Chloe Williams gave me the names of some pilots who have signed on with the believers' co-op."

"What are you saying?" Judd said.

"If I can arrange a flight back to the States, I'm going ahead. You can come if you want."

Judd felt his face flush with anger. "Can't you wait until we bury my friend? Don't you even care?"

Lionel sighed. "I know this is a rough time to bring it up. This may be our best shot."

"Fine," Judd said. "Make your plans."

Judd briskly walked into a beautiful New Babylon sunset. The buildings glistened with light. The sight was stunning. But with the death of his friend and an uncertain future, it was more than he could bear. Judd stopped and tears rolled down his cheeks.

He met Nada at the corner of the building and they walked across a plaza and found a bench behind a row of shrubs. Nada put her head on Judd's shoulder. "I'm so sorry."

"It's just beginning to sink in," Judd said. "I know he's in a better place, but it went so fast."

"You can be happy you were part of the reason he's in such a good place," Nada said. "You were the one who told him about God."

"It was one of the best things that's happened to me since the vanishings," Judd said.

As they sat together, Judd spilled everything. He told her Lionel's plan to return to Illinois with Sam, Pavel's words to Judd the last time he had seen him, and what Judd had seen outside Dan Nieters' door.

Nada pulled away. "We have to go to Dan's apartment."

"Lionel thinks it's a trap," Judd said.

"Perhaps," Nada said. "But maybe someone's there who knew Kasim. We could find out for sure about his decision."

Judd tried to talk her out of it, but Nada said she would go alone if he didn't come with her.

"All right," Judd said, "let's go."

Vicki grabbed Conrad's arm. "What are you going to do?"

"Watch," Conrad said.

Vicki followed him into the office. Pete was in the middle of a sentence but stopped. "What?"

Conrad looked closely at Traickin's forehead, then stepped back. "I know you used to be a senator, but I've got my doubts about you being one of us."

"Conrad!" Pete shouted.

Chris Traickin held up a hand. "It's okay. I don't blame you for being suspicious."

Pete was enraged. "How can you think . . . ?"

"I have my reasons," Conrad said, "and the first is that mark on your forehead. There's something weird about it."

"Looks the same to me," Pete said, leaning forward.

"What do you see on my forehead?" Conrad said.

The man squinted in the dimly lit room. "The same thing I see on everybody else, a cross."

"When did you first see yours?"

Traickin smiled. "I've never seen my own. Not even in a mirror. But I suppose it looks like yours."

"This will stop right now!" Pete said.

Before Conrad could say anything, Traickin held up a hand. "You're probably wondering about this suit I'm wearing too."

Conrad nodded. "Let's see you take it off and take one step ouside."

"That's enough!" Pete shouted.

Traickin stopped Pete again. "It's a fair question. Two answers. Number one, I think it would be better for all of us if I wear this protective gear."

"So you won't get stung," Conrad said.

"No, in case we get stopped by the GC," Traickin said, "I might be able to bluff my way around them in this costume."

"What's the second reason?" Conrad said.

"It's kind of embarrassing," Traickin said.

"Humor me."

Traickin smiled. "Ever since I was a kid, I've had this fear of bugs. Maybe a spider crawled on me when I was little, I don't know. When I first got a look at those locusts, I was terrified. Even though I'm a believer, even though I'm an adult, I'm scared. I've stayed inside most of the time. I just can't stand the thought of having one of those things touch me."

Conrad stared at the man. After an awkward silence, Traickin sighed. He unsnapped and unzipped his protective suit.

"What are you doing?" Pete said.

"It's obvious there's only one way to prove I'm the real thing. I'm going to take this off and head outside for a little chat with those slimy—"

230

"No, you're not," Pete said. "This is ridiculous. You're one of us and that's that."

Conrad turned away. Traickin put a hand on his shoulder. "Look at me."

Conrad turned.

"I believe in God," Traickin said. "My wife disappeared and I searched for answers. I found them on Tsion Ben-Judah's Web site. I asked God to forgive me and I gave him my life."

Pete stood and hugged the man. "That's enough for me." He looked at Conrad. "Are you satisfied?"

Conrad glanced at Traickin, then walked away.

Traickin looked at Vicki. "You believe me, don't you?"

Vicki smiled. "Of course. Conrad's been through a lot." Pete grabbed more supplies and headed for the truck. "We'll leave as soon as Roger gets back."

Judd and Nada rode the elevator and found Dan Nieters' apartment. They stood in the shadows by a stairwell and waited.

"Maybe I could get some tools and we could pick the lock," Nada suggested.

"They'll hear us. Does Kweesa have an extra uniform?"

"A bunch."

"What if we find something to deliver? A letter or a package?"

"And I could dress as a GC worker and get a look at whoever's in there," Nada interrupted.

"I was thinking I would go."

231

Nada smirked. "You wouldn't look good in her uniform."

Judd watched the hallway while Nada went to Kweesa's room to change. She returned a few minutes later with a small package under her arm. "How do I look?"

"Pants are a little long, but I'd hire you," Judd said. "What's in the package?"

"One of the GC handbooks autographed by Nicolae Carpathia himself."

"You're kidding!" Judd said.

Nada smirked again. "Just signing the name made me feel powerful."

"I'll wait here," Judd said. "Promise you'll do what we agreed. Put the package on the floor, knock, and get out of there."

"Why are we doing this if I can't talk with them about my brother?" Nada said.

"Let's see who opens the door. And remember to put the package in the hall so the person has to step out to get it."

Nada kissed Judd on the cheek. "Just let us Global Community workers do our job, okay?"

Nada straightened her uniform and walked down the corridor. She slowed when she came to the apartment and put her ear to the door.

Come on, Judd thought, *just knock and get out of there.*

Nada placed the package on the floor a couple of feet from the door.

Good job.

Nada knocked lightly and put her eye to the peep-hole.

"Nada," Judd whispered, "get out of there!"

She put a finger to her lips and pointed toward the door. "I think somebody's coming."

Judd's heart beat faster. The elevator dinged. A man and woman got off the elevator and headed down another corridor.

A lock clicked. Judd glanced at Nada. She picked up the package as the door opened. "Someone at the front asked me to deliver this," Nada said.

Her voice trailed as she straightened and looked at the person. Judd strained to see but couldn't.

Suddenly, Nada cried out and crumpled to the floor. Judd rushed to her. A man stepped out and said, "Help me get her inside."

Judd dropped to the floor to help Nada but she was out cold. He stole a glance to see what had shocked her.

24

JUDD couldn't believe his eyes. The man in the apartment had a dark beard and a mustache. On his forehead
was the mark of the true believer.

The man picked Nada up and hurried inside. Judd
closed the door and looked through the peephole. "I
don't think anybody saw us."

"Good," the man said, placing Nada on a couch in
the living room.

The apartment was dark. Blinds were drawn, and a
flickering light came from a computer screen down the
hall.

"She's out cold," the man said, putting a hand to
Nada's face. "I hope she didn't hit her head." He hurried
into the kitchen and brought ice in a plastic bag. He lifted
Nada's head and gently placed the ice underneath. "Are
you her boyfriend?"

"I guess you could say that," Judd said.

"What do you mean, you guess?"

"Yes, I'm her boyfriend. What's your problem?"

The man gritted his teeth. "If you really cared about her, you wouldn't have brought her here." He brushed hair from Nada's face and knelt beside her. "She should have stayed in Israel."

"How did you know she was from Israel?"

Nada stirred. The man propped her head on his lap and whispered something in her ear. Finally, Nada opened her eyes.

"Is it really you?" Nada said. She reached out and touched the man's face.

"You're not dreaming," the man said softly.

She pushed his hair away, revealing the mark of the true believer. Nada hugged him.

Judd paced. *How does Nada know this man? Is this one of her old boyfriends?*

Nada sat up and slapped the man hard across the face. "Why didn't you tell us?"

The man caught her hand and she tried to hit him again. He pulled her close. "Shhh, it's all right. I'm sorry. I couldn't let you know."

Nada wept. When she had composed herself, she reached for Judd's hand and squeezed it tightly. "I want you to meet my friend. This is Judd Thompson from the United North American States."

The man put out his hand. "Pleased to know you."

Judd shook his head. "I'm sorry. I don't know who you are."

"I'm Kasim. Nada's brother."

236

Vicki followed the others to the new truck. Chris Traickin knelt to tie his shoe before he climbed into the passenger seat. Pete drove and Vicki, Shelly, and Conrad rode in the sleeper.

As Pete always did, he said a brief prayer before they pulled out. "And we thank you, Lord, that you've brought a new brother to us. Protect his friends who are in custody, and release them soon."

"Amen," Traickin said softly.

Vicki watched for any GC vehicles, but none came. Traickin took off his helmet but kept the rest of his protective suit on.

"I've heard there are groups of believers springing up all around the country," Traickin said. "How many would you say are in Johnson City?"

"More than a hundred," Pete said, "and that was just one cell."

"Where did you guys hide?"

"There's a cave up in the hills behind the gas station," Pete said. "We hid there, then spread out to people's houses." Pete explained how he had crashed the truck in order to get away from the Global Community Peacekeepers.

"You're a genius," Traickin said. "You coordinated everything through that guy at the gas station?"

Pete nodded. "Roger Cornwell. Fantastic guy. If we hadn't met him, all those people would be in jail right now."

Conrad frowned and leaned close to Vicki. "I wish Pete would shut up."

"Tell me about the believers back in Illinois," Traickin said.

"Well, there's—"

"Let me," Conrad interrupted. "There's only the four of us and a little old lady and her dog. And the dog's the smartest of the bunch."

Pete shot Conrad a look.

"It's OK," Traickin said. "You don't have to talk to me."

"Why don't you tell us more about yourself?" Conrad said.

"What do you want to know?"

"How long have you had that mark on your forehead?"

Chris Traickin smiled. "The same time it showed up on everybody else. Look, why don't I give you my story?"

"You don't have anything to prove," Pete said.

"I like telling it. I had a wonderful wife who tried to tell me the truth. But I was caught up in the political world. I thought I was really important. Then my wife vanished into thin air."

"You were with her?" Pete said.

Traickin nodded. "Dana and I had an apartment in Washington, D.C., and a house in Maryland. I picked her up at the apartment late that night. She went to sleep as we drove home."

Traickin glanced out the window. His lip quivered as he continued. "I record talk shows and listen later. Dana always hated them, which is probably why she went to sleep.

"I was exiting the interstate when I saw something move. Her clothes went flat and her shoes fell to the floor. Her door was still locked, so there was no way she could have gotten out. I pulled over and looked in the backseat. She wasn't there."

"I bet it made you think, didn't it?" Pete said.

"It made me crazy," Traickin said. "One minute she was there; the next she had vanished. I retraced my route. I looked along the side of the road. Then it hit me. She had told me about God coming back for the good people, but I didn't listen."

"So that's when you believed?" Pete said.

"I went to the house and found a Bible and a book Dana had tried to get me to read."

"What book?" Conrad said.

"*Mere Christianity*," Traickin said. "It's by C. S. Lewis."

Vicki looked at Conrad. He shrugged and leaned forward to listen.

"How did you find other believers?" Shelly said.

"First, I got involved with the militia movement. It felt weird because I was always against guns and war, and here I was working next to people I'd been against.

"It was there that I met my first believer. He showed me Dr. Ben-Judah's Web site and helped me find a group to meet with."

"Where's this guy now?" Conrad said.

Chris Traickin shook his head. "He was killed at the start of World War III."

"Figures," Conrad muttered.

Vicki didn't know what to believe. Traickin sounded

genuine, but the part about God coming back for "good people" made her wonder. She glanced in the side mirror and thought she saw someone behind them. She kept watch as the truck rolled toward Illinois.

Judd sat hard on the couch and stared at Kasim. He remembered pictures Nada had shown him of vacations when they were younger. He had seen a couple of Kasim in a GC uniform, but in those, Kasim had no beard or mustache. *No wonder Nada fainted*, Judd thought.

Nada was clearly upset with her brother. They spoke in a different language until Judd said, "English, please."

"I was just asking how he could do this to his family," Nada said, turning to Kasim. "Why not send us an e-mail or pick up the phone?"

Kasim put a finger to his lips as footsteps sounded down the hall. "Let's move into the next room."

When they were settled in the computer room, Kasim began his story. "I was questioning my loyalty to the Global Community. I met a man named Dan who—"

Nada interrupted and explained they had talked with Dan in a GC prison. "He's the one who told us to come here."

"So that's how you knew," Kasim said.

Judd explained how they had read the computer files embedded in his daily log.

"You read my diary?" Kasim said.

"We thought you were dead," Nada said, "and you never gave us any reason to doubt it."

240

"I'm getting to that," Kasim said. "I met with Dan several times. I don't know why he trusted me, but he told me the truth. On the morning of the earthquake, I made my decision. I was on security detail on the ground floor of Carpathia's building."

Kasim took Nada's hands in his own. "You have to understand. I was not just choosing God; I had to choose against Nicolae. He was my whole life, everything I had hoped for. To turn from him was so difficult, but after reading and researching, I had to do it.

"I walked outside and prayed the prayer Dan had written for me. Afterward, I felt like a weight had been lifted from my shoulders, and yet, another one had taken its place. How could I be against Nicolae and work for the Global Community?"

"What happened?" Nada said. "How did you survive the building collapse?"

"I went inside but noticed something strange. Dogs barked. People walking them were being dragged down the street. Then I remembered that animals can sense the vibrations of the earth.

"I ran inside and told everyone to get out. They stared at me. I said there was an earthquake coming. One woman got on an elevator. She was laughing. They all thought I was crazy."

"Did you run?"

Kasim nodded. "But before I went outside, I took off my radio and my badge and left them in the lobby. I ran as fast as I could. At the time there was a field a few blocks from the building."

"Where the park is?" Judd said.

"Yes. I ran there, hoping no buildings would fall on me. The earth opened up and nearly swallowed me. I spotted the helicopter on top of Carpathia's building and figured he made it out. Then I saw people falling from the chopper. It was terrible."

Nada put a hand on Kasim's shoulder. "Judd heard he kicked people off the helicopter who were trying to get on."

"I believe it," Kasim said.

"So, how did you get here?" Judd said.

"When I left my badge and radio in the building, I knew I was walking away, but I hadn't fully formed my plan. I knew I was a believer in Christ. That meant I was an enemy of the Global Community. When the building collapsed, I knew I would be counted along with the other dead."

"So you disappeared," Judd said.

Kasim nodded again. "Getting out of the country was impossible. I found Dan and he let me stay here."

"They didn't find you when Dan was arrested?" Judd said.

Kasim held up a hand. A radio squawked in the hall. Kasim switched the power off in the apartment, and the computer went dead.

"Quickly," Kasim said, "follow me." He raced to a back bedroom. Judd noticed there was nothing out of place in the apartment.

Kasim lifted the carpet in a closet. Underneath was a door. He opened it, and the three climbed down a ladder mounted to the wall. Someone was putting a key in the door to the apartment as Kasim repositioned the carpet and closed the trapdoor.

The room below was long and narrow. Kasim told them to keep quiet and showed them a video monitor hooked to a small television.

"Where are the cameras?" Judd whispered.

"In the smoke detectors," Kasim said.

Two GC Peacekeepers moved furniture and searched the apartment. One opened the blinds. "What was the report again?" the man said.

The other Peacekeeper was right above Judd, inspecting the closet. "Neighbor across the hall heard a scream. She looked out and saw somebody coming in here."

The Peacekeepers moved to the other end of the apartment. Kasim whispered, "Dan knew they would try to catch him one day, so he built this hideout. Then he rented the apartment above and cut the hole. The people who moved in here never knew the back bedroom was supposed to be four feet wider."

Judd noticed a refrigerator and cans stacked in the corner. "You must have enough food to last a month."

"Two," Kasim whispered. "It was packed so full I could hardly crawl in when Dan was arrested."

"Why didn't you call us?" Nada said. "Mother and Father were so upset."

"Dan found the GC files confirming my death," Kasim said. "I was afraid an e-mail would be traced, and the same with a phone call. Dan was arrested before I could get phony identification. Without that, there's no way I can get out of the country."

The Peacekeepers moved to the kitchen. One opened the refrigerator. "No food in here. Why don't we just rent the place to somebody and let them keep an eye on it?"

The other Peacekeeper walked into the living room and sat on the couch.

"Oh no," Nada said.

"What?" Kasim said.

"We forgot something."

"Hey, look at this," the Peacekeeper said, bending over and picking something off the floor.

Judd gasped. The man held up the ice pack Kasim had brought to Nada.

"The ice is still frozen," the Peacekeeper said. "Secure the building. We're not letting them get out of here."

25

JUDD and Nada huddled close to Kasim as they watched
the Peacekeepers on the monitor. Two more officers
arrived to inspect the apartment.

"Why didn't you go to Kweesa after Dan was
arrested?" Nada said.

"How do you know her?" Kasim said.

Nada explained that she had stayed with Kweesa since
arriving in New Babylon. "Kweesa gave us your minicom-
puter."

Kasim nodded. "I couldn't confide in her. She was
even more into the Global Community than me. As soon
as I made my decision to follow Jesus, I had to go underground."

Nada shared her conversations with Kweesa. "She's
been asking questions about God."

Kasim scratched his beard. "We don't dare trust her
yet."

245

As they watched the Peacekeepers comb the apartment, Kasim asked about their parents. Nada told him everything. Kasim asked Judd how he had come to Israel.

Judd began with the night of the disappearances and told Kasim about the Young Tribulation Force. Kasim listened closely. He raised his eyebrows when Judd told him about his speech at Nicolae High School. When Judd told Kasim what had happened during the earthquake, Kasim said, "Incredible."

"Why didn't you work from inside the Global Community?" Judd said.

"I've been loyal to the potentate and his ideas for a long time," Kasim said. "Once I believed in Christ, I didn't think I could fool anyone. When Dan was arrested, I had to hide until I could find a way out."

Another Peacekeeper entered the room above them. He put on plastic gloves and asked to see the bag of ice.

"What are they doing?" Nada said.

"Fingerprints," Kasim said.

"You both handled the bag," Judd said.

Kasim nodded. "And if they find even one print of mine, they'll match it with the database at headquarters."

"What does that mean?" Nada said.

Kasim held up a hand and pointed toward the monitor. Another GC official ordered the Peacekeepers into the hall. "We'll do an apartment-by-apartment search. A security camera in the stairwell shows a young man and woman were on this floor. We've sealed the front, so they couldn't have gotten out. Let's find them."

Kasim stood.

"Where are you going?" Nada said.

"We have to get that bag before they take it to the lab," Kasim said.

As Pete drove, Vicki thought of her friends back at the schoolhouse. She couldn't wait to talk to Mark and Darrion and find out how Charlie was doing. Tolan had probably grown since they had been gone. Then she thought of Judd. Where was he? Would he ever come back to Illinois, or was he stuck in the Middle East with Lionel forever?

Chris Traickin asked about other believers in Johnson City. Pete told him what he knew. Vicki, Conrad, and Shelly kept quiet.

Vicki spotted a motorcycle behind them and told Pete.

"He's coming up fast," Pete said.

Vicki craned her neck and saw a skinny man on the cycle. His scraggly beard blew in the wind. When he pulled up next to the truck, he waved at Pete to pull over.

"He's not GC," Chris Traickin said, snapping on his helmet, "but this might be a trick."

"Good thinking," Conrad muttered.

Shelly shouted, "It's Omer!"

Pete stopped and rolled down his window. "What's up?"

Omer glanced at Chris Traickin as a few locusts flew inside. "I need to talk with Vicki."

Chris Traickin spoke into his microphone hidden

under his shirt. "We're on official Global Community business, son."

"It won't take long," Omer said.

"What do you want with her?" Traickin said.

Omer hesitated. "I want to say something. I-I think I'm in love."

As Kasim climbed the ladder, Judd grabbed him. "If the GC catch you, you're dead meat. They'll charge you with deserting or worse."

"Judd, *you're* not going up there," Nada said.

"Why not?" Judd said. "If they catch me, I'll tell them—"

"If anybody should go, it's me," Nada said. "If they catch us, who has the best chance of getting out?"

"They'd hammer Kasim," Judd said.

"And they'd probably find out you were staying with Pavel and his father," Nada said. "You don't want that."

Judd shook his head. Nada had a point. He couldn't drag Pavel's father into this.

"She's right," Kasim finally said.

Before Judd could protest, Nada was up the stairs and into the room above. Judd and Kasim moved to the monitor. Nada ran into the living room. She gave a mock Global Community salute to the camera.

"Hurry up," Kasim said.

Nada placed the bag of water in the sink and grabbed oven mitts from the counter. She found another plastic bag and filled it with the ice from the first bag, then switched the bags and headed for the hideout.

Suddenly, the door to the apartment opened and a GC officer backed in. Nada ducked and scampered into the back bedroom. The GC officer turned. "Did you hear something?"

"Don't think so," the man outside the door said. "The room's been locked."

The GC officer walked through the apartment. Kasim enlarged the screen and focused on the bedroom where Nada was hiding. The officer walked into the room and slowly moved to the closet. He grabbed the handles of both doors and swung them open.

A few more locusts got inside the truck when Vicki climbed out, but Pete got rid of them. Conrad gave Vicki a wink as she followed Omer behind the truck. Omer looked at the ground and shifted from one foot to the other.

Vicki shook her head. "Why did you drive all the way out here?"

Omer turned his back to the truck. "You guys are in big trouble. This Traickin fellow is dirty."

"What?" Vicki said. "How do you know that?"

"I finally talked with your people in Illinois. I was on-line with your friend Mark, when that Roger guy from the gas station came to the house. He said you were taking Traickin back to Illinois, and Mark told us Traickin's a GC plant."

Pete yelled for Vicki, "We need to get moving!"

"Give me another minute!" she yelled back.

"Mark also told me to warn you that Traickin might be wearing a wire," Omer said.

"You mean the GC are listening to everything we're saying?"

Pete honked the horn.

"Go," Omer said, "and get rid of this guy before you get to Illinois."

Vicki hugged Omer. "Have you thought any more about what we talked about?"

"Maybe we can talk when you get home."

Vicki got back in the truck. Conrad and Pete teased her and she blushed. "He ask you to marry him?" Pete said.

Vicki ignored them and scribbled a note to Conrad. She hid it when Chris Traickin took off his headgear and turned. "What did your friend want back there?"

Vicki shook her head. "I spent some time at his mom's house, and I guess he has a crush."

When Traickin turned, Vicki passed the note to Conrad. His mouth dropped open and he passed the note to Shelly.

What do we do? Shelly mouthed.

Vicki put a finger to her lips. After a few miles she pecked Traickin on the shoulder. "Can I see your helmet? I've wondered what it feels like to wear one of those things."

Traickin hesitated. "I'd rather not. If it gets damaged . . ."

"You're not working for the GC," Conrad said. "That thing's only for show, right?"

250

Traickin chuckled. "You're right. But only for a minute."

He passed the helmet to Vicki. She looked at it, then leaned forward and hit the window button by Pete's arm.

"What are you doing?" Pete said.

"Taking care of a little business," Vicki said. She threw the helmet out the window. The helmet slammed onto the road and cracked.

Chris Traickin cursed.

"What did you do that for?" Pete said.

"Roll up the window!" Traickin yelled. Pete hit the button.

Vicki said, "We're going to see if our friend here is telling the truth."

Judd leaned closer to the monitor. "Is she in the closet?"

Kasim stared at the GC officer. "If he finds her, we'll have to rescue her."

The officer backed away, scanned the room again, and walked into the living room. He picked up the bag of ice and left.

"Whew," Judd said, "that was close."

Nada crawled out from under the bed and crossed to the closet. She was almost to the trapdoor when three GC officers bounded back inside the room, yelling and pointing their guns.

Nada screamed. Judd jumped from his seat, but Kasim grabbed him. "Wait."

The officers led Nada into the living room. She broke

free and kicked the door closed. The officers screamed and dragged her back to the living room, throwing her onto the couch.

Kasim frantically loaded information onto a disk from his computer. When he was finished, he ran a program that destroyed all the information on the computer. "This is it. One way or another, we're not coming back here."

Vicki stared at Chris Traickin as Pete pulled to a stop at the side of the road. Locusts swarmed around the windshield yelling, "Apollyon!" Traickin looked terrified.

"Are you wearing a wire?" Vicki whispered.

Traickin glanced at Pete, then back to Vicki.

"What's going on?" Pete said, squinting.

Vicki explained what Omer had said. Pete ripped Traickin's uniform open and found a tiny microphone. Pete tore the microphone away and smashed it against the dashboard.

"They're going to be here any minute!" Traickin screamed. "They're onto you!"

Pete grabbed Traickin's head with one hand and rubbed at the man's forehead with the other. The mark smudged a little.

"How did you know how to fake this?" Pete said.

Traickin pulled away. He reached for the door handle but spied the swarming locusts and shrank back.

"You're not going anywhere," Pete said. "Talk."

Traickin shook his head. "I'm not telling you anything!"

"Fine," Pete said. He reached for the window button. "Maybe letting a couple of locusts in will change your mind."

"No!" Traickin shouted. When Pete removed his hand from the button, Traickin said, "I serve Nicolae Carpathia. When the militia uprising started, under the command of President Gerald Fitzhugh, I was asked to go undercover and expose the rebels."

"And you got a lot of people killed," Pete said.

"A lot of guilty people who were trying to overthrow the Global Community," Traickin said. "It was our one chance at a peaceful world."

"So the war ends and you're looking for different work?" Conrad said.

"The war ends and I volunteer," Traickin said. "I want to expose anyone who's against Nicolae."

"You're a traitor to your wife," Pete said. "She tried to tell you the truth."

Traickin smiled. "My wife is dead. I honor her memory by following a man of peace."

"How did you learn about the mark of the believer?" Vicki said.

"I stumbled onto one of those—what do you call them?—house churches. One of the kids drew a picture of the mark. A friend helped me put it on."

"You got those people in Maryland arrested," Shelly said.

Traickin smiled again. "And any minute, the GC will catch up to you."

Pete started the truck and gunned the engine. "Not if I can help it."

Kasim and Judd quietly crawled into the apartment above. Somehow the bedroom door had closed when the GC led Nada from the room. Judd put his ear to the door and listened. Kasim moved to the window.

"How did you get into the apartment?" a Peacekeeper said.

"I told you," Nada said, "I came in by mistake."

"What were you doing with the bag?" the officer said.

"We have to do something," Judd whispered.

"I'm working on the windows," Kasim said. "They won't open."

"We can't climb down from here," Judd said.

"That's not the plan," Kasim said. "It's going to take some time to break it. Lock the door and put your body in front of it."

Judd locked the door quickly. Kasim picked up a wooden nightstand and smashed it against the window. The glass didn't break.

"What's that?" the GC officer said from the next room.

"Hurry!" Judd said.

Kasim retreated a few steps and ran at the window with the nightstand above his head. The window shattered but didn't break.

Someone jiggled the doorknob. "Open this door!"

Judd stood his ground as someone ran against the door. The hinges cracked, but the door stayed in place.

Kasim threw the nightstand against the window again, but the glass wouldn't break. There was a fluttering outside the window, and Judd finally figured out Kasim's plan.

Kasim picked up the nightstand once more and raised it over his head.

From the other side of the door Judd heard a Peace-keeper say, "Stand back. I'll shoot the lock!"

26

JUDD jumped out of the way as a gun fired. Seconds later a burly GC officer crashed through the door.

Judd threw his hands above his head. "Don't shoot!"

The officer looked past Judd and raised his gun. "Stop!"

Kasim threw the nightstand. It crashed into the window, and glass scattered on the floor.

Another officer ran in just in time to see the first locusts fly inside. The two men screamed and tried to pull the door closed, but it was off its hinges. Frantically they scrambled into the living room as the locusts landed on their backs and stung them.

Judd raced past them and found Nada. She was handcuffed. Judd found a key on a man writhing on the floor and set her free.

In the hallway, Judd, Nada, and Kasim found other Peacekeepers on the ground, gasping and moaning. They stepped over several of them to get to the stairwell. Locusts surged into the stairwell as Nada opened the door.

"Which way?" Nada yelled.

"Kweesa's apartment," Judd said.

"No," Kasim said, "we have to get out of the building!"

Kasim propped the door open. Locusts seemed to follow the three as they raced to the first floor.

Kasim paused at the bottom. "Let's put on a good show."

Again Kasim propped the door open and the three went screaming into the lobby. An alarm pierced Judd's ears, and the locusts shrieked, "Abaddon! Abaddon!" Two Peacekeepers at the entrance drew their guns, then scrambled under a table.

"Lock it down!" someone yelled on the radio. "Lock down every floor so these things don't get into the tunnel!"

It was too late for the Peacekeepers on the floor. Judd opened an emergency door and another alarm rang. More locusts poured into the building, sensing their opportunity to sting unbelievers.

"Hold it open!" Kasim yelled as he ran to an access panel near the back of the lobby. He flipped a few switches and the alarms stopped. The door Judd was holding began to close.

"Hurry!" Judd yelled.

Nada stuck a foot against the door, but it pushed them back inside. Kasim lunged at the door and opened it enough for them to escape.

"Why'd you do that?" Judd said.

258

"I locked the stairwell doors and the floor we were on," Kasim said. "No sense in letting everybody in there get stung."

"If they get in the air ducts, it won't matter," Judd said.

Kasim looked at the building. "I hope Kweesa's all right."

"Let's get out of here," Nada said.

"Either of you know a safe place?" Kasim said.

"I do," Judd said.

Vicki watched the countryside roll by as Pete raced west. Shelly was the first to notice a car following.

"They're not closing in," Conrad said. "I wonder if they're tracking us somehow."

Pete looked at Chris Traickin. "Did you put something in the truck that tells them where we are?"

Traickin looked away. Pete grabbed him with one hand. "Tell me or I'll open this window right now."

Traickin trembled. "I stuck the transmitter they gave me under the step on my side."

"You stopped to tie your shoes before we left," Vicki said.

Pete shook his head. "We have to get rid of it."

"What do we do with him?" Conrad said, pointing at Traickin.

"I'd like him to see the truth," Pete said, "but I don't suppose—"

"I know the truth," Traickin said. "Nicolae Carpathia is god and I'll serve him."

"What would it take to convince you we're right?" Vicki said.

Traickin sneered. "Nothing you could ever say would convince me. I've met the man face-to-face. I know Nicolae Carpathia is the leader we need, and he's going to bring peace to the world. Follow him or one day you'll die."

"That's the mark of a man of peace," Conrad said. "Follow him or he kills you."

Pete looked at Traickin. "We don't want to hurt you or see you get stung. But we have to put you out of the truck."

"They're going to catch you, no matter—"

Pete held up a hand. "I want to give you one more chance. If you get stung by those things, you'll suffer pain for at least five months. God doesn't want that. He's trying to get your attention. The Bible says—"

"Stop," Traickin interrupted. "If you're going to throw me out of here, do it. Don't preach."

Pete bit his lip. He pulled to the side of the highway and pointed to a frontage road that paralleled the interstate. "You're wrong about Carpathia and the GC. I've read the end of the story. They don't come close to winning."

"I'll take my chances," Chris Traickin said. With that, he opened the door and stepped out. A swarm of locusts surrounded him. He flailed at them, but a locust landed on his neck. Vicki turned her head as the man ran toward a guardrail, lost his balance, and fell into a ravine.

Conrad quickly got out, grabbed the transmitter, and ripped it from the truck. "What should I do?"

"Throw it close to that road," Pete said. "That'll keep the GC busy awhile and they'll find Traickin."

Conrad threw the transmitter as far as he could and jumped back inside. Vicki looked for the GC but didn't see their car. As they drove away, Vicki spotted the crumpled body of Chris Traickin at the bottom of the ravine.

Lionel sat with Sam in Pavel's apartment. Since the boy's death, they hadn't heard from Mr. Rudja or Judd. Lionel wanted to help the man in his grief, but he didn't know what to do.

Lionel had sent several e-mails trying to find a flight home. He used Pavel's computer and was excited to find a message from Chloe Williams.

Lionel,

I don't have good news. I can't help with your request to get back to the States or to Israel right now. Buck's still in Israel himself, and we're hoping he'll make it home for the birth of our baby. I'm slowing down a little with my work here. I feel as big as a barge.

There are new pilots and drivers signing up with the co-op every day to help move supplies, but air travel is almost impossible with the locusts taking out most of the ground crew. If I find a way for you to get home, I'll let you know. Please keep working every angle you have there. Maybe Mac will have an idea.

Tsion sends his love. We're praying for you and the others. Dad and I were talking about the Young Trib

*Force the other day. We're excited about the new Web
site you've put together. Tsion raves about it. Whoever is
heading that up is doing a great job.*

*We wish we could have you all with us, but space is
pretty tight here. We've added a doctor to the Force who's
helping me with the pregnancy. You may remember the
flight attendant, Hattie Durham. She's staying with us
too. She was stung and Doc Floyd is trying to help her,
but nothing seems to work. She's skin and bones.*

*If there's anything you want us to pray about or help
with, please let us know. And be careful in New Babylon.
I know the locusts have changed things for a while, but
Nicolae will be back to his old tricks in no time.*

Love in Christ,
Chloe

Sam asked about Chloe and the others. Lionel
explained how they had met the Tribulation Force.

"Wow," Sam said, "I can't believe you actually know
Tsion Ben-Judah."

Lionel forwarded Chloe's message to Mark back at the
schoolhouse and typed a note to Mac McCullum, Nicolae
Carpathia's pilot who had flown the kids to New Babylon.

Moments later the front door opened. Judd, Nada,
and a bearded man rushed inside and slammed the door.

"What's going on?" Sam said.

Judd put his hands on his knees and gasped for air.
When he caught his breath he said, "I want you to meet
Nada's brother, Kasim."

Lionel couldn't believe it. Kasim told his story of

becoming a believer in Christ just before the worldwide earthquake. Judd explained what had happened with the Peacekeepers in Dan Nieters' apartment. "We barely got out of there," Judd said.

"What about the girl you were staying with?" Lionel said to Nada.

"We're not sure," Nada said. "She may have been stung."

Nada reached for a phone, but Judd shook his head. "I don't want to take the chance of them tracing the call here."

"But I have to tell Kweesa where I am or she'll be suspicious," Nada said.

Judd scratched his head. "Just hold off until things settle. If she was stung she won't be able to talk."

"What about Mom and Dad?" Nada said to Kasim. "We have to tell them you're alive."

"Not now," Kasim said. "We have to wait for the right time. I want to get some sleep."

Lionel told Judd and the others what Chloe had written. The kids decided to wait for Mr. Rudja to return and help them figure out what to do.

———

Vicki and the others prayed God would protect them from the Global Community Peacekeepers as they traveled. Though Pete was exhausted, he kept driving. Vicki fell asleep at nightfall and didn't wake up until the sun was coming up the next morning. Pete finally pulled into a truck stop for fuel and coffee.

Vicki ran inside and found a phone. She dialed the secure phone in the schoolhouse, and Lenore answered.

"Mark's still asleep," Lenore said. "He was talking with Carl in Florida half the night, getting updates about you."

"Carl heard about us?" Vicki said.

Lenore explained that the Peacekeepers' plan was to have Traickin expose as many believers as possible. "Word is, several of the believers in Johnson City have been tracked down and arrested."

"Oh no," Vicki said. "It was a trap and we fell for it."

"Just get back here as fast as you can so we can regroup," Lenore said.

"What's going on?" Vicki said.

"Those guys from South Carolina wrote, and we put their messages on the Web site. Now kids from around the country are writing and asking if the Young Trib Force can come to their area!"

"Unbelievable," Vicki said.

Judd fell asleep on the couch and was awakened a few hours later by Mr. Rudja. Judd explained about Kasim, and Mr. Rudja said, "He'll want to get back to Israel and reunite with his parents."

Judd nodded. "That seems like the best plan, but how?"

Mr. Rudja put his head in his hands. "I won't be able to arrange anything until after the funeral."

"We understand," Judd said. "We wouldn't want to leave before then anyway."

Judd still felt guilty about Pavel. He had neglected the boy because he had been so caught up with Nada.

"What kind of service will you have?" Judd said.

"With the locusts, nothing is normal," Mr. Rudja said. "I notified my superiors about Pavel's death, and they have arranged a memorial service. I told them it wasn't necessary, but they insisted."

"What will they do?" Judd said.

Mr. Rudja took a deep breath. "We'll meet in a secure room at the Enigma Babylon Cathedral. They wanted Pontifex Maximus to be there, but he's still suffering from a locust sting.

"I don't want to be there, but it would be a slap in the face to the Global Community not to go. And I would dishonor my son."

"What do you mean?" Judd said.

"I made a promise to him before he died, and I'm going to keep it."

27

JUDD listened as Nada and Kasim spent hours talking, laughing, and crying at Mr. Rudja's apartment. They relived childhood memories and adventures. When Kasim asked about their parents, Nada couldn't hold back the tears. She told Kasim about meeting Judd and their father's anger toward him.

"He doesn't like the thought of losing you," Kasim said.

Judd met with Lionel and Sam about returning to Israel or the States. Mac McCullum had e-mailed Lionel and said it was too risky to take them, and he could only do it if he received word from his superiors.

Rather than bother Mr. Rudja with questions, Judd and the others let him grieve his loss. At dinner the night before the funeral, Mr. Rudja seemed upset. Judd asked what was wrong.

"I guess I'm having doubts," Mr. Rudja said. "I believe

in God with all my heart, but how do I know for sure
where Pavel is?"

Judd nodded. He had tackled the same questions after
Ryan's death. Where was his soul? Was it somewhere
waiting in limbo? Could Ryan talk with Bruce Barnes or
God anytime? Could Ryan see what was going on with
the Young Trib Force?

Lionel excused himself from the table and went to
Pavel's computer. He returned with a printout. "This is
from Tsion's Web site. This section deals with the most
frequently asked questions about death and what
happens to people."

Lionel handed the paper to Mr. Rudja, but the man
waved at him. "You read it."

"OK," Lionel said. He spread the pages out before
him on the table and read.

"For the believer in Jesus, heaven is a place of rest
from sorrows. We are told that God will swallow up
death forever. Isaiah writes, 'The Sovereign Lord will
wipe away all tears. He will remove forever all insults
and mockery against his land and people.'

"This is a wonderful thing to look forward to, no
matter what way we experience that home going. We
will find there a total happiness and joy. We will
know each other there. We will have work to do.
And there will be a place for us.

"Jesus himself said, 'Don't be troubled. You trust
God, now trust in me. There are many rooms in my
Father's home, and I am going to prepare a place for

you. . . . When everything is ready, I will come and get you, so that you will always be with me where I am.'

"That is such a comfort for those who have had loved ones disappear or know believers who have died. We are told in God's Word in 2 Corinthians that if we are absent from our bodies, that is, when we die, we will be at home with the Lord. So take comfort in this if you have lost someone who is a believer. They are in a place of beauty and splendor. They are with God right now."

Mr. Rudja put up a hand and asked for the pages. He hugged Lionel and carefully folded the paper and put it in his pocket.

Nada called Kweesa and discovered the girl hadn't been stung. Nada told her she was staying with friends from Israel and wouldn't return to Kweesa's apartment.

Nada and Kasim stayed at Mr. Rudja's place when it came time for Pavel's funeral. Judd followed the others into a secure area of the Enigma Babylon Cathedral. Soft music played through speakers. Several of Mr. Rudja's employees attended, many on the tail end of the effects of the locust stings. Judd kept his head down and stayed out of sight.

Judd glanced at Pavel's body and wondered if he and Ryan were together talking about the Young Trib Force. Judd wiped away a tear as a GC technician came into the room and opened curtains revealing a giant screen. The man adjusted several controls and focused a camera on the small gathering. Whoever was on the other end of the video link would be able to see the entire room.

Mr. Rudja leaned toward Judd and the others and whispered, "When I give you the signal, go as quickly as you can back to the apartment."

"What are you going to do?" Judd said.

Mr. Rudja put a finger to his lips and sat back.

A woman dressed in a long, colorful robe came forward. She wore the emblem of Enigma Babylon One World Faith. Judd noticed a welt on her neck. She smiled as she talked about Pavel and his father, but the smile seemed fake.

"As I understand, it wasn't long ago that the Rudja family faced a similar tragedy with the disappearance of Pavel's mother," the woman said. "Many in the same situation simply gave up. But not Pavel and his father. They persevered. They moved on with their lives. And now, with the loss of Pavel, we all face a similar choice.

"The loss of a child, one taken so young, tears at our hearts. We long to know what Pavel would have done in the future. We ponder the contributions he could have made to the Global Community."

Judd glanced at Mr. Rudja. He thought the man was going to be sick.

"She never met my son," Mr. Rudja whispered to Judd.

The woman gave a signal to a man in the back. "And now, if I'm correct, we have a very special guest joining us via video link. None other than the Supreme Commander of the Global Community, Leon Fortunato."

Leon Fortunato sat in front of a black cloth, his hands folded. Judd ducked his head and listened. Even though Judd had grown a beard since seeing Fortunato at Nicolae High, he didn't want to take a chance being recognized.

"My friends and loyal servants of the Global Community and Nicolae Carpathia, it saddens me to have to join with you at a time such as this."

Mr. Rudja tensed when he heard Leon's voice. The man bit his lip and seethed with anger. Judd put a hand on the man's arm to calm him.

"Pavel Rudja will be remembered as a fighter," Leon continued. "He fought the disease that eventually took his life. He fought the good fight and kept the faith in the ideals of the Global Community. There will always be a place in our hearts for this courageous young man."

He showed more courage than you'll ever know, Judd thought. *And he told more people about the true God than you'll know.*

Fortunato held up a piece of paper. "I have here a certificate of merit honoring Pavel Rudja that is signed by none other than the potentate himself, Nicolae Carpathia."

Audience members around the room *ooh*ed and *ahh*ed. Leon nodded knowingly and smiled. "This will be given to you as soon as possible, Anton, as a keepsake."

As soon as you come out of your underground bunker, Judd thought.

"Our greatest natural resource in the Global Community is our young people," Fortunato continued. "I am pleased to see teenagers in the audience, and I hope you will all try in your own way to take Pavel's place."

Fortunato said a few more words, then closed by recognizing Mr. Rudja and the work he had done for the "cause of world peace." Mr. Rudja restrained himself and gave a sigh when the screen went blank.

The woman with Enigma Babylon One World Faith stood and welcomed Mr. Rudja to the podium. "I know this is a very difficult time for you, but we would love to hear any thoughts you have about your beloved son."

Mr. Rudja hesitated, then walked forward. Judd glanced around the room. Except for Lionel, Sam, Mr. Rudja, and himself, no one had the mark of the true believer.

"I want to thank you for coming to this memorial for my son. I have struggled with what I should say to you. What I am about to share is something you may not be ready to hear."

Judd shifted in his seat. What was Mr. Rudja up to?

"The supreme commander's words were very nice, as are all the words coming from the leadership of the Global Community," Mr. Rudja continued. "But just because something is nice, doesn't mean it is right. The supreme commander and our representative of Enigma Babylon One World Faith would have us believe that once this life is over, that's it. Pavel is no more. When he died, he simply ceased to exist."

Mr. Rudja scanned the room. "Do you really believe that this life is all there is? Isn't there something deep inside that tells you this is not all there is?

"Our spiritual leader with us today speaks of Pavel as

if we will never see him again, but that's not true. Pavel is more alive today than he has ever been."

A few shifted in their seats and whispered to those around them. The woman from Enigma Babylon still smiled, her hands clasped as if in prayer.

Mr. Rudja took a wrinkled piece of paper from his pocket. "Pavel wrote this a few days ago. He asked me to send it to certain people he hadn't been able to contact. I did that, but I think what he wrote fits here. If you will indulge me."

Mr. Rudja opened the paper and spread it before him on the podium. "'Dear friend,'" he read, "'if you're reading this, it's because I'm dead. Believe me, I'm in a much better place now, though I know I'll miss you. That's why I'm writing this. I want you to know the truth.'

"'The truth is, God is real and wants to know you. He created us to be with him. But we all sinned and a holy God can't allow that. So God gave us his Son, Jesus. He lived a perfect life and paid the penalty for our sin by dying for us.'

"'The terrible things happening in our world are designed by God to get our attention. Don't let anyone fool you. If you'll ask God to forgive you of your sins, he will. And you can be as sure of heaven as I am. I'm not living with God because I was a good person, but because I asked Jesus to forgive me.'"

The woman from Enigma Babylon One World Faith stood. Mr. Rudja put up a hand. "I'm almost finished."

"Yes," the woman said nervously, "but you need to hurry."

Mr. Rudja kept reading. "'I prayed a simple prayer with a friend of mine over the Internet. Wherever you are, you can do it right from your seat.'"

Mr. Rudja read the prayer, then told anyone who had prayed it to read material on Tsion Ben-Judah's Web site.

Judd glanced around the room. Some people were sniffling. Others seemed angry. Judd counted four other people in the room who had received the mark of the believer.

"My son concludes with this," Mr. Rudja said. "'There is one king, one ruler who deserves your devotion and loyalty. His name is Jesus. May my life praise him and him alone for all eternity.'"

Mr. Rudja folded the paper and looked at the audience. When he saw those with the mark on their forehead, he smiled. "Amen," he said. He looked at Judd and nodded.

Judd, Sam, and Lionel rose and followed Mr. Rudja out a side door. The audience watched them leave, clearly stunned.

"We have to hurry to the airport," Mr. Rudja said. "I've chartered a plane. You're getting out of here."

———

It was late when the truck pulled up to the schoolhouse. Vicki jumped out and hugged Lenore and Tolan. The others came out to greet the kids and Pete.

"Where's Charlie?" Vicki said.

"Asleep," Mark said.

Pete found a place to rest. Conrad and Shelly sat in

the kitchen and told everyone what they had been
through. Vicki grabbed a sandwich and met with Mark in
the computer room. She typed an e-mail to Omer in
Tennessee and asked him to call their secure phone.

"If it hadn't been for him," Vicki said, "we would have
brought that Traickin guy right here."

"How much did you guys tell Traickin before Omer
caught up to you?" Mark said.

Vicki shook her head. "Too much. I can't remember
everything Pete said, but the GC knows a bunch of us are
working together."

Mark opened a file of e-mails and Vicki shook her
head. Kids from around the country had read what the
Gowin brothers in South Carolina had written about the
Young Trib Force's teaching. As Vicki read the e-mails, the
phone rang. It was Omer.

"I'm glad you made it home," Omer said.

"I can't thank you enough for helping us. We heard
there were some arrests."

"Yeah, I was up on the hill when they came for my
mom. There was nothing I could do."

"I'm so sorry, Omer."

"They got that guy at the gas station too."

"Roger?"

"Yeah," Omer said. "When I get over the sting, we're
going to get them out, one way or another."

"What do you mean?" Vicki said.

"I believe what you said about the GC being mean
and all. A few of us are here at the house making plans.
We're getting them out of there."

"Omer, they'll kill you," Vicki said.

"Maybe, but it beats sitting around like scared rabbits."

"What about the other stuff I told you?"

"I don't see how a God who's supposed to love his people could allow them to be hauled off to jail like they did my mom."

"Please," Vicki said, "you have to listen—"

"No, I have to go. I'll let you know how we make out."

Vicki hung up and told Mark what Omer had said. "I've got a bad feeling about this. . . ."

Mark held up a hand and nodded toward the door. Charlie stood in the darkness. Vicki ran and hugged him.

"See anything different about me?" Charlie said.

Vicki shook her head.

Charlie stepped into the light. "I finally got that old mark," he said, beaming.

Vicki stared at Charlie's forehead and couldn't hold back the tears.

28

JUDD and the others rushed to pick up Kasim and Nada. They went straight to an airfield on the outskirts of New Babylon.

"Where are we going?" Judd said.

"I didn't want to tell you my plans before the funeral," Mr. Rudja said. "I made arrangements before Pavel died to find a pilot and get you back to Israel."

"You're going to be an enemy of the GC now," Judd said.

"Yes," Mr. Rudja said as they pulled onto the tarmac and sped toward a private jet. "Pavel's last wish was for his funeral to tell the truth about God. I couldn't let him down. And you saw there were at least four people who became believers."

"But if Fortunato or Carpathia hear about what you said—," Lionel said.

"I have friends who still need this message. I'll be careful, but if it means I am arrested for my faith, so be it."

The kids hugged Mr. Rudja and got on the plane. Their pilot was a believer named Hank Keller. He had known Mr. Rudja from previous military service and was the newest member of the Commodity Co-op organized by Chloe Williams.

As they flew toward Israel, Hank told his story of becoming a follower of Jesus shortly after the disappearances. "There were so many theories about what had happened. My father drove a cab in New York and was working the late shift. He'd just picked up a couple from a club in Greenwich Village when it happened. The car went out of control and slammed into a store window. The couple lived. I tracked them down from a news story I found."

"What did they say?" Judd said.

"It was just like all the stories," Hank said. "My dad was there one second and gone the next. He was talking to the couple about God. I guess they were pretty drunk and just laughed at him."

"When did you put it all together?" Judd said.

"I went through his stuff at his apartment. He and my mom had been divorced for about fifteen years. I found notes he had made and letters my mom returned without opening. He said he was sorry for messing up their lives. He had found God at some big church in town and wanted the rest of his family to find the same kind of peace.

"The scariest part was finding the place where my dad

made a prediction about what was going to happen. He wrote something like, 'One day Jesus is going to come and take his children away. I just want the rest of you to be there with me.'"

Kasim became quiet as they neared Israel. Nada held his hand.

Lionel asked Hank what the chances were of getting a ride back to the States.

"I might be able to take you at some point, but I'm not headed that way for a few weeks." Hank gave them his card and told Lionel to contact him.

When they landed, they thanked Hank and rented a car. Only compacts were available, so the five squeezed into one and headed for Jerusalem.

Nada helped them navigate the streets. Finally, they found Yitzhak's house. Kasim took a deep breath.

"You're not the one who needs to be worried," Nada said.

Kasim smiled. "They'll be happy to see us all."

Kasim knocked on the door. Someone peeked through a side window. Finally, Yitzhak opened the door and hurried them inside.

"Where are my parents?" Nada said.

"We had to move them," Yitzhak said. "Neighbors were becoming suspicious about the number of people staying with me."

"Who's been here?" Judd said.

"Many witnesses from around the world. We have a network of safe houses now."

Yitzhak took them to a downstairs room filled with

cots. Three men slept soundly. "These arrived two days ago and have told us extraordinary things. I want you to meet them when they awaken."

"We need to find my parents," Nada said.

Yitzhak wrote an address on a piece of paper. "Would you like to call before you go?"

"No," Nada said. "I want to surprise them."

Vicki met with the others at the schoolhouse while Pete drove to meet with Zeke at his gas station. Pete said he would be in touch before he made his next supply run.

Lenore took Vicki aside and asked to speak privately. "Thank you again for taking care of Tolan and me. I'm learning so much that I'm afraid I'm not doing enough to earn my keep."

Vicki smiled. "Mark says you're the best thing that's happened to us since we found the schoolhouse."

"I appreciate that, but I'm wondering if I could do more."

"Such as?"

"Have you seen the girls downstairs?"

"Melinda and Janie? I was going to but . . ."

"You put it off," Lenore said. "You're just as scared as the rest of us are to go down there and see what they've become."

Vicki nodded. "I've heard them moaning and screaming. Gives me the creeps."

"Well, I felt the same way for a long time. Had to make myself go down there. Then a strange thing happened. I felt drawn to them. I felt God calling me to talk with them. I think I gave them a little hope in a hopeless situation."

"So, what do you want to do?"

Lenore leaned closer. "I feel like God wants us to open this place up to anybody who's hurting. I know it's a risk. But once people see how much we love them and try to help them, maybe they'll believe our message."

Vicki blinked. "You mean, make the schoolhouse like a hospital?"

"We could keep the teaching area separate from the people who've been stung. If they show an interest in God, we'll teach them. If not, we help them get better and let them go."

"Where would the people come from?" Vicki said.

"There are lots of people in town who need help. And I know of a station wagon we could use to bring people back."

"Let me think about it and talk with the others," Vicki said. "Right now I need to do something."

The kids had cleaned up the basement and tried to make the rooms more comfortable, but Janie had torn down lights and coverings for the walls. Vicki knocked and opened the trapdoor that led to the deepest part of the hideout. The last time she was here the locusts were after Lenore and Tolan.

Melinda sat on a bed, her back against the wall. Her hair hung in front of her face. Janie stood in the corner, arms folded. She looked like she hadn't eaten in weeks. Her skin was pale, her lips chapped. Janie stared at Vicki.

The girl's eyes seemed vacant, like the lights were on but there was no one home.

Janie stared at Vicki but didn't respond when Vicki said hello. "Don't look at me that way—you're creeping me out," Vicki said.

Janie's voice was hollow. "Are you here to rescue us or to keep us locked up?"

"What do you mean?"

"They're torturing us. It's not enough that we're in pain; they lock us in the dark."

"From what I heard, you were dangerous to yourselves and the others."

"She almost burned the place down," Melinda said.

"Shut up!" Janie shouted.

Vicki backed away. The girls looked like someone from a bad horror movie had done their makeup. Only this was real.

"Take a good look at us!" Janie shouted. "You think your God can save us now?"

Before Vicki could answer, Melinda said to Janie, "Leave her alone. She hasn't done anything but try to help."

"Help?" Janie said. "She tried to shove her religion down our throats."

Vicki sat on Melinda's bed. "Are you feeling any better?"

Melinda swallowed hard. "I don't know whether the pain has lessened or if I've just gotten used to it. I keep thinking about Felicia and how much better off she is—"

"Who's Felicia?" Janie shouted.

"The Morale Monitor she came here with," Vicki said. "She drank some water that was poisoned and died."

"I wish I had drunk that water," Janie said.

Vicki spoke softly to Melinda. "God's still trying to get your attention. In a few weeks, you won't feel as bad. You'll be tempted to forget what you've gone through."

"I'll never forget this," Melinda said.

"How do you know we're going to get better?" Janie sneered.

"Tsion Ben-Judah says the sting's effect lasts a few months; then it wears off. Pretty soon those locusts will be gone and something else is going to happen. Something terrible."

"What?" Janie said.

Vicki shook her head. "You're not ready to hear it."

Janie rushed toward Vicki and screamed, "Tell me!"

"I've tried," Vicki said. "If you really want to know, come to me after this is over."

Janie muttered something and retreated to her bed.

Vicki turned to Melinda, but the girl asked her to leave. "I can't listen when I feel this bad."

Vicki found the others and explained Lenore's plan. Everyone seemed open to the idea except Mark. "It sounds good, but it's a huge risk. We're the hub of the Young Trib Force. If somebody rats us out, the GC could be here in no time. They'd seize our equipment and find out about Carl. The Web site would be history. Why do you want to make us vulnerable?"

"We're not trying to make the schoolhouse vulnerable," Lenore said. "We're trying to help people come to know the truth."

"From the start, that was my dream for this place," Vicki said. "I didn't see it as a clubhouse for us, but a training center and a place where anyone truly seeking could find answers."

"It's that now," Mark said. "We're reaching people around the world on the Internet—"

"But we could do more," Lenore interrupted. "I was a risk and you guys still took me in. I could have ratted you out, but I didn't. God brought me here."

Mark smiled. "I can't argue with that." He scratched his neck and winced. "I'm not saying I don't like the plan; I just want us to count the cost of doing this."

"Let's vote," Darrion said. "All in favor, raise a hand."

Slowly, everyone in the room raised a hand, even Mark.

"Then it's settled," Vicki said. "We'll make our first run into town tomorrow."

While Lionel and Sam stayed with Yitzhak, Judd rode with Nada and Kasim through the darkened streets of Jerusalem. The streets were deserted. With the windows rolled down, Judd heard sobbing and howling from people inside their homes who had recently been stung.

As Kasim drove, Judd's mind wandered to his friends in Illinois. Were the locusts as thick there? He wondered if Vicki had heard about his friendship with Nada and that things were getting more serious. *But how serious?*

Judd thought. Nada's father might hold a grudge against him, blame him for taking Nada to New Babylon. Would the safe return of Kasim be enough to ease the man's anger at Judd?

Kasim parked on a darkened part of the street and waited. When they were sure they weren't being watched, the three got out of the car and walked toward an alley.

Suddenly, a GC squad car approached with its lights flashing.

"In here," Judd said as he pulled Nada toward a doorway.

The squad car flew past them. Judd noticed the two officers wore protective clothing. Kasim motioned for Judd and Nada to follow him. They located the correct apartment and pressed the buzzer in the lobby.

A woman spoke in a different language through a tiny speaker by the door. Then in broken English she said, "Who you?"

Nada gave her name. "I'm looking for my mother and father."

"Who with you?" the woman said.

Judd looked in the corner of the tiny lobby and saw a camera. He whispered to Nada, "She might think it's a GC trap and you're being used."

"My name is Nada. I've come to see my parents. I have very good news for them."

"Third floor," the woman said. The door buzzed. Nada and Kasim went through first and headed upstairs.

Judd took a deep breath and followed.

29

JUDD couldn't remember feeling so nervous. When he made the speech at Nicolae High he was scared, but he felt peaceful because he was doing the right thing. He had no idea how this would turn out.

Both Nada and Kasim wore bulky clothes and hats pulled low. Nada knocked on the apartment door. A wiry, older woman opened it a few inches and checked them out.

"Are my parents here?" Nada said.

The woman nodded. "They know you, not man with beard."

Nada put her arm around Kasim. "This is a friend and brother. Let us in."

The woman unlatched the door and the three went inside. The apartment smelled musty, and there were old pictures and trinkets on every shelf and table. Nada's mother rushed from the kitchen and the two embraced.

The woman led them through the kitchen to a back

room. Nada's father, Jamal, stood in the doorway with
his arms folded. When he saw Nada, he took her in his
arms. "I didn't think we'd ever see you again."

"I'm so sorry. I shouldn't have put you through this.
But I learned God can even use my mistakes."

"Quiet," Jamal said, "you're home now."

Kasim watched the scene and wiped away a tear. His
mother and father glanced at him, but it was clear they
didn't recognize him.

Jamal led Nada and her mother into the bedroom. He
returned and glared at Judd. "At least you brought her
home safely. I thank you for that. Since you came to us
we've seen no end of trouble. The GC have impounded
our house!"

Judd wanted to defend himself, but he held his
tongue.

"I can't have you stay with my family any longer."

Kasim put a hand on Judd's shoulder. Kasim's lips
trembled.

"I'll have to ask you and your friend to leave," Jamal
said. "I'm sorry."

"Father, you don't understand," Nada said from the
bedroom.

Kasim put a finger to his lips and stepped forward. He
tried to speak but couldn't.

Kasim's father stared at him, going over his features.
"You have to forgive me. There's something about you
that reminds me . . ."

Kasim took off his hat and put a hand on the man's
arm.

288

"You look so much like my son, except for the mark of the believer, of course."

Judd felt like an intruder. He wanted to look away or move into the next room, but he stayed.

Kasim glanced down, wiped his eyes, and finally looked into Jamal's eyes. "Father."

When Kasim spoke, Jamal's mouth dropped open.

Nada pulled her mother close. "Kasim?" the woman whispered.

Then the tears flowed. Jamal embraced Kasim. Kasim's mother fell to her knees and the two men followed.

Nada knelt beside the three. "You see, Father, I told you something good happened while I was in New Babylon."

"Yes," Jamal said as he embraced his son. He rocked back and forth, as if holding a baby. Kasim's mother wept. Every few moments she touched her son's face or ran a hand over the mark on his forehead.

The old woman, who had been watching from the kitchen, came up behind Judd. "Move. Too much noise."

Judd followed the others inside. Nada, Kasim, and their parents wept several minutes before Kasim could tell his story. Judd didn't want to interfere with the reunion, but he couldn't help listening to Kasim's story again. Kasim had gone from loyal Global Community worker to follower of Christ. To his parents, he had come back from the dead.

Kasim's mother wanted to know why he hadn't contacted them. Jamal asked how he had survived, once his roommate had been arrested by the Global Community. On and on they talked. When there was a lull in the conversation, Nada would hug Kasim or her parents. Finally, Kasim turned the questions on his parents.

Jamal shook his head. "We've tried to stay ahead of the GC, but even with the locusts, they find a way to harass us. We went back to our home a few days ago and found it has been boarded up and condemned."

"What will you do now?"

Jamal smiled. "We have our son back. We will find an answer to that question together." But Jamal's smile vanished when he finally looked at Judd.

"Father, Judd was a great help to us in finding Kasim," Nada said. "And while we were there he lost his friend."

Jamal stared at Judd. "I'm truly sorry for your loss. Let's step in the next room."

Judd followed the man into the kitchen and sat at the table. The old woman offered them coffee but both refused.

"Nada said you had nothing to do with her going to New Babylon."

"That's right."

"I find that hard to believe."

Judd took a breath. "Sir, your daughter loves you and your wife very much. When we discovered her on the plane, I suggested she call you."

"I appreciate that."

"Your daughter is very strong-willed. When she decides to do something, it's very hard to talk her out of it."

Jamal smiled and nodded.

"Nada and I are good friends," Judd continued. "I'm not exactly sure where that will lead us, but I know she feels strongly about me. If you try pushing me away, it would hurt both of us."

"You believe she would choose you over her own family?"

"I'm not sure. I don't want to force her to make that choice. She needs her family, and right now we both want to spend time with each other."

Jamal scratched his beard and thought. Finally he said, "You're an exceptional young man. I admit I felt you were responsible for luring her away. I was wrong." He stood and reached for Judd's hand. "Thank you for helping us find our son. You have permission to see Nada as much as is safe. I only ask that you not stay with us during this time."

"Agreed. Thank you."

Judd walked back into the room and said good-bye to Kasim.

Kasim stood and hugged Judd. "We've been through a great adventure together. I hope we see each other again."

"You will," Nada said, smiling. She walked Judd to the front door. "What did my father say to you?"

"It was what I said to him that was the most important," Judd said.

"What?"

"I told him he has a muleheaded daughter who's madly in love. And if he wants to keep her around, he ought to let us see each other."

"Muleheaded?"

Judd smiled. "I know it's not fair to the mules, but he understood."

Nada punched Judd on the shoulder and laughed. "Call me."

The two embraced before Judd quietly slipped out the front door.

Vicki and the others decided Darrion, Vicki, and Lenore should go into town. They would start walking before sunup and try to make it by lunch. If they weren't back before dark, Mark would come after them on a motorcycle.

The others began moving the computer equipment and stored files to the second-floor office. That room and the room next to it would become the nerve center for their Internet operation.

Mark showed Vicki e-mails that had come in since she had returned. There were at least a hundred requests from kids around the country to have the Young Trib Force visit their cities.

"No way we could go to all those places," Vicki said. "The GC could be monitoring the Web site."

"True," Mark said, "but there might be a way to tell people you're coming but not let them know specifics until the day of the meeting. With the locusts still out there, it could work."

"You usually tell me to be cautious. Why are you convinced this will work?"

Mark turned in his chair. "I've read what those guys in

South Carolina said. We've gotten some e-mails from Tennessee too. What you taught them really made a difference. God is using you in this soul harvest predicted in the Bible."

Vicki shook her head. "I appreciate your confidence, but what you're talking about is something God does through Tsion Ben-Judah and the witnesses. Who am I?"

"Pray about it."

Mark patted Vicki on the shoulder and left the room.

Before she went to bed, Vicki tried calling Omer's place in Tennessee. There was no answer.

The next morning Vicki, Darrion, and Lenore left for town. Lenore gave instructions to Shelly for Tolan's feeding times and naps.

The air was crisp, but Vicki thought it felt good to be outside. A few locusts still buzzed around them, but there didn't seem to be as many as before.

As they walked, the girls prayed out loud for people and situations. Vicki prayed for Omer and the believers in Tennessee. Darrion prayed for the believers in Maryland who had been arrested. Lenore prayed for Chris Traickin and others who had been stung by the locusts. "And, Lord, we ask you to prepare some people right now, the people you want us to meet. Show us which ones we can trust, which ones want to hear the message, and which ones just aren't ready."

When they reached town, Lenore led them to a friend's house. A station wagon was sitting in the driveway. Lenore knocked at the front door but there was no answer.

Vicki heard pecking and found a tiny window in the basement just above ground. She rubbed dirt from the window and spotted two women inside. One was older with gray hair, and the other was middle-aged.

"Is that you, Connie?" Lenore shouted.

"Who is that?" the middle-aged woman yelled.

"Lenore Barker! Is your mother with you?"

"Yes!"

"Have you been stung?" Lenore said.

"Both of us," Connie shouted. "But only once. We're hiding down here, but the food's about to run out."

"We've come to help you," Lenore said.

Lenore told Vicki that Connie and her mother had given her food when no one else would. "I think these two would be perfect for the schoolhouse."

Vicki and Darrion nodded.

Lenore coaxed the women upstairs and promised the locusts wouldn't sting again.

"We're in bad shape," Connie said as they made their way outside. The two were pale as ghosts and squinted at the sunlight. They had been bitten the first day of the locust attack and hadn't been outside since. They both felt that the effects of the stings were wearing off a little.

Connie and her mother cowered as locusts buzzed around them saying, "Apollyon."

"They won't bite you twice," Lenore said.

"How is Tolan?" Connie asked. "We haven't seen you since the big freeze."

Lenore told them about her husband's death and how the kids had rescued her. "We'd like to use your car to take people to a hospital we've set up. We'll help take care of you until you get your strength back."

Connie and her mother agreed to go but said their car was out of gas. While Lenore helped clear junk out of it, Vicki and Darrion went to a gas station for fuel.

On the way, Vicki and Darrion discovered two teenage girls wandering the street. They seemed in so much pain that they could hardly listen to Vicki's questions about wanting help. Finally, she convinced them to follow her to the station wagon.

By the time they made it back to the car with fuel, Lenore had met another middle-aged woman who wanted to go to the schoolhouse.

"God is working it out," Lenore said. "We have a whole carful without even trying."

"Should we say anything about God before we leave?" Darrion said. "Just to see their reaction?"

Lenore shook her head. "Let's show them God's love by our actions. Take them in, give them a place to recover, and eventually they'll ask us why we're doing this. Then we tell them and invite them to study the Bible with us."

Others in the neighborhood heard people were offering help and came running. A group gathered around the station wagon and pleaded to be taken to the makeshift hospital.

"This could get out of hand," Darrion said.

"We have to be ready to help them no matter what they do with the message," Vicki said. "If they reject it, we'll help them get better and they'll be on their way in a few weeks."

A few others wandered onto the scene, asking what was going on. Each had been stung. Vicki saw some with bloody marks on their wrists. One man had a rope burn around his neck.

Vicki turned and walked a few steps away. Darrion followed. "What is it?"

Vicki wiped away a tear. "I was just thinking about that place in the Bible where Jesus looked at the crowds of people around him and saw all their problems. He felt pity for them. The people had no idea where to go for help."

"Just like these people," Darrion said.

Vicki nodded. "I memorized this part. Jesus told his disciples, 'The harvest is so great, but the workers are so few. So pray to the Lord who is in charge of the harvest; ask him to send out more workers for his fields.'"

Darrion looked at the people. "You know what's weird? With everybody we've talked to today, I haven't seen one believer. Is everybody hiding while these people suffer?"

Vicki put her head in her hands. "Good point. You've helped me make two decisions. We have to take in as many people at the schoolhouse as we can."

"What's the other decision?" Darrion said.

"We have to get this message out," Vicki said. "I have to meet with as many groups as possible."

30

VICKI returned to a flurry of activity at the schoolhouse. Mark and the others had moved the computer equipment and had set up cots throughout the first floor. Shelly had convinced the others to let Melinda come upstairs. Janie had screamed at them and remained downstairs.

Conrad made a schedule and handed it to everyone when they arrived. Breakfast, lunch, and dinner were at specific times, and each person was asked to help with some duty, no matter how small. Some couldn't help because their stings were more recent, but many were nearing the end of their suffering.

Mark came up to Vicki. He looked worried. "We forgot something."

"What?"

"We didn't tell Z. This is his family's place, and we've just opened up a secret."

"I'll call him," Vicki said.

Z answered on the first ring with his familiar drawl. He was a big man, burly, with tattoos, but his voice was high-pitched. Vicki had liked Z from the moment they had met.

"Pete told me about your trip south," Z said. "We saw a report last night that the GC had caught up with that Traickin guy. He's in custody."

"He fooled a lot of believers, but he won't anymore."

"Pete wants to talk with you."

"Wait. I have news." Vicki explained Lenore's idea and how many people they had brought to the schoolhouse. "We want to open up the schoolhouse to anyone who needs help."

Z paused. "And you want to know if I'll go along with the plan?"

"Will you?"

Z gave a belly laugh. "Little lady, from the moment you told me about your dream to set up a training center, it was only logical that you'd bring in unbelievers at some point."

"Really?"

"Of course, it's risky. If the GC gets wind of it, they'll be crawling all over that place and taking our supplies. That's why Dad and I located a couple of warehouses closer to us."

"So you think this is a good idea?"

Z chuckled. "You've got a good heart, you care about people, and you want to do what God wants you to do. I'm with you."

Vicki nearly cried when Z finished. Pete got on the

phone and apologized for not being at the schoolhouse
sooner. "We're going over my routes. Looks like I'm
headed your way with some things for the people who've
been stung; then I'm headed east."

Vicki frowned. "We were hoping you'd take us with
you out west." She explained the idea about talking to
other groups of believers around the country.

"You're always welcome in my truck," Pete said, "but
it might be better for you to go this alone." Pete told her
he would be at the schoolhouse in the next few days with
supplies.

When she hung up, Vicki gathered the others in the
computer room upstairs. They couldn't find Charlie but
decided to go ahead without him. Shelly suggested they
use the station wagon for the trip.

Conrad questioned whether the car would hold up.
"That thing's so old it'll probably break down before you
get to Iowa."

"If Pete can't take us, what other option do we have?"

Conrad stood. "Maybe somebody knows of another
car. I'll check."

Darrion opened a map showing cities and towns west
of Illinois. Roadways were highlighted in yellow. "This is
a list of areas where most of the requests are coming
from. These roads are all in operation. Assuming we
could contact the people, we could head out tomorrow."

Mark sighed. "I know this was my idea, but I've been
thinking about the risks. You're probably going to reach a
few hundred people."

"Try a few thousand," Darrion said.

"Hang on," Vicki said. "God's more concerned with people's hearts than big numbers. He used a little boy's lunch to feed thousands, right?"

The kids nodded.

"For a long time I've concentrated on how small I am, how little I have to offer," Vicki continued. "That's not the point. The point is how big God is and what he wants to do."

Shelly nodded. "I wish I knew about God before all this happened. I would have told as many people as I could."

Conrad came back into the room out of breath. "You're not going to believe this. Come with me."

Lionel awakened when Judd returned to Yitzhak's house. He wanted to talk about their next move, but Judd fell into bed and went to sleep.

Things had happened so quickly after Pavel's funeral in New Babylon. Lionel was glad to get away from there, but he really wanted to get back home, not only for himself but also for Sam, who seemed to be getting more and more concerned about being in Israel.

Lionel was also upset about Judd and Nada. He had gone back and forth about confronting Judd. Was it any of Lionel's business what Judd did with his personal life? Finally, Lionel had talked with Judd and told him what he thought. Now that they were relatively safe from the Global Community, Lionel feared they would stay put.

Sam awoke and met Lionel at the breakfast table. The boy looked troubled. "I've been having dreams," he said.

"About what?" Lionel said.

"My father. He is running after me in his GC uniform. He has a weapon and yells at me to stop. He says he wants me to tell him where Tsion Ben-Judah is hiding. They catch me and put me in prison."

"What happens then?" Lionel said.

Sam looked away. "That is what scares me most of all. In the end I tell him. Dr. Ben-Judah is found and arrested."

"But you don't even know where Tsion is," Lionel said. "None of us do."

"I know that," Sam said, "but it still frightens me."

Judd finally awoke and came to the table. He told them about Nada's parents' reaction to Kasim.

When he was finished, Lionel said, "I'm happy for Nada's family and that you're back together, but we need to talk about Sam." Lionel shared Sam's nightmares.

"How long have you had these?" Judd said.

"For the past three nights. I wake up sweating because they're so real."

Judd pursed his lips. "I used to think dreams came because of something you ate, but now I pay more attention. Do you think God's trying to tell you something?"

Lionel smirked. "Yeah, he's telling us to get out of here and go home."

Judd ignored Lionel and turned to Sam.

"I assume God's telling me I'm in some sort of danger. My fear is that my father will come through the door any minute and arrest all of us."

"I wouldn't worry about that," Judd said. "This place is safe. Just keep praying for your dad."

"Since I came with you, I've prayed for him every day." Sam stared at the floor.

"What is it?" Lionel said.

"I have a confession. I went out earlier to find a pay phone and called the hospital."

"You what?" Judd said.

"What did you find out?" Lionel said.

"I didn't tell them who I was. They would only say that my father was released some time ago."

Judd shook his head. "You can't make contact. Like you said, it's dangerous, not just for you but for all of us."

Sam nodded and Lionel asked to speak with Judd privately. When they were alone, Lionel said, "You can't bring him back here and expect him not to wonder about his own flesh and blood. You'd do the same thing if it were your dad."

"Don't lecture me," Judd said sternly.

"I'm not lecturing," Lionel said. "I've been telling you we need to take Sam to the States, but you won't listen. You're too . . ."

"Too what?" Judd said.

"You don't seem with us anymore," Lionel said. "You're more concerned with your love life—"

"That's it," Judd said. "I don't have to take this."

"Maybe I'm wrong," Lionel said. "Finding Kasim was a good thing, but it just feels like we've lost you as leader of the Young Trib Force."

Judd ran a hand through his hair. His beard was fuller

now, and his hair was getting longer. "We're not going anywhere right now. There aren't any commercial flights, and the pilots with the co-op aren't giving rides."

"If I could find one, would you go back with us?" Lionel said.

"I don't know," Judd said.

———————————

Vicki and the others followed Conrad downstairs. Several of the unbelievers who were suffering greatly had moved into a darkened room down the hall. But in the old computer room they found Charlie talking with one of the teenagers Vicki and Darrion had met the day before. The girl sat with her back to the door, and Charlie looked up when he saw Vicki and the others. He excused himself and came into the hall. "She wanted to know more, so I told her! Her friend didn't want to hear it, but she did. I borrowed your Bible, Vicki; I hope that was OK."

"What are you talking about?" Vicki said.

"I think she's going to pray the prayer!" Charlie said. "I was just about to read her some of the stuff from the Bible."

"Wait," Mark said. "I thought we were going to take this slow and make sure—"

Vicki interrupted. "You talked with her about God?"

"Oh yeah," Charlie said, "I told her how I really wanted one of those things on my forehead, and I thought I had to do stuff to make God like me. And Jenni said, that's her name, she spells it with an *i* instead of a *y* . . ."

"What did she say?" Mark said.

As Charlie talked, he became more excited. "She always felt left out with kids at her school and her church, and she was always trying to do stuff to fit in but it never worked."

"OK," Vicki said. "Go back and talk to her."

Charlie smiled and ran back into the room. The other kids went back upstairs, but Vicki stayed by the doorway and listened.

"Those were my friends," Charlie said. "They're cool. Now, you said that after you got stung, you just kind of walked around and didn't know where to go, right?"

"Yeah," Jenni said. "I was in so much pain I didn't even care what happened to me."

"Look at this verse," Charlie said. "The words in red are the ones that Jesus said. He's the guy I told you about."

Jenni placed a finger on the Bible and read the words slowly. "'I am the way, the truth, and the life. No one can come to the Father except through me.'"

"See," Charlie said, "Jesus doesn't just tell us the way to go; he *is* the way. And if we believe the truth about him and about ourselves, he'll give us life."

"What do you mean, the truth?" Jenni said.

"The truth about God is, he's perfect. The truth about us is that we've all done bad stuff. To be with God we have to be perfect, but we've messed up, so we can't."

"I believe that," Jenni said.

"But God loved us so much that he made a way for us. Read this."

Charlie flipped a few pages and Jenni read, "'For God

so loved the world that he gave his only Son, so that everyone who believes in him will not perish but have eternal life.'"

"See," Charlie said, "God made a way for us to be forgiven for the bad stuff we've done. Anybody who believes the truth and asks God to help them, God promises to give them life."

"You mean, when we die?"

"Both then *and* now," Charlie said. "Since I prayed that prayer I told you about, you wouldn't believe how much more alive I feel. And I know I'm going to heaven because Jesus said it. You can trust him because he's the truth."

Jenni wiped a tear from her face. "I want to believe that so much."

"God will hear you if you pray to him, I promise."

"OK," Jenni said. "What do I do?"

"Well, I got down on my knees because . . . well, I guess that's the way I always saw people do it."

Jenni slipped out of her chair and Charlie knelt beside her. "Just tell God you know you've messed up and you believe that Jesus is the way."

"God, I've done a lot of bad things, and I'm sorry," Jenni said. "I believe Jesus is the way and that he died for me. Please forgive me."

"Good. Now just give your life to God and ask him to change you."

"God, I want you to change me. Whatever is left of my life, I give it to you. And thank you for these people who are giving me a place to stay."

305

Phoenix walked up beside Vicki and licked her hand. Vicki patted his head.

Charlie helped Jenni to her feet and pointed to his forehead. "Do you see this?"

Jenni did a double take. "When did you put that there?"

"I didn't. God did. And look at this." Charlie opened the Bible to Romans and read another verse. "'For if you confess with your mouth that Jesus is Lord and believe in your heart that God raised him from the dead, you will be saved.'"

"That's what I just did," Jenni said.

Charlie saw Vicki through the open door. He turned Jenni around.

Vicki covered her mouth with a hand. On Jenni's forehead was the unmistakable mark of the true believer.

31

JUDD thought about what Lionel had said and couldn't sleep. He wished he could talk to someone who would understand what he was going through. He had feelings for Nada, no question. But was Judd chasing after something he needed to let go of? He admired and respected Nada, but was he ready to commit himself to her?

Judd prayed that God would give him someone to talk to about his dilemma. He peeked into the room where Lionel and Sam were sleeping and noticed Sam's cot was empty. He woke Lionel and the two searched the house. Finally, they went back to the bedroom and found a note under Sam's pillow.

> *Lionel and Judd,*
>
> *I know you won't like this and you may not under-stand it, but I have to talk with my dad. I keep having*

the dream and it scares me. One of the verses I've read lately is in 1 John. It says, "Such love has no fear because perfect love expels all fear." So I think God wants me to face this. If I don't, I'll live the rest of my life wondering about my dad.

You don't have to worry about me giving you guys up. The GC can do anything they want, but I'll never give them any information about the Force.

In case something happens, don't come looking for me. If I can make it back to you, I will. I still dream about visiting the schoolhouse in the States.

God bless you. Thank you for showing me the truth and for being my friend.

In Christ,
Sam

Lionel sat on the cot. "This wouldn't have happened if you'd agreed to go home."

"Don't blame me for this."

Lionel shook his head. "You think we can catch him before he gets to his house?"

"It's hard telling how long ago he wrote this. He could already be there."

Someone pecked at the back door, and Judd rushed to see if it was Sam. He opened the door and gasped. "Mr. Stein!"

––––––––

Vicki and the others talked with Jenni about what it meant to be a follower of Jesus. Charlie had done well.

He had explained the gospel clearly but hadn't revealed
too much to the other people living with the kids. When
Jenni heard that the kids needed a different car than the
station wagon, she told them about her parents' minivan. It was still in the garage where her parents had
left it.

"What happened to them?" Vicki said.

"They were visiting some friends when the earthquake
hit," Jenni said. "They didn't make it."

"Could we use it?" Vicki said.

"It's yours."

Conrad volunteered to walk into town and get the
van the following day while the others prepared. Since
Shelly had driving experience, the kids decided she
should go with Vicki. Darrion also wanted to go,
but Lenore said she would need her help at the schoolhouse.

"It's not fair," Darrion said, "but if I'm needed here,
I'll stay."

"You need at least one guy along," Conrad said.
"Once the locust stings wear off, there's probably going to
be a lot of weird stuff going on."

The others agreed, and the kids voted that Conrad
should go with Vicki and Shelly. The three looked over
the route Darrion had mapped out. Mark said he would
begin e-mailing people to set up meetings.

"How long do you think we'll be gone?" Conrad said.

Vicki looked at her calendar and jotted a few notes.
"If we follow this route, it could be weeks. Maybe
months."

Judd and Lionel greeted Mr. Stein and woke Yitzhak to tell him the news. Everyone wanted to hear Mr. Stein's story, but the man was exhausted. He promised to tell them what had happened when he awoke.

"Before I sleep," Mr. Stein said, "how is our young Israeli friend, Sam?"

Judd showed him Sam's note.

Mr. Stein closed his eyes and prayed, "Father, I ask you to protect our friend and keep him from harm. Make him a bold messenger of your gospel."

While Mr. Stein slept, Judd contacted Nada. They had agreed to call each other once a day and meet face-to-face once a week. She was excited about Mr. Stein's return but concerned for Sam. "We're not that far from his house. I could go there and give you a report."

"No," Judd said. "Sam asked that we not follow him. I'm hoping he'll be back soon."

"I want to see you," Nada said.

"Me too," Judd said, "but you know what we agreed to. I want to show your mom and dad that we can stick to this."

As Vicki prepared for the trip, she felt sure this was something God wanted them to do. She knew they couldn't travel and teach without God's help. There were many obstacles to overcome. The three would only have phone contact with their friends for a long time. They would need to camp at night, which Vicki didn't care for. And the traveling looked grueling.

Conrad returned with the van the next day, and Vicki went out with the others to meet him. To her surprise, four other people got out of the van.

Conrad shrugged. "I don't know how they heard about the schoolhouse, but they did. They wouldn't let me leave without them."

Darrion took the four inside and found places for them to sleep. All had been stung by the locusts and were weak. Charlie carried blankets and pillows to their rooms, while Lenore fixed a light meal for those who were hungry.

Vicki turned to Conrad. "This is really working. Everybody's pitching in."

Conrad nodded. "The more people we get, the more hands on deck we'll need. Maybe Judd and Lionel will come back soon."

Vicki leaned against the minivan. "Maybe they'll stay over there."

Conrad smiled. "They'll be back."

Mark joined them and helped get the van ready. "We've almost maxed out our living space."

"You can use my bunk," Conrad said.

"What if these people scream at night like Janie?" Mark said.

"God won't give us more than we can handle," Vicki said.

Pete arrived the next morning with fresh supplies and two more people who had been stung by the locusts. "Zeke said they were good candidates for the schoolhouse."

Mark rolled his eyes and went back upstairs.

Pete was heading east to move food to a warehouse that would supply believers in New England. He handed Vicki an envelope that contained several thousand Nicks.

"I wish we could go back to using dollars," Shelly said. "I hate spending something with that guy's face on the front of it."

"I know what you mean," Pete said, "but you'll need this to keep fueled up. Keep it hidden."

Pete helped them load their things, and the kids gave each other hugs. Vicki took a deep breath and closed the sliding door. She wondered what the world would be like the next time she saw her friends. Would the next judgment of the horsemen occur by then? How would kids respond to her teaching?

Shelly pulled out and Vicki watched the schoolhouse slowly disappear in the trees.

Though Judd couldn't wait to hear about his trip, Mr. Stein slept for nearly twenty-four hours. When he finally awoke, he was starving.

"I anticipated your hunger," Yitzhak said from the kitchen. "Come and tell us what God has done while I make breakfast."

Mr. Stein's face lit up as he talked of his travels. "There is so much to say, so many reasons to praise God. First, Judd must tell me what happened when he returned."

Judd quickly explained how his plane had been

attacked by locusts as they touched down in Israel. Lionel gave his perspective and added that they were able to see Moishe and Eli, the two witnesses at the Wailing Wall.

"How I long to hear their voices again," Mr. Stein said. He took his time eating, savoring every bite. When he finished, he wiped the stray food from his beard and moved to a comfortable chair.

Judd, Lionel, Yitzhak, and the others staying in the house crowded into the room. They all tried to get as close as they could.

"Before I begin, I want to pray," Mr. Stein said. "Father, for what I am about to say, I give thanks, and I pray that you alone would receive the honor and glory for what you have done."

Lionel said, "We've heard from Judd about what happened the first week in Africa. Pick up the story from there."

"As I traveled farther into the country, things became spiritually darker. In one village, I noticed there were very few young people. I learned that these people had been terrified by the Rapture of their children. They knew nothing of the true God and believed a spirit had stolen their children in the night.

"So, when the other judgments came—the earthquake, the stars falling from the sky, the darkened sun, and so forth—they believed the spirit wanted their older children. To please this angry god, they planned to sacrifice one child each day."

Judd shook his head. "That's awful."

"I spoke to them and told them that the Great Spirit

was almighty God and that he took their children because he was kind and loving. Their sons and daughters who had vanished were safe in heaven."

"Did that make them happy?" Lionel said.

"They were confused. I explained that God had become a man and lived a perfect life. He gave his life as a sacrifice. They understood the concept of sacrifice and wanted to hear more."

"What happened?" Judd said.

"Every one of them believed in Jesus and received the seal of God on their forehead," Mr. Stein said. "Then an amazing thing happened. A mother of two teenagers rushed up to me. She literally pulled me toward a mountain. We walked more than an hour. I had no idea where we were going."

"I'll bet she wanted you to talk to some friends in another village," Lionel said.

Mr. Stein smiled. "This will show you the goodness of God. On the night before the villagers were to perform their first sacrifice, the woman was awakened by a voice. She said it sounded like many waters coming together. The voice told her they must not kill their children. Someone was coming with wonderful news.

"She got up immediately, awakened her teenage sons, and quietly they rounded up all of the young people. She told them what the voice had said and that they were to hide.

"When we reached the edge of the mountain, the young people came streaming out to meet me. I told them the news that God loved them and didn't want them to die. Before I had finished my first few words, the boys and girls fell on the ground and cried out to God for mercy."

Mr. Stein had tears in his eyes. "I can't describe the look on the faces of their parents when I led their children back to them. The parents had believed the evil spirit had taken their older children in the night just as their young ones had vanished. When they saw their sons and daughters coming toward them, the parents rushed to them and embraced them."

The room fell silent. No one moved.

Mr. Stein sipped a hot drink and continued. "The people wanted me to stay but I had to keep going. God showed me each step to take. He took me to villages so remote that there were only a handful of people. But everywhere I went, I found people ready for the message. God had prepared their hearts to hear long before I arrived."

"Were you ever afraid?" one of the other witnesses said.

Mr. Stein smiled. "There were times when the people came at me with spears and clubs, thinking I was there to harm them, but each time God gave me the language of the people to speak. Men clutching sharp knives stopped in their tracks when they heard my voice.

"But what did I have to fear? If I die, I am with Christ and my family. If I live, I do the will of God." Mr. Stein paused. "Before I became a believer in Jesus, I was so concerned with what people thought of me. I chose my words carefully. I made sure I put forward the right image. I was so proud. Now I don't care what people think. If they believe I am a madman, so be it. I am a madman for Christ. If they think I am a fool, that I am loony, it is OK. I would rather be considered a fool and show people the way to God than be thought of as intelligent and respectable and allow people to go to hell."

"There aren't any flights right now," Judd said. "How did you get here?"

Mr. Stein took a deep breath. "That is the most incredible part of my story."

32

JUDD hung on every word Mr. Stein said. He knew how much Mr. Stein had resisted the gospel and how he had treated his daughter, Chaya. If a man that opposed to the things of God could be used to tell others the message, Judd thought God could use anyone.

Mr. Stein described how he woke up each morning and felt God leading him to a new place. "Some mornings there would be nothing to eat, and I would praise God that he was the Bread of Life. There were times when I came to great rivers or impassable canyons, and I would praise God that he was the way. Every day I learned something new about trusting him."

Mr. Stein said, "To me, this is the most miraculous part of my story. I spoke in languages I have never heard before, watched God do things I couldn't begin to tell you, and yet, how he brought me here is most amazing to me.

317

"As I spoke and traveled, I realized God was leading me in a northern direction. The Sahara Desert lay to the east, and I was glad he didn't lead me there. But I was going farther and farther away from Israel, and I desperately wanted to come back here if it was God's will.

"After the locusts came, there were fewer people to speak with. So many had been stung and were in such great pain. Some people listened and received the mark of the believer.

"But God was leading me. I no longer had anyone with me, so it was quite lonely. I walked, borrowed vehicles, rode with some believers in a caravan, and kept pushing toward the coast. When I finally came to the shore and looked out on that vastness of blue water, I thought of the ocean of God's love. It is so wide and so deep."

"Did you know where you were going at that point?" Judd said.

"I believed God would give me the desire of my heart to return to Israel. There were no flights leaving and I had very little money, but I found a believer with a small fishing boat who agreed to take me to Casablanca."

"The same place as in that old movie?" Lionel said.

Mr. Stein smiled. "I've seen that, but I never dreamed I would visit under these circumstances. Locusts had attacked everyone and the city was nearly shut down.

"I spoke on the street corner and even went into the bars. I had proclaimed the Good News to people who lived in villages and wore almost no clothing. Now I was in a city telling people that same news.

"I didn't have the same success, but God was still with

me. I was speaking to people gathered near a hospital, and a man approached and said he was the captain of a fishing vessel. He was looking for men who were able to work in spite of their injuries.

"I told him I had no injuries, that the Lord God had spared his servants. The man cursed at me but I followed him. The next day the boat headed for the Mediterranean Sea. . . ."

"And you were on it?" Lionel said.

"I was. But I discovered this was no fishing vessel. I was sent belowdecks on an errand and found the cargo hold. There were no fish. This boat carried millions of dollars' worth of drugs. I later discovered that hundreds of cartons were filled with heroin and cocaine."

"How could the men on the ship work after being stung?" Yitzhak said.

"Their greed was greater than their pain. I saw men doubled over, writhing on deck, and others would simply step over them. They set their minds on the money they would receive, thinking that would ease their troubles."

"Did you tell them about God?" Judd said.

"I told them so much they threatened to throw me overboard. I spoke to them individually; I preached from the bow, the mess hall, and anywhere there was someone who would listen. Sadly, it took a disaster to get their attention."

Mr. Stein shuddered and continued. "We were a hundred miles off the coast of Malta when the storm hit. I have seen movies about such waves and violent winds, but I have never experienced anything so powerful.

"I was asleep belowdecks when I heard the screaming. Men who had already felt the pain of the locusts were now fearing for their lives. I ran onto the deck and saw a sight I'll never forget. Black clouds as thick as soot and waves three times higher than the mast. Waves crashed against the deck. Some men simply leaped into the sea, trying to take their lives.

"Of course, I knew they would not die. The Scriptures are clear that even if a person wants to die during this period he will not. I knelt and asked God to give me something to say, something to comfort the crew. Then I realized again that nothing we do is by chance. Nothing that happens to us is a mistake. God can use us in any situation.

"God brought to my mind the passage about Jesus asleep in the boat when a terrible squall came up on the Sea of Galilee. The disciples feared for their lives and woke him. Do you remember what happened?"

"Isn't that where Jesus spoke and made the wind die?" Lionel said.

"Exactly," Mr. Stein said. "God had led me onto the deck and I called the men forward. The wind howled around us. Somehow God gave me the strength to speak above the noise."

"What did you say?" Lionel said.

Mr. Stein closed his eyes and put both hands in the air. As he spoke he gestured, as if he were back on the deck of the ship. "You have heard the message of God, and you have not believed. You have survived an earthquake and meteors and freezing temperatures, and you

320

have not believed. The stinging locusts came, and you have not believed.

"Hear me, not one of you will perish because of this storm. But you will all surely die if you do not accept the one and only Son of God."

Mr. Stein opened his eyes. "They shouted at me, 'How do you know we won't be killed?' I said that it was prophesied in the Bible.

"The captain stepped forward. He was such a hardened man. He knew the ship wasn't going to make it without some kind of miracle. 'Can you save us?' he shouted. I told him only God can save, and each one of them must come to him for forgiveness."

Mr. Stein stopped talking and knelt on the floor. He put his face in his hands. "I tell you this not to boast, but to rejoice in the power and goodness of God. I have no power of my own. But God impressed on me to raise my hands and shout at the wind, 'The Lord God wants to use each of you for great and mighty things which you know not. So you will know that God alone has the power to save, I say, Peace, be still.'"

Mr. Stein wept until tears streamed through his fingers. The other witnesses and Yitzhak knelt beside him, hands on his shoulders, praying and weeping.

Judd looked at Lionel and whispered, "Wonder what happened?"

Lionel put a finger to his lips, and they waited until Mr. Stein stopped crying. He sat in a chair and wiped his eyes. "As God is my witness, the wind stopped almost immediately. Within a minute or so, the waves stopped and the sea grew calm. A yellow spot about the size of my hand broke through the dark clouds. It widened until the sky was a brilliant blue. The sun was out, and it was the finest day I have ever seen."

Judd shook his head. He had read about miracles like that in the Bible when he was a kid, but he never expected anything like that to happen in his lifetime.

"Again I hesitate to tell you this for fear you will praise me, but this has nothing to do with me. This is God's miracle. He alone is worthy. He alone deserves glory and honor!"

A chorus of amens rang throughout the room. Judd felt goose bumps on his arms. "What happened to the men?"

Mr. Stein laughed. "That is the best part of the story, not that God performed a miracle with the sea, but God changed their hearts.

"First one, then another fell to his knees. Then others on deck did the same and cried out to God for forgiveness. As they did, they received the mark of the believer on their foreheads. When they looked at each other, they were amazed at what God had done. And so was I."

"Every one of them believed?" Judd said.

"I counted every man there except the captain," Mr. Stein said. "I have never seen anyone with such anger in his soul. He disappeared belowdecks before I could get to him. Then a few minutes later he returned holding something. He rushed past me to the railing and ripped open a package. A white powder spilled out and spread across the surface of the sea."

"The drugs!" Lionel said.

322

"Yes," Mr. Stein said. "Later he told me he prayed for forgiveness as he ran into the belly of the ship. After he spilled the first bag into the water, the others raced to the cargo hold and dumped the entire load. A fortune was lost that day, but many precious souls were won."

"Did they bring you straight to Israel after that?" Judd said.

"We talked about what they should do as we studied the Scriptures and prayed. Many of the men couldn't study because of the pain from their stings, but in spite of that, I have never seen people so hungry for God's Word. After a few days they decided they would go to Greece as planned and explain what had happened to them."

"But they destroyed all the drugs," Lionel said. "They could be killed for that."

"The men said they wanted to tell the buyers what they had seen and experienced," Mr. Stein said. "They believe, as I do, that no one is so bad that God's love can't reach them."

"What about Carpathia?" someone said. "Is he too bad?"

Mr. Stein grimaced. "Nicolae will soon be indwelt by Satan himself. With all the Global Community has unleashed, I fear we have not yet seen the evil he is capable of."

"What happened in Greece?" Lionel said.

"Someone had tipped the authorities about the deal. GC Drug Enforcement officers were at the dock waiting for us with their bulky protective gear. They seized the ship and searched it. When they found nothing, the captain asked to speak. With all of the officers lined up on that ship, he gave the clearest presentation of the gospel I have ever heard. Most of the GC officers scoffed at him, but I saw a few who prayed and received the mark."

"Unbelievable," Judd said.

"And that is just my story," Mr. Stein said. "There are 144,000 witnesses who are preaching the Good News. Each one of them has a story of God's working."

"How did you make it here?" Lionel said.

"The GC had no reason to hold the ship, so the crew asked to escort me to Tel Aviv. As we sailed, I told the men about the commodity co-op of the Tribulation Force. They want to be fishermen by day, helping the co-op obtain food, and fishers of men by night, building the kingdom of God."

Mr. Stein slapped his knees with his hands and stood. Everyone around the room joined hands and stood in a circle. Mr. Stein looked at each one of them. "Now I am back with you in this great city. I am ready to serve however God leads, wherever he wishes. And I tell you that he wants to do something great and mighty through each of you. He wants to accomplish more than you can dream. And I pray that you would let him do it and that none of us would hinder God's work or become distracted from our true mission."

Mr. Stein bowed his head. Yitzhak prayed; then others joined in. Judd couldn't hold back the tears. To think that God would allow him to be part of his plan for reaching others was too much for him.

Judd walked alone later to see Nada. The things Mr. Stein had said were exciting, but troubling as well.

Nada told Judd how difficult it was staying in the small apartment with her family and the others. Her father didn't want them moving in and out for fear they would be reported. Kasim struggled with whether to call Kweesa and talk with her about God.

Judd told Nada about Mr. Stein's return and everything he had seen and done. Several times he had to stop and compose himself as he described how God had worked.

"I wish I could have been there with him," Nada said.

Judd nodded. "I want to be just like him. He's single-minded and won't let anything get in the way of doing what God wants."

Nada stared at Judd. "What does that do to us? Am I a distraction?"

Judd smiled. "You're a good distraction. But I've been thinking a lot about Pavel and Sam. Lionel's called me on this a couple of times and I think he's right. I've let down my friends. Being with you is great. Our friendship means a lot to me, but right now it just seems . . ."

"Selfish?"

"Yeah, exactly." Judd paused and looked into Nada's eyes. "Maybe God wants us to work together. Maybe he wants us apart. I don't know which it's supposed to be. But whatever God wants, that's what I want."

"I understand," Nada said. "Me too. But I would be lying if I said I wasn't hurt. I felt like we were growing together. Let's not tell anyone about this until we're sure what God wants us to do."

"Agreed," Judd said. "Let's be totally committed to doing what God wants us to do from now on."

33

VICKI watched the miles roll by as the kids headed west in the minivan. Shelly had driven first on an old tollway coming from Chicago. In places, concrete slabs rose straight up and Shelly had to drive off the road, but mostly the driving was slow, watching out for potholes or separated roadways.

Pete had warned them not to drive too fast. "You'll hit smooth spots and think you can drive the old speed limit. That's when people bust a tire and get themselves stranded."

The kids were aware of news reports of roving bandits. Before the locusts had come, groups of bandits had taken over lonely stretches of roads. They stopped cars, robbed the occupants, and stole vehicles. Sometimes the people inside the cars were even killed. But now reports of these bandits had dwindled.

At night, the kids pulled the van away from the road

and slept in it. It took them nearly two days to get to their first meeting in Iowa. Mark had given directions to a college about fifty miles from Des Moines. They found the campus in ruins, most of the stone buildings destroyed by the earthquake. Huge trees had been uprooted and lay strewn between piles of rubble. A few of the older buildings were still standing but looked dangerous.

"Where do you think everybody is?" Shelly said.

"The meeting isn't supposed to start until sundown," Vicki said. "Let's get something to eat."

They hid the minivan behind some shrubs and ate sandwiches. Vicki used the cell phone to call Mark but couldn't get a signal. When the sun went down, the kids got out and walked the campus.

"I don't see anybody," Conrad said.

Something moved in some trees. At first Vicki thought it was the wind blowing leaves; then she realized the movement was young people walking toward them. Soon the campus was full of teens and young adults.

A girl a little older than Vicki stepped forward and shook hands. "I'm Kelly Bradshaw. I sent the e-mail inviting you here. Are you Mark?"

Conrad shook his head and introduced himself. "Mark stayed behind. Vicki is the one who does the teaching."

"Come on," Kelly said, "we're meeting in Darby."

Darby had been a combination gymnasium and computer center for the college. Kids with flashlights illuminated the room. The floor was cracked. Bleachers sat at an angle and looked unsafe. What hadn't been destroyed by the earthquake had been wrecked by looters.

328

Kelly led them down a set of concrete stairs to a locker room. "We'll be safe down here."

"Do you all stay together?" Vicki said.

"Some of us took over my family's farm a couple of miles away," Kelly said. "We're trying to grow our own food so we can live when we can't buy it. Others are people we've met from the area. Some came all the way from Missouri. Everybody's a believer."

Some kids sat on benches, others on the floor. Vicki did a quick count and estimated there were almost a hundred in the room. She looked for something to write on, and Kelly handed her a black Magic Marker. "Just write on that wall."

"My name is Vicki Byrne," she said, her voice echoing through the locker room. "I believe we're living in one of the most exciting times in the history of the world. By the end of the soul harvest, there will be more Christ followers than at the time of the Rapture.

"That's the good news. The bad news is that Nicolae Carpathia and the Global Community are in control. There is so much evil, and that's only going to get worse. That's where we come in. Our job is to tell as many as we can about God's message."

Mark tried to contact Vicki and the others about their next meeting but couldn't. He had fallen asleep at the computer and was awakened by the phone.

"You won't believe how well the meeting went," Vicki said. "We're staying another day at a farm nearby and going through the rest of the teaching. These kids are really learning."

"Great," Mark said, "but you'll have to drive tonight if you're going to get to Minnesota by tomorrow evening."

"We can do it," Vicki said.

While he talked with Vicki, Mark opened an e-mail from Lionel.

"Read it," Vicki said.

"*We're back in Israel,*" Mark read, "*but our friend Sam is missing. He went to see his dad a couple of days ago and hasn't returned. We're trying to decide what to do.*

"*Mr. Stein is back and you should hear his stories. He could write a book about all that God's done! But my main reason for writing is Judd. He's been seeing . . .*" Mark stopped and read the rest of the message silently.

"What is it?" Vicki said. "What about Judd?"

"It's . . . nothing," Mark said.

"Tell me," Vicki said.

Mark read on. "*Judd's been seeing a girl ever since we came here. We went to New Babylon because his friend was dying, but I wound up spending more time with Pavel than he did.*"

"I remember Judd talking about him," Vicki said. "Pavel's dead?"

"I guess so." Mark kept reading. "*Some good things came out of him being with her, but I'm afraid we're going to lose him. He and Nada are getting serious.*"

"Her name is Nada?" Vicki said. "What kind of name is that?"

"Almost finished," Mark said. "*Please pray for Judd and*

Sam and that we'd find a way back to the States as soon as possible. I want to get back and help you guys with the schoolhouse."

Vicki took a deep breath.

After a few moments Mark said, "You all right?"

"Yeah, I'm fine," Vicki said quickly. "Have you heard anything from Carl?"

"He's checked in a couple of times. He's still in good with the GC and they don't suspect anything. He did say they found Traickin along the side of the road somewhere in Tennessee. He'd been stung."

"What a surprise," Vicki said.

"They must have gotten some information from you guys because they arrested a bunch of people from Johnson City, and they're looking for a hideout in Illinois, but Carl doesn't think they're even close to us."

"Is there anything we can do for the people in Tennessee?"

"Carl said they're waiting to be processed as rebels."

"What will the GC do with them?"

"Maybe some kind of reeducation facility. Or the GC could try to make an example of them and put them in prison. Or worse."

Vicki groaned.

"You can't blame yourself. You rescued those people from the GC once."

"Yeah, but what good did it do? They're in jail. Can you do me a favor?"

"Name it."

Vicki gave Mark Omer's name and asked if Carl could

find out any information. "I'm afraid Omer might try something stupid to get his mom and the others out."

"I'll get on it and check back with you when you guys are on the road tonight."

Vicki tried to teach in the afternoon but felt distracted. She had the kids break into small groups to pray and come up with questions.

She took a walk in a cornfield to clear her head. The people in Tennessee were on her mind, but it was the news about Judd that had her stomach tied in knots. She had talked with him before her trip with Pete, but he hadn't said anything about Nada.

Vicki argued with herself as she walked. She and Judd fought like cats and dogs. He was a couple of years older and from a different background. Still, Vicki had to admit she cared for Judd. There were times when things went well. Now, with news of Nada, Vicki felt frustrated. *Don't you see what this is doing to you? There are a hundred kids waiting to learn more about God, and you're out here in a cornfield acting like a schoolgirl!*

Shelly found Vicki and asked what was wrong. "You didn't seem yourself this afternoon."

Vicki told her about Mark's call. "Believe me, I don't want to waste energy on something stupid like this."

"But it feels bad, doesn't it?" Shelly said.

"It feels like somebody punched me in the stomach. I know I don't need Judd. Since he's been gone I've grown a lot; I've been able to do more things. But there's still part of me that misses him."

"Maybe God separated you for that reason," Shelly said. "He wanted both of you to grow so that when you get back together—"

"How's that going to happen if Judd's married? I told you what Lionel said."

"If Judd gets married, which is pretty unlikely, then you can move on." Shelly put out a hand and stopped Vicki. "It's not like you're the only one who has these kinds of feelings."

"You like Judd too?" Vicki said.

Shelly laughed. "Judd's not my type. But when you're thrown together with so many people, you naturally have feelings for them."

"Who?" Vicki said.

Shelly rolled her eyes. "No way. I'm not getting into this. But I want you to know you're not alone with your feelings."

"Thanks," Vicki said. "Do you like Mark?"

Shelly shook her head. "Come on, let's get back to the group."

___

When Sam didn't return or call, Judd went to Mr. Stein and asked his opinion.

The man scratched his beard. "I've been thinking a lot about him," Mr. Stein said. "Before we left for Africa I told Sam I would talk with his father if I ever had the chance. Perhaps that time is now."

333

Mr. Stein decided it would be best to go to Sam's house late at night. Even those who had already been stung by locusts avoided going out at night because of the eerie sounds. Mr. Stein agreed that Judd and Lionel could come along if they stayed out of sight.

As they walked, Mr. Stein told them more details about his travels. There seemed to be no end to the miracles God had performed.

"The temptation is to think that I can do great things for God in my own strength, but that is not true. I can only do what Christ strengthens me to do. I found that the long hours of travel prepared me for what was ahead. I would pray as we walked or rode and asked God for his intervention." Mr. Stein stopped. "This is a perfect example. As we walk, let's bring this situation before God."

Mr. Stein went first and prayed for Mr. Goldberg. Judd asked protection for Sam, and Lionel prayed that Mr. Stein would be kept safe. They continued praying as they walked.

"Our Father, Mr. Goldberg is a servant of Nicolae Carpathia," Mr. Stein prayed. "He has been blinded to the truth, and we ask that you might open his eyes tonight and accept the message we bring."

When they came in sight of Sam's house, Lionel said, "What are you going to say to him?"

Mr. Stein smiled. "I imagine Sam has used every argument he can think of with his father. At this point, I believe the only thing that can change Mr. Goldberg's mind about God is God himself."

Judd pointed to the house. A light was on in the living room, but the blinds were closed. Judd and Lionel slipped into the shadows beside the house as Mr. Stein stepped to the front door.

Mr. Stein paused before knocking. Judd saw the man's lips move in one final prayer. He knocked twice and stood back.

Judd glanced at the street, thinking they might have walked into a trap, but there were no Global Community squad cars in sight. A shaft of light hit Mr. Stein in the face as someone opened the door.

"Yes?" Mr. Goldberg said.

Mr. Stein stood like a stone and stared at the man.

"What do you want? Don't just stand there; tell me!"

Mr. Stein stepped forward. "Is your son here?"

Mr. Goldberg's voice trembled. "You're one of them, aren't you?"

"I am a servant of the most high God. I have come to find out about your son."

"He . . . he isn't here," Mr. Goldberg said. "They took him away."

"Who?"

"I called them when he came back."

Mr. Stein said nothing.

"I have had second thoughts. He is a good son. He's mixed-up."

"He is trying to tell you the truth."

Mr. Goldberg stepped outside. Judd could tell the locust sting had weakened him. He looked thin and his

335

hair was much grayer. Judd guessed he was at the end of the cycle of pain the locust had inflicted.

"I have bad dreams," Mr. Goldberg whispered. "Can you help me?"

Mr. Stein nodded and glanced at Judd. "Pray."

34

JUDD told Lionel to keep watch at the back of Mr.
Goldberg's house; then he found an open window at the
side.

Mr. Goldberg asked Mr. Stein if he wanted anything
to drink, and Mr. Stein refused.

"Why haven't you been stung? Everyone I know has
been."

"Not your son," Mr. Stein said. "God does not punish
his children in these judgments."

"How could those things possibly distinguish
between one person and another?" Mr. Goldberg said.

"You will see greater miracles than that. Now tell me
about your dreams."

Mr. Goldberg sat back and put a hand to his forehead.
"How could you possibly help me?"

"Throughout the centuries God has used dreams to
draw people to himself. Tell me."

"It's the same one each time. There is a hideous beast attacking people. I don't see its face, but I see the terror in the eyes of the people being attacked. For some reason, I can't help them. This monster continues until it devours everyone I love.

"Then I see my son. He is running toward me, calling out my name. He runs straight toward the beast and tries to fight him with a sword, but he is so small. I try to move but I can't. I'm stuck. That's the end of the dream. I wake up in a cold sweat."

"Did you tell your son this dream?" Mr. Stein said.

"Of course not! Besides, he was taken away so quickly, I didn't have time."

Mr. Stein bowed his head in prayer.

Mr. Goldberg leaned forward. "Do you think this dream means something?"

Mr. Stein nodded. "I'm not sure you're ready to hear it."

"I am. Please."

"Sometime ago I told your son I would speak with you about these things if the time was right. If you will open your heart to the truth, you will understand."

"I'm ready to hear," Mr. Goldberg said.

"Then hear the interpretation. The beast in your dream is the Global Community. You are powerless to move because you have been deceived by this monster. Your son carries the sword of truth, which is the Word of God. Though he is small and outnumbered, he battles the beast because he knows one day God will be victorious."

"Why is he fighting? If he would simply join us . . ."

338

"He battles for your soul," Mr. Stein said. "He kn⁓
if you do not believe in the only Son of God, your sou⁓
will be lost forever."

Sam's dad stood and walked a few steps. Judd
couldn't see the man's face, but he could hear the anger
in his voice.

"It's because of you that my son turned on me! You
and those boys took him away."

"His friends shared the truth with him and he
accepted it. As I said, it appears God is drawing you to
himself. Do not wait."

Judd prayed for Mr. Goldberg as he listened. Suddenly
someone moved behind him. Judd turned and saw Lionel
waving wildly. "Get back here! I think the GC are
coming!"

Judd ran to the front of the house and saw two GC
squad cars pull in. The men inside were wearing bulky,
protective suits.

Judd banged on the side window and joined Lionel at
the back. Mr. Stein threw open the back door and rushed
down the steps two at a time. "Into the alley!"

Sirens from the squad cars blared as Judd, Lionel, and
Mr. Stein reached a cross street. A few minutes later they
found a row of trash cans and scurried behind them to
rest.

"Goldberg must have alerted the GC," Lionel said.

"So it seems," Mr. Stein said, "but I thought I was
getting through."

Mr. Stein told them about the conversation. "As the
GC came near, Mr. Goldberg put his head in his hands

---

said, 'Maybe I have made a mistake.' It was then that alerted me."

"Did he say where Sam is?" Judd said.

"It must be GC headquarters because he said Deputy Commander Woodruff is still questioning him."

The three caught their breath and hurried back to Yitzhak's house. Judd wondered if they would ever see Sam again.

The talk with Shelly made Vicki feel better, and she was able to concentrate on her message. When they got on the road later that night, Mark called and gave them information about the next stop.

"It's Mankato, Minnesota," Mark said.

Vicki wrote down the directions. Mark gave her the next three groups and their locations as well. "We're getting more requests. I'm having to tell them no unless there are at least a hundred people."

"That doesn't sound fair," Vicki said.

"If we said yes to every small group, you'd be on the road for a couple of years," Mark said. "We don't have that much time."

Mark gave her an update on the schoolhouse and how everyone was doing. Melinda was still upstairs, but Janie was causing problems. "We caught her the other day trying to open the door to the tunnel that leads away from the house."

"I wanted to keep that a secret from the unbelievers," Vicki said. "Does she know what's down there?"

340

"I think she was just trying to cause more trouble."

Vicki relayed the information to Conrad and Shelly. Shelly said, "We're going to Mankato!?"

"What's so big about it?" Vicki said.

"I used to read the Little House on the Prairie books when I was small. Mankato was one of the towns nearby."

Conrad rolled his eyes. Vicki admitted she hadn't read the books.

As they drove through the night, they tried to keep the driver awake with conversation about books and movies. Their lists had changed when the kids had become believers, but as expected, Conrad liked action and adventure films while Vicki and Shelly liked dramas.

"I like it when guys risk their lives to save people," Conrad said, "but if it's supposed to make you cry, leave me out."

Vicki shook her head. "What if the guy trying to save people gets killed? Aren't you supposed to cry then?"

"I guess you could feel a little sad," Conrad said, smiling.

The kids arrived in Mankato in time to eat something and hurry to the meeting place. There were almost two hundred gathered in an abandoned video store. The kids had moved shelves against the wall until there was enough room for everyone.

Vicki took a megaphone from the organizer and looked at the audience. She no longer thought of how high her voice was or what she was wearing. She thought about what she was teaching. This wasn't just a seminar about Bible knowledge. Anybody could give people facts and figures. Vicki was trying to do the same thing Tsion Ben-Judah was doing with his writing. He was preparing his readers for the future and trying to set their hearts on fire for God.

As she spoke, she had to resist the temptation to just say the words. She couldn't go on autopilot. This material had to come from her heart.

Toward the end of the evening Vicki passed out small slips of paper Mark had asked the organizer to bring. "I want you to write down the name of a person who doesn't know God."

Kids shared pens and pencils and scribbled down names. One boy held up a hand. "Is it OK if we put two down?"

Vicki smiled and nodded. "Now let's spend two minutes praying for that person whose name you've just written down. Thank God for bringing that person into your life. Ask him to open their eyes to the truth. If there are things that person is going through, like a locust sting or family members who have disappeared or have been killed, ask God to use those things to create a hunger in that person's heart."

When the two minutes were up, Vicki asked for everyone's attention. "God is the one who will speak to your friend. From today on, each time you sit down to eat, pull out this slip of paper and pray for two minutes for your friend. Pray for opportunities to show love and kindness. Ask for a chance to speak about God. Then, when your friend becomes a believer, get a new slip and write down another friend's name. And teach the new believer how to do the same."

A thin girl raised a hand. "My dad disappeared. My brother and me are alone and we only get one meal a day. Sometimes none. When should we pray?"

Vicki bit her lip. To think of other believers without enough food nearly broke her heart. Before she could answer, a young man in the back stood. "We've got more than enough at our place. See me after the meeting and we'll work out something."

"Thank you," Vicki said. "You don't have to wait until mealtime to pray, of course. You can pray at any point in the day, for as long as you'd like. I just find that if there's something that can help me remember to pray, it's easier."

The next day the group was back. The man who had offered food brought the thin girl and her brother packages of vegetables, bread, and canned food.

When Vicki finished that afternoon, she took questions. Though she had told them about the end of the locusts and what was coming next, the kids wanted to know specifics. What will the horsemen be like? Will they kill any believers? What will Nicolae Carpathia tell the world about this judgment from God?

Vicki answered the questions as best she could and referred them to Tsion Ben-Judah's Web site as well as the kids' Web site located at theunderground-online.com.

The thin girl came up to Vicki after the meeting and handed her a piece of fruit. "Thank you for coming. You changed my life." The girl pulled out the slip of paper from the day before. "I wrote down the name of a friend who doesn't know God on this side, and I wrote down your name on the other. I'll pray for you every day."

Judd and the others prayed each morning about Sam. Though he wanted to storm Global Community headquarters and rescue him, Judd knew that wasn't the best plan.

"God will sustain him," Mr. Stein said. "I feel such compassion for him, like he is my own son. But to try and deliver him from that prison would only endanger more believers."

Judd took a call from Nada. She was upset about her brother. "Kasim and my father argued about his relationship with Kweesa in New Babylon. Kasim wants to call her and tell her the truth, but my father won't let him."

"Is he afraid Kweesa might rat him out?" Judd said.

"Exactly. My father says it puts us at too great a risk. Now my problem is that I know Kasim called Kweesa and talked with her."

"You're kidding," Judd said. "What did she say?"

"She didn't believe it was him for a long time. Then he told her things that only the two of them knew."

"Did Kasim tell her about God?"

"She let him talk for a long time, but we don't know how she responded. We're praying she'll believe. Should I tell my parents?"

"If you do, Kasim's going to hit the roof."

"I'm sorry?"

"It's an expression," Judd said. "He'll be really upset with you."

"Yes. But if I keep this from my parents, they will punch the roof."

344

Judd laughed.

"It would be much easier if I didn't have to live in t]. tiny apartment." Nada sighed.

"No matter where you go or who you're with, you're going to have these kinds of problems. Talk with Kasim. Maybe he'll tell them himself."

"Have you thought any more about us? I miss you."

"I wish we could exercise together again," Judd said. "Yitzhak is letting Lionel and me help pack and ship materials for unbelievers. I think we ought to stay apart for now and see where things go."

"All right," Nada said. "I have to go."

Judd hung up and wondered if he was doing the right thing. He missed Nada's friendship and their talks. But if he was kept from doing what God wanted, their relationship had to be put on hold.

Judd thought of his friends in Illinois and wondered about Vicki. They had both come a long way since meeting Bruce Barnes at New Hope Village Church. God had done so much to and through them. What would he do next?

35

THE next few weeks were a blur to Vicki as they traveled west to visit more groups of believers. From Minnesota they drove through South Dakota. Since it was only a few miles out of the way, they stopped at Mount Rushmore to see what was left of the faces carved into stone. The earthquake had ruined the national monument, and the park was closed.

Mark directed them south, through Wyoming and into Colorado. They spent a few days in a small ski town west of Denver, then continued south to Colorado Springs. The mountains were beautiful, but when Conrad pointed out Pikes Peak, Vicki nearly cried. The once towering mountain had crumbled in the great earthquake.

They followed Mark's directions to an abandoned Christian ministry. The earthquake had destroyed all but the main building.

Conrad led them through a service entrance and up a

flight of stairs. Paintings and posters hung from the walls. They found a huge room with scattered metal chairs. A few dozen people sat in the chairs. Someone had rigged a crude public-address system.

When the crowd realized who Vicki was, they clapped. Vicki walked onto the stage and was surprised to find out they were a day early. When news about the meeting spread, people who were living in different parts of the building filed in. The organizer took Vicki aside and explained there would be a few hundred people within minutes.

"How did you guys find this place?" Vicki said.

"Most of the people who are here lived in the area," the woman said, "but some traveled a great distance. We'd all heard about this ministry through the radio, and when our families disappeared, we thought we might find some answers here.

"We found books and pamphlets that explained about a relationship with God. People came and learned. Sadly, when the earthquake hit, a lot of people in the warehouse and the lower buildings didn't make it out."

Vicki was amazed at the people's organization. In most meetings she had been in, people came from miles around and straggled in. Here, they filed in and took their seats, ready to learn. Between sessions the group was served a meal from the cafeteria.

"This is an even bigger training center than the schoolhouse," Conrad said. "We should remember this place if we ever leave Illinois."

The kids worked their way through Utah and reached

their farthest destination in the Northwest—Olympia, Washington. It was there that they noticed the locusts were gone.

After a few days, they turned south through Oregon and into California. They made five stops in California, concluding with a stay at the coastal town of Chula Vista, near the old Mexican border. Mark had told Vicki to expect a translator for those who couldn't speak English.

Conrad pulled into a parking lot near a beach and pointed. In the distance were hundreds of kids gathered by a bonfire.

Vicki shook hands with Rosa, the one who had e-mailed Mark and set up the meeting. "We have many who know both English and Spanish, but I'll translate for those who can't understand you."

The meeting was like nothing Vicki had ever experienced. The smell of the salty air, the sounds of the seagulls squawking overhead, and the crackling fire made the teaching even more special. Vicki watched the glowing faces of the participants as she spoke. Rosa translated. It was difficult to get used to stopping and waiting for someone to say your words in a different language, but soon Vicki got the hang of it.

Many unbelievers just getting over their stings strolled by. Some stopped, curious about the meeting. When Vicki mentioned "God" or "Jesus," a few walked away. Others lingered. She guessed there were about fifty who stayed.

Vicki felt God wanted her to give these people the message. She spoke through a loudspeaker and asked

...iose on the outskirts of the group to gather closer. Vicki clearly explained the message of God's love and prayed. When she finished, she saw many had received the mark of the true believer.

Vicki looked at the kids sitting in the sand. "Find a new brother or sister and welcome them to the family."

The next day the group had grown. Vicki, Shelly, and Conrad decided to postpone the next meeting in Arizona a few days. God was doing something special in California, and they didn't want to miss any of it.

Judd and Lionel had thrown themselves into whatever work needed to be done. Every day new witnesses arrived in Israel. Mr. Stein helped write new materials to print and deliver, and spent much of the time poring over Tsion Ben-Judah's Web site.

Though they prayed for Sam, they had heard nothing from him. Mr. Stein held out hope that he would return. "Perhaps God will speak to Sam's father, and the boy will be released."

When the locusts vanished, Judd feared the Global Community would increase their efforts to arrest believers. Slowly, airplane flights resumed as more and more people returned to their daily lives.

"We still have a great opportunity to spread the message," Mr. Stein said. "Many are still suffering from stings they received just before the locusts disappeared."

"You still want to head back to the States?" Judd asked Lionel.

"I'd go in a second if Sam were here. But I can't lea him."

Judd had been in touch with Nada once a week. She hadn't talked with her parents about Kasim's call to Kweesa. The apartment was still crowded, but Nada said she had learned to cope.

A few days after the locusts disappeared, Judd called Nada but got no answer. He tried again later in the day, but still no answer. Finally, he told Lionel he was going to check on her after dark. Lionel went with him.

When they reached the building, Judd saw something strange. There were no lights on in Nada's apartment. Lionel pointed to the stairwell, and Judd saw a strip of yellow tape covering the door. "Looks like a GC crime scene. They could be waiting up there."

Judd closed his eyes and leaned against the lobby door. The tape meant one thing. Nada and the others in the apartment had been arrested. "Go to the other side of the street and wait."

"Judd, you can't—"

"Just do it," Judd said, gritting his teeth.

Lionel backed away and found a safe spot across the street. Judd pushed the doorbell and ran. He and Lionel crouched behind a railing and watched. Minutes later a GC squad car pulled up and two officers got out. They checked the front door and walked to the back. When they returned, an officer radioed a message to headquarters.

"A neighbor heard the buzzer and called us," the man said. "Nobody's here."

When the squad car left, Judd and Lionel scampered

...t of their hiding place and rushed to Yitzhak's home.
...udd didn't look at Lionel.

"Come on," Lionel said, "you don't know that the GC
got them."

"I feel it," Judd said. "They must have traced
Kasim's call to Kweesa. Nada should have told her
parents."

Judd and Lionel explained what they had seen to Mr.
Stein and the others. Mr. Stein put his head in his hands
and prayed.

"I have feared this type of thing would happen to *us*,"
Yitzhak said. "The GC is offering rewards to those who
turn in rebels."

Someone knocked at the door. Yitzhak put a finger to
his lips and turned off the lights. He ruffled his hair, put
on a bathrobe, and opened the door. "I'm sorry it took so
long for me . . ." Suddenly, Yitzhak threw his arms
around the person at the door and pulled him into the
darkened room. Judd stood.

"We must have a celebration," Yitzhak shouted. "Our
wayward lamb has come home."

Lionel turned on the lights, and Judd couldn't believe
his eyes. It was Sam Goldberg.

Vicki took a call from Mark as they drove into Arizona.
She told him about the success of the Chula Vista meeting.

Mark's voice quavered. "I'm afraid I have some bad
news."

Vicki immediately thought of Judd and Lionel. Had something gone wrong?

"We got an e-mail from Tsion this morning about Chloe Williams. Buck's still not back from Israel and she's about to give birth any day. I know how close you two were."

"Yeah," Vicki said, stunned.

"Tsion says there may be something wrong with the baby too. Tsion asks us all to pray."

"I will." Vicki remembered when Chloe had first shared the news of her pregnancy. Everyone was excited, and Vicki had wanted to be nearby so she could baby-sit. That clearly was impossible now. Vicki longed to talk with Chloe and ask her questions.

Mark told her about the schoolhouse and how many of the new people had become believers. Some had left as soon as the effects of the stings were over, but most had stayed.

"What about Janie and Melinda?"

"Melinda is back to normal. She helps Lenore a lot with Tolan. Janie's another story. She won't do anything. She says she still has pain and can't help."

Vicki shook her head. "Sounds like Janie."

Mark explained that their next meeting was near Tucson, Arizona. "The meeting is small, less than a hundred," Mark said, "but the pastor who started the house church there begged for a visit after seeing our Web site."

Vicki sighed. "OK, but we sure are tired. I wish we could just come home."

Judd and the others were so happy to see Sam that none of them could speak. They simply hugged him and laughed and wept. Mr. Stein was the most moved. He kept calling Sam, "My son . . . my son."

Finally, Sam told how he had met with his father at their home. "He didn't question me about where I had been or who I was staying with. He just listened. I explained the message clearly and even showed him verses from the Bible. I was so excited. Then GC officers arrived and I realized I had been tricked."

"Your father may have listened more than you realize," Mr. Stein said. "I believe God is working on his heart."

"You talked with him?"

Mr. Stein nodded. He told Sam about his father's dreams.

"What happened at GC headquarters?" Lionel said.

Sam smiled. "Woodruff kept asking where the Tribulation Force was and who I had been staying with. I told them nothing."

"Why did they let you go?" Judd said.

"Three reasons. They wanted to follow me. I found a tiny transmitter in my wallet. I've been out three days, and I'm sure they have no idea where I am."

"Good," Judd said. "Why else did they let you go?"

"It may have something to do with my father. I overheard someone at the front desk mention his name as I was released. Perhaps he convinced Woodruff to let me go. But the best reason they wanted me out of there was the number of people who believed in Christ while I was there."

"In the prison?" Mr. Stein said.

Sam nodded. "I never stopped talking about God to the guards and other prisoners."

"Wonderful," Mr. Stein said.

Sam looked at the floor. "There's only one bad thing to report."

"What?" Judd said.

"Before I was released, I saw them bring in Nada and her family. The GC have them."

Vicki met with the pastor in Tucson, a thin man in his early thirties. He had set up the house church after becoming a true believer, and many in his congregation were starting their own groups.

"We have about twenty teenagers who really need some good teaching," the pastor said. "But there will be others here who don't know Christ. And a few adults as well."

"My normal presentation just deals with believers, but we'll make it work."

Vicki followed the man to his basement. Walls had been knocked out to make room for chairs. About fifty people were scattered throughout the room.

Conrad motioned for Vicki and told her she had a phone call.

"Thought you'd want to know," Mark said. "We got an e-mail early this morning from Tsion."

"Oh no," Vicki said. "Chloe and the baby?"

"Relax," Mark said. "Chloe gave birth to a son this

.iorning. Kenneth Bruce Williams. He's doing fine and Chloe is too. Oh, and get this—Buck made it back before he was born."

Vicki sighed. "Thanks for telling me."

When Vicki hung up, the pastor introduced her. People applauded politely. She tried to concentrate and give the message, but she kept thinking of Chloe and the baby. When she came to the subject of how much God can change your life, she told the story of Buck Williams and how he had been a hard-nosed newspaper reporter. As a journalist he searched for the truth about news stories. Finally, after a long time of searching and many questions, Buck believed and accepted God's forgiveness. His life changed forever.

Vicki ended her time of teaching before 10 P.M., and the pastor invited anyone who wanted to accept Christ as Savior to pray with him.

As people filed out of the meeting, a middle-aged man came up to Vicki and shook her hand. He looked slightly familiar, but Vicki couldn't place him. He was not a believer.

"I want to thank you for coming and talking," the man said. "I was especially interested in the journalist you talked about."

"Mr. Williams has a great story," Vicki said.

"Yeah, I've heard it before. Too much, as a matter of fact."

Vicki folded her arms. "What do you mean?"

"My name is Jeff Williams. Buck is my brother."

ABOUT THE AUTHORS

Jerry B. Jenkins (www.jerryjenkins.com) is the writer of the Left Behind series. He owns the Jerry B. Jenkins Christian Writers Guild, an organization dedicated to mentoring aspiring authors. Former vice president for publishing for the Moody Bible Institute of Chicago, he also served many years as editor of *Moody* magazine and is now Moody's writer-at-large.

His writing has appeared in publications as varied as *Reader's Digest, Parade, Guideposts,* in-flight magazines, and dozens of other periodicals. Jenkins's biographies include books with Billy Graham, Hank Aaron, Bill Gaither, Luis Palau, Walter Payton, Orel Hershiser, and Nolan Ryan, among many others. His books appear regularly on the *New York Times, USA Today, Wall Street Journal,* and *Publishers Weekly* best-seller lists.

Jerry is also the writer of the nationally syndicated sports story comic strip *Gil Thorp,* distributed to newspapers across the United States by Tribune Media Services.

Jerry and his wife, Dianna, live in Colorado and have three grown sons.

Dr. Tim LaHaye (www.timlahaye.com), who conceived the idea of fictionalizing an account of the Rapture and the Tribulation, is a noted author, minister, and nationally recognized speaker on Bible prophecy. He is the founder of both Tim LaHaye Ministries and The PreTrib Research Center. He also recently cofounded the Tim LaHaye School of Prophecy at Liberty University. Presently Dr. LaHaye speaks at many of the major Bible prophecy onferences in the U.S. and Canada, where his current prophecy books are very popular.

Dr. LaHaye holds a doctor of ministry degree from Western Theological Seminary and a doctor of literature degree from Liberty University. For twenty-five years he pastored one of the nation's outstanding churches in San Diego, which grew to three locations. It was during that time that he founded two accredited Christian high schools, a Christian school system of ten schools, and Christian Heritage College.

Dr. LaHaye has written over forty books that have been published in more than thirty languages. He has written books on a wide variety of subjects, such as family life, temperaments, and Bible prophecy. His current fiction works, the Left Behind series, written with Jerry B. Jenkins, continue to appear on the best-seller lists of the Christian Booksellers Association, *Publishers Weekly*, *Wall Street Journal*, *USA Today*, and the *New York Times*.

He is the father of four grown children and grandfather of nine. Snow skiing, waterskiing, motorcycling, golfing, vacationing with family, and jogging are among his leisure activities.

areUthirsty.com

well . . . are you?